PAID TO THE PIRATE

PAID
TO THE
PIRATE

UNA ROHR

Paid to the Pirate

ISBN: 979-8-9882794-4-0

Published by:
Bound & Crowned Press

Content Expectations including Potential Triggers

Dark Romance (Spoilers)

This book contains dubious consent during some sexual acts, as well as non-consent during punishments. Please do not read this book if these are your triggers. There are many spicy scenes which include BDSM.

This novel is part bodice-ripper, part dark romance *first* and historical fantasy *second*.

Potential Triggers:

- Rather than reveal her plans/schemes, the protagonist experiences non-consensual punishments, including a spanking with a belt and the whipping of intimate regions with a crop
- Edging, humiliation, degradation, shame, figging, anal sex, bondage, forced deep throating, and sex (first time) under dubious circumstances
- Attempted rape by a nameless character (very brief/not detailed)
- Death of a parent
- Dubious use of power imbalance

If you have any questions about material not covered, please do not hesitate to email me at unarohr@gmail.com

PROLOGUE

I DON'T REMEMBER MY life before the accident, but surely, I was a lady.

Everyone insists.

With sharp cheekbones, an hourglass figure, and wild curls cascading down my back, I possessed all the marks of a highborn girl.

If my hair had been miserably knotted and my skin sunburnt to a crisp when they found me on the beach two years ago, *well,* that was only to be expected after tumbling ashore like... *rubbish,* I thought, cheeks pinking at the memory.

I might not understand the state of my overly-callused hands when I'd awoken, and my *occasional* manner of selecting a rather indelicate word in times of frustration, but a reasonable explanation must exist. I was in possession of a lady's education, after all, and my grace and intelligence were inarguably an asset in helping the Penninghams run the inn. I knew exactly how to pour tea and charm any well-bred patron passing through our door—though sadly, none of whom ever recognized me.

That wasn't surprising; we were but a tiny settlement, after all.

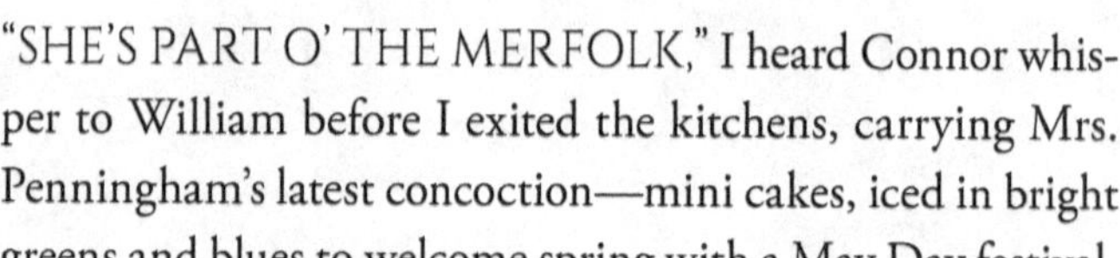

"SHE'S PART O' THE MERFOLK," I heard Connor whisper to William before I exited the kitchens, carrying Mrs. Penningham's latest concoction—mini cakes, iced in bright greens and blues to welcome spring with a May Day festival, a tradition the governor brought from his Swedish homeland.

"A selkie," William agreed, voice full of wonder.

I bit back a smile and pressed myself against the wall, listening. Since no one in our small town knew from whence I came, the mystery gave rise to ever more magical origins. Sometimes they'd even say I was a handmaiden of Aphrodite herself.

"Aye, those freckles across her nose came from long days in the sun with the other sea-folk, luring men to their deaths with their sweet voices," William said, as wistfully as if he wished such a fatal demise upon himself.

Self-consciously, I turned my head to my shoulder. I would have covered my nose if my hands weren't full of the sweet tray. Each morning, I steadfastly powdered my face, but after a long day helping Mr. and Mrs. Penningham serve guests, those vulgar specks stubbornly shone through.

"I've heard her sing many a night. She might have lost her tail, but she didn't lose her voice," Connor agreed.

I straightened my spine. I *was* a talented singer. Most nights the men begged and cajoled me to entertain them as they drank. Sometimes it was a bawdy tavern ballad that colored my cheeks just to think upon; other times I sang a melancholic sea shanty which—if I really gave it my heart— brought tears to the eyes of even the hardest man.

Perhaps Daniel could be persuaded by this tale of my lethal siren voice, I thought, wryly. *Perhaps then he'd stop pestering me to marry him.*

Unlikely, as he'd been enamored ever since he found me on the beach.

Bare as a babe, I thought, cringing at my indecent state. *Thank God he was a gentleman. Not to mention, ostentatiously coming up in the world.*

I could do worse for a husband.

When I heard the front door to the inn swing shut, indicating William and Connor had left, I shimmied out into the main dining area and deposited the tray of sweets onto one of the wooden tables by the window. Thinking over the boys' musings of my past, I absent-mindedly caressed the necklace dangling nearly to my breasts.

Only one piece of evidence remained from my life before the sea spit me out onto the beach—a golden locket engraved with the name *Charlotte* on the back.

But, save a strange smear of dirt along the locket's edge, the inside was as bereft as my memory.

PART I
CAPTURED

CHAPTER 1

CHARLOTTE

"PIRATES!" DANIEL SHOUTED, rushing through the inn's door. "A ship's anchored just inside the bay and the men are coming into town as we speak."

My stomach dropped and my gasp was echoed in every man, woman, and child stuffing the inn's many tables. There wasn't much else to do in our tiny settlement and most evenings villagers gathered for company and gossip, like moths to our torchlights. Mrs. Clayton, the governor's wife, clutched her pearls. Then, wisely, she unfastened the necklace and slid it into the safety of her ample bosom.

"Is there time to mount a defense?" someone asked.

I held back a near-hysterical snort. *What defense could we manage against pirates?*

"They'll be here any minute," Daniel protested, sounding even more frightened than I felt. "The night was too black and misty to spy the incoming ship until it was too late."

"Calm down, everyone please, calm down," Mr. Clayton said, raising his voice above the chatter. Our little settlement was barely a proper enough town to have elected a governor, but Mr. George Clayton served as our de facto leader since long before I'd arrived.

"They're not here to attack or they would have done so already. They're simply here to-"

"Extract payment," Mrs. Penningham harrumphed.

George grimaced both at her interruption and its certainty. "We'll have to decide what kind of town we aim to be, one who pays tribute to these pirates or-"

"A town who ceases to exist," Mrs. Penningham interrupted again. This time, Mr. Penningham jabbed her in the ribs. She pursed her lips but didn't wipe the hard look from her face.

"Which black heart is it? Did you get a look at the colors?" Someone's panicked shout rose above the rest and everyone turned to Daniel, holding their breath.

He slid one hand along his sandy hair, smoothing it back into the ribbon tied low at the nape of his neck. "Couldn't tell in the dark. There's no moon and the skies are cloudy."

Grumbles and groans came from the crowded inn, but Mr. Clayton held up his hands. "Leave the boy alone, he did his watch as best he could."

An older lady in the corner piped up, "Just give 'em whatever they want and be done with it!"

That's the problem, I thought. *Once we gave it to them, we'd* never *be done.* If the pirates came demanding tribute, they'd extract regular payment henceforth, in exchange for "protection." Our settlement would bear a mark, a symbol of such safeguarding and a warning for other pirates to leave us alone. In theory.

I didn't see how we had a choice. Mr. Clayton hesitated because the crown despised such arrangements. It meant monies potentially lining *their* coffers would be redirected into pirate hands, funding and encouraging the practice. But while our overseers in London reclined on their pillowed sofas eating candied delights safely across the sea, we faced monsters with daggers held to our throats.

"They're here!" a young girl shouted, peering outside the curtained window.

The room sucked in another collective breath and everyone stilled. Mrs. Penningham suddenly appeared by my side.

"Get to the kitchens," she whispered. "They'll be wanting ale and lots of it. Serve it 'round and don't stop lest I give you the signal."

I nodded, hurrying out to do as I was bid and secretly grateful. I didn't want to admit it, but the notion of pirates filling our inn made a terrible shiver run down my spine.

"HOW THOUGHTFUL OF YOU ALL to gather for our visit," I heard a man announce to the room. He spoke with a more eloquent tone than I expected from such a band of scoundrels. "May I present to you our captain, Colton Pearce," he said, with relish.

Colton Pearce. My heart thudded and I gulped. *This is bad.*

Colt the Cruel, he was called, or just Captain Colt. *Why had one of the nastiest pirates plaguing the coast turned to trib-uting? Wasn't his method slash-and-dash?*

That answered the question as to what Mr. Clayton would decree. No one feared the disappointment of the crown more than Colt's blade.

We'd pay. Whatever he asked.

I heard shuffling and the scrape of wooden chair legs as the pirates took seats, evacuating jumpy patrons previously occupying those same chairs, I assumed. As the men sauntered into the room, the air changed. Inhaling, it was almost as if the scent of flint and danger accompanied the sweat and sea air clinging to their bodies.

Buried deep beneath my terror, something familiar mingled with the odor.

"What is it you want?" I heard our governor ask, and I admired that he kept fear from infecting his voice.

"We seek a business relationship, *a partnership*," the pirate-emissary replied. I couldn't see beyond the kitchen door, but so far, his was the only voice speaking on behalf of the crew. Elected, I supposed, because he bore such an elegant manner of speech.

"I'm sure we can come to a friendly arrangement. We don't want to have to turn… unfriendly. At the sun's rise," he specified, in warning. "Our ship is anchored not a stone's throw from your inn. You haven't the time to call for reinforcements from Charles Town."

Charles Town, to our north, was the nearest proper village. With its wall of protection and dense numbers deterring any attacks, it wasn't surprising Colt turned his eye on our sleepy settlement instead.

Quietly, I pushed the kitchen door ajar and peeked into our crowded inn. Immediately, I found the man addressing our townsfolk—he stood tall in the center of the stuffy room, whilst most everyone else sunk into a chair or slouched along the walls, as if wanting to disappear. I caught Molly, a curious girl of four or five, reaching for the shiny handle of one bald-headed pirate's gun, strapped to his waist. Flashing a crooked grin, he leaned over to allow her exploration, but Mrs. Bestly noticed her daughter's attention and quickly yanked the girl back.

Craning my neck, I scanned the room for the infamous pirate, but when I found the imposing figure to whom everyone cast sly glances, he was seated facing the opposite direction. I only caught a head of dark hair, partially obscured by a lanky member of his crew standing behind him.

"So what you're saying is, if we pay you what you want tonight, you won't attack tomorrow."

I bit back a smirk at Mrs. Penningham's blunt tongue.

Can't put it off any longer, I thought.

Taking a deep breath, I pushed the kitchen door wide and slid out into the main room of the inn, now crammed with vile pirates alongside our peaceful townsfolk.

"I'm sure we can come to an arrangement," Mr. Clayton grumbled. "Gold, I'm assuming, though you'll find little of it here. We've had good years of indigo and tobacco crops recently…"

Nervous, I tuned out Mr. Clayton as I began serving flagons and tankards of ale haphazardly, ensuring the room had enough to go around, regardless of whose glass was empty or who'd ordered more. Spirits could raise tempers or soothe them, depending, but I wouldn't question Mrs. Penningham's orders.

No one paid me any mind as Mr. Clayton and the pirate emissary held the room. Rounding a particularly crowded table, I caught sight of Colton from the corner of my eye, though I still couldn't see him fully. *He's a towering beast of a man.* Just *looking* at him made my stomach flip, and that wasn't all. Inside my chest, something tightened.

Run, said a voice in my head. *Run away from this dangerous stranger.*

His hair reached just to his ears—not long enough to tie back, yet not short enough to stay out of his way, as if he'd neglected to cut it in a timely manner or couldn't decide whether to keep it long or short. Colt tossed his head, once, flinging back the hair from his eyes, his face.

Coming to the other side of the small table, I stood directly, unwillingly, in the pirate captain's line of vision. Already in possession of a tankard of ale he must have swiped from another patron, he lifted it to his lips, smiling and drinking deeply. But when he saw me, our gazes locked.

Colton's eyes widened and he froze. He had the momentary appearance of someone who'd seen a ghost, but it was there and quickly gone. In that moment, it was as if time stood still and the rest of the room faded away. His cold, near-black eyes banished any hope of Colton being a "gentleman pirate," as some were called who extorted tribute, rather than attacking. I began to sweat in a very unladylike manner.

Run, repeated the voice in my head. *You should have run when you had the chance.* Following their captain's lead, I felt the eyes of the crew upon me and thought I heard someone swear beneath their breath, *"well, I'll be..."*

Finally, Colton moved, striking out a hand to silence the increasing whispers of his crew. Slowly, he placed his tankard back on the wooden table. Still, he didn't stop *staring.*

I studied his face—long, but not overly so. His features were sharp, his eyes hooded and dark. To be fair, it was a pleasing face. His full lips turned just a hair upwards, as if they resisted a smirk. Arguably, he could be called quite handsome.

That cruel gaze seemed to pin me to the floor, but Colt's resumption of movement worked as a strange release on some of my own limbs, as if they mimicked his. My hand flew to my collarbone, rubbing in a familiar, anxious habit.

"Change of terms," Colton said, speaking for the first time. Those pitiless eyes bore into mine. "I want the girl."

CHAPTER 2

CHARLOTTE

MY HEART STOPPED and my blood ran cold. No mistake could be made about whom Colton spoke. Everyone turned in my direction.

But… he can't mean me.

"The girl?" Mrs. Penningham asked, voice quaking in a manner I'd never before heard from her throat.

"Her. Miss Charlotte," Colton said, narrowing his eyes. "Unless she calls herself something else now."

He knows my name. A tremor ran down my spine to hear it spoken on the pirate captain's cruel lips. *How does he know?*

"Are you saying you want Miss Charlotte instead of our bumper crop?" Mr. Clayton asked, incredulous. "That if we give her to you, your men won't attack tomorrow?"

Colton's severe expression remained unchanged as he replied, "I'm saying that if you hand her over right now, my men won't slaughter all of you this instant and burn this fledgling village to the ground."

Mrs. Penningham, *bless her,* stood in front of me, blocking me from the pirates. "We will do no such thing," she swore. "What could you possibly want with our Charlotte? Nothing good, I'm sure. Do you think we'd hand her over to you to be… to be… *mistreated?*"

My cheeks grew hot as I knew exactly what she implied—and so did the crowd present. I was positive everyone, patron or pirate, now pictured something unspeakably indecent—be it my naked flesh or worse, Colton's touch despoiling me back in his captain's quarters.

My hand flew to my décolleté again, rubbing, and I noticed my skin had turned as pink as my gown. Far too fine for work at the inn, I couldn't refuse wearing the dress at Daniel's request. It was a gift, after all, and the iridescent blush-and-coral silk busk was like nothing else this side of the Atlantic.

Serves me right, I thought, cursing myself. I'd paraded around in the eye-catching gown all day. Suddenly, I couldn't shake from my mind that its color resembled the pinks of… other parts. *I should have worn that brown, smocked dress.*

As if he could read my mind, Colton's mouth quirked upwards. I gulped.

Had Mrs. Penningham noticed?

"Charlotte," she said carefully. "I want you to go to your room and prepare your things. You're in my employ and this is my inn. I'll be the one discussing your staying or leaving with Captain Pearce. Alone."

I couldn't tell if Mr. Clayton looked relieved or affronted. It seemed he couldn't decide himself, either.

Shifting only his eyes, Captain Pearce considered Mrs. Penningham for a moment, then gave one curt nod.

"Everyone out," shouted the tall, eloquent emissary who'd done most of the speaking on behalf of the pirates. Eager to depart, some people jumped from their chairs and scurried through the door. Others looked around, reluctant to abandon me, God bless them. Only Mrs. Penningham's gentle encouragement helped them move out into the balmy night.

One more nod by Colt and his men shuffled outside as well, until only Mr. and Mrs. Penningham remained. Mrs. Penningham whispered something to her husband, and he too departed.

"Daniel, please escort Charlotte to her room."

I blinked. I hadn't realized I'd been rooted to the ground, wide-eyed, until Mrs. Penningham commanded Daniel to help me move. I felt his arm around my shoulder and allowed myself to be guided.

That I could *feel* his touch meant this wasn't a nightmare. It was truly happening.

I didn't think I could make my shaky legs move without his assistance. I trusted Mrs. Penningham with my life, but I was too shocked to walk on my own.

What on God's good Earth could a criminal like Colt want with *me?*

CHAPTER 3

COLT

I WANTED TO WRAP my hands around her pretty little neck and squeeze the life from her.

One part of me did, anyway.

Another part of me inwardly smiled, grateful for Mrs. Penningham's insistence on her well-being, on a certain standard of treatment. It gave me the perfect excuse to tell the crew that we *not* kill her or lash her with the cat o' nine tails until she wished we did.

I wasn't capable of that.

Not even that fateful night when she challenged me to do it. Or perhaps she'd thrown out the request in desperation. I could never sort out what went through her beautiful head those evenings. *And for two bloody years I'd been wondering.*

But seeing her sashaying blithely around the tavern, passing out ale as if she hadn't a care in the world—processing her nonchalance in seeing *me*—caused me to temporarily indulge the fantasy of wringing her elegant neck.

That was a lie. I'd indulged the daydream many times over the years. Almost as many times as I'd indulged… other fantasies.

What did it mean that she still wore the locket?

I ran a hand down my face, forcing my thoughts back to business. I needed to get a handle on how much of my crew felt the same. Conks and Johnson wouldn't be any trouble. Robert the Red would be a problem, no doubt, living up to his name.

My hands found my belt, adjusting.

Oh, she'd be punished alright. After I got the story from her own lips as to what she'd been up to these past two years. Nay, *before.* She'd speak more honestly after a belting.

This was clearly yet another game of Charlotte's but what was the purpose this time? I informed the innkeeper that Charlotte belonged to *us,* and she countered by alluding to a more refined upbringing Charlotte had before they'd met.

Nonsense.

Perhaps Charlotte was lying to this woman as well? She was skilled at deception, after all.

"She's like a daughter to me. I won't be seeing her harmed," Mrs. Penningham insisted, after a long, strange line of questioning I couldn't make heads or tails of. Mrs. Penningham's story about how Charlotte came to work at the tavern didn't add up. The details were vague and evasive. The outspoken old innkeeper had been hiding Charlotte, that much was clear. But she was hiding something else too, and I didn't think it was the Crimson Eye.

Mrs. Penningham obscured something *about* Charlotte. I gritted my teeth, fist clenching beneath the table as I guessed it might have something to do with that Daniel boy who freely touched her as he escorted her up the stairs.

Charlotte might be *like* a daughter to Mrs. Penningham, but no one could misbelieve her to be the spawn of this dowdy woman and her timid husband.

But what did it mean that she still wore the locket?

Charlotte had further bloomed into a stunning woman. My cock twitched at the memory of those intimate glimpses. Too few, but seared into my brain nonetheless. Time had only fleshed out the curves of her hips and breasts, separating her even more from the scrawny girl I knew before.

What her rear looked like; I couldn't tell beneath the voluminous skirts of her ridiculous gown. But I'd find out soon enough.

CHAPTER 4

CHARLOTTE

"I WON'T BE SOME prize for this pirate," I whisper-shouted, hands curled into fists, tears threatening to spill. More calmly, I continued, "If I had some association with the scoundrel in the past, I'm *sure* it was unwilling on my part. And I don't care to know it, in any case. If my past involves any contact with these horrible men, I won't stand to hear of it."

Even as I hurled the declaration, I knew I lied. I was *dying* to know anything at all about who I was before I lost my memory. I just didn't want it to be anything less than perfect. Less than my fantasies.

My mother and father were supposed to show up and claim me. Noble, respected, gentle. Or—or—a well-to-do aunt, at least. That was the way it was meant to happen. Not some swarthy pirate captain thinking he knew anything about me.

"Shh… my beautiful, sweet, Charlotte," Daniel soothed, though he seemed even more rattled himself. "It's obvious you escaped this black-hearted captain sometime in the past. Most likely he kidnapped you. What passes by a woman's attention is observed, man-to-man," Daniel intoned, and I frowned at the casual slight. "I caught the look in his eyes and I could see right through to the vulgar images in his mind."

"You don't mean… you don't think…" I couldn't finish the shameful sentence. Was Daniel implying I'd *known* Colt, as a wife knew a husband?

"Shh, my sweet Charlotte, I would never suggest that," Daniel replied, gently squeezing my shoulders. I was too distressed to shake him off. "Put that thought from your mind. *I* know in my heart you're pure as the lilies by Isaac's farm. But I'm saying that I know when a man's eyes darken with desire, and I could see that monster wants you for himself."

No. I was untouched. I knew it. Felt it.

Wasn't I?

I was saved from having to say more by Mrs. Penningham bursting into my small room above the inn. Daniel and I turned to her in unison, holding our breath.

"The captain knows you," she announced, frowning. "I don't know how that filthy pirate knows you, but he is undoubtedly from your past."

Impossible. My head resumed its maniacal shaking.

"Child, you know I can tell when a man is lying," Mrs. Penningham insisted.

I did know; it was her talent. She'd honed the skill over pitchers of ale throughout the years, conversing with all sorts of men who sat a stool, seeking a sympathetic ear or a regaling chat.

"That man knows you from before your accident, as sure as I'm standing here today."

I whimpered and she quickly added, "But I can tell you that he doesn't intend to kill you and I don't think he means to… violate you. He seems to want… something else."

Mrs. Penningham's assurances sent mixed feelings shooting through me, almost too fast to process.

Captain Colt doesn't mean to rape me, and her words implied he hadn't, in the past. It was some relief, at least, to know I remained unspoilt. But she hadn't negotiated my release and he intended *something* with me.

"I don't understand," I cried. "Why does he want me?"

"I'm not sure, exactly. He's hiding something and I couldn't sort it out without giving away that you lost your memory, child. And I don't think that's a secret he should know." Mrs. Penningham's eyes held mine. "He could easily use it to manipulate you. Make you believe falsehoods about your history. Far better you should find out everything you can about your past, while pretending you never forgot."

"But... how am I supposed to act when I don't know anything?"

"He thinks you've been putting on an act here in your pretty gown. Pretending to be something you're not, some kind of highborn lady."

I am, my mind insisted. *At least, I might be.*

"Keep with it," Mrs. Penningham advised. "As if you refuse to stop pretending."

My only reply was to drop my jaw. She truly wanted me to go with him?

"I've negotiated a sort of check-point, a confirmation that you're unharmed on his ship. Captain Colt plans to return to these parts in a few weeks time, ferrying sugar and coffee from Nassau up the coast. The man's got a dizzying mix of piracy, extortion, and legitimate trade, I'll tell you that."

Mrs. Penningham fixed me with what I knew to be her "encouraging" smile. "Captain Colt will return here, we'll see each other again, and he promises you will be able to confirm to us that you haven't been..." she trailed off.

"Raped or killed!" I finished for her.

Both Daniel and Mrs. Penningham fell uncomfortably silent.

What other options had I, than to trust Mrs. Penningham's words? If I didn't agree to go peacefully, nothing stopped the bloody pirate from taking me by force. And God only knew what else he'd steal along with me.

I covered my face with my hands. "I *have* to go," I whispered, collapsing into bed. "You've been so kind to me, I can't risk all your lives to save mine."

I felt the weight of Mrs. Penningham sink into the mattress beside me. She wrapped one comforting arm around my shoulders as I struggled not to weep. The helplessness of my situation enraged me more than anything else. It should have been fear—and that was unmistakably crawling up my spine—but the idea that I was at Colt's whim, that I had no power over—

Suddenly, a thought occurred to me. I raised my head from my hands.

"We've lived under the thumb of these criminals for too long. Extorting us, tormenting us, killing us. Why do we allow them to shape this new world the way they want when we can take back the power to shape it another way? What if I used this opportunity? For *us?*" I shot to my feet and before they could stop me—before *I* could stop myself—and a plan came tumbling out.

"What if I feign cooperation whilst I learn their ways? In a few weeks' time, I could report back to you everything I learn about the inner workings of their piracy. When I return, I might know enough so that we can take them down. Why,

I could do it myself," I said, jutting my chin. "If I'm close to this Captain Colt, I could easily slip poison into his drink one night. Into the whole crew's."

My heart beat terribly fast by the time I'd finished, but my eyes shone, feeling like I'd wrested some control over my plight. *Not that I know where to find poison,* I thought. But I pushed the objection from my mind. Mrs. Penningham's mouth turned down at the corners, but to my surprise, Daniel stared with rapt attention.

"Yes…" he said, eyes bright, and my heart gave a small leap to see that he respected my scheming. Using his palm, he smoothed back a loose strand of sandy hair that had fallen free from its ribbon. "Yes, my sweet Charlotte, this is a won-derous plan. We shall rendezvous at the agreed-upon time, and you can report back to us everything we need to know about these scoundrels. We'll use the information to entrap Captain Colt, putting an end to his piracy, and hopefully, his life."

Grateful for an ally, when Daniel clasped my hands and met my eyes, I saw him in a new light.

"And then, once you're safely returned to us, perhaps you'll do me the honor of becoming my wife?"

Daniel's blue eyes glittered with hope. He was handsome. He was newly-rich and growing richer every day. *And* he respected my idea.

I couldn't see a reason to deny him any longer.

I stammered but replied with sincerity, "I—I shall con-sider your offer."

CHAPTER 5

COLT

S HE TOOK HER sweet time gathering her belongings. If I hadn't men posted at the base of the stairs and outside her window, I'd have thought she intended to give us the slip.

I knew from experience how good she could be at escaping notice.

But then why had she sauntered into the room as if *wanting* to get caught?

I told Johnson to ensure the crew obeyed orders—no one but myself was to engage Charlotte. No questions, no accusations, no probing of the past. She'd floated into the room like a goddamn ghost and they were going to treat her as such until I got to the bottom of her lies.

I had a plan. I had it under control.

Which was *my* lie, but they'd never know. The important message to convey was that anyone stepping out of line would face my wrath.

Near a half-hour later, Charlotte descended the stairs like a bloody duchess, shoulders squared and chin jutting stubbornly. Her face, however, was the pale of death, and I caught the quiver of her lower lip. She was scared.

Good.

I'd instructed the crew to keep their distance. I didn't know who had the best or worst intentions for *Miss Charlotte,* as she apparently called herself, and I wanted ample space to sort out whether or not my own intentions ran more on the side of protection… or punishment. More than once my fingers dug into my thighs, itching to encircle her neck and squeeze.

Unsure whether or not I had my impulses under control, I temporarily kept my distance as well.

Surrounded by my men, Charlotte had no choice but to be led into the jolly boat and deposited securely in the middle bench. Head high, she faced *The Dread Night,* anchored safely in the bay and guarded by the remainder of the crew. I sat at the stern, watching the waves and wind sweep strands of honeyed curls from her pins and sending them in disarray down her neck. She tried to reassemble them—she actually tried to tidy her hair as I rowed her to her doom. I didn't know whether to laugh or to throttle her.

Hair pins would be the least of her concerns when I was through with her.

Though they obeyed my orders not to engage Charlotte, I could see the crew's curious eyes steal glances as we rowed, and once we boarded *The Dread Night,* whispers ran from man-to-man.

In the brief moment I took to silence them with a stern look, Charlotte dared to wrest command by wheeling to face me, eyes blazing and speaking first.

"I demand to know what it is you want from me," she declared with her pouty pink lip jutting.

Unbelievable. She spoke as if she didn't already know. She spoke as if she wasn't practically asking me to firmly put her in her place in front of my crew.

Well, then. I'd oblige. With pleasure.

"I think we're going to be wanting a lot from you." I paused, letting her mind race with the implication. "But we'll start with that preposterous dress. Hold her," I ordered. A quick jut of my chin in the direction of Robert and James and both men eagerly grabbed Charlotte's arms as I stalked forward.

She dropped the indignant lady act when I withdrew my dirk from its scabbard and held the glistening tip close to her rounded eyes. She knew the damage I could do with it. Perhaps her mind flashed back to all those men I'd gutted with the same blade. The rise and fall of her chest told me she wasn't sure I wouldn't gut her, as well.

Good.

She'd certainly earned it.

Slowly, I dragged the flat side of the blade down the column of her neck. I smiled as her rapid breathing grew even shorter when the knife crossed the expanse of flesh exposed by the gown's low cut and headed toward her breasts.

What did it mean that she still wore the locket?

I blinked at the golden oval dangling low on her chest, before shaking my head to clear it.

Using one hand, I grasped the top of her dress to hold it taut and was rewarded by her small squeal. With a quick swipe downward, I used the dirk to cut the ties on her bodice. The tear would decrease the gown's value at our next port, but it was worth it for the fear in her eyes.

Stepping back, I said, "You can remove the rest yourself or we can do it for you."

I not only wanted her stripped in front of my men, I needed it.

There could be no questioning my authority on my ship and my intent to make her pay. I'd have had no qualms about removing every thread of clothing on her body and marching her fully naked to my cabin, but for some who might find it distasteful. And it was only for those who might sympathize that I showed restraint. For soft old men like Conks, who'd grown protective of her.

Looking around in wide-eyed fright, Charlotte's trembling fingers reached for the top of her dress and she pushed it downward from her torso, revealing the pristine white chemise beneath.

"All the way," I commanded. "And step out. You won't need it anymore."

"You're vile," she swore between clenched teeth, as if she'd expected mercy. As if she expected to be served tea for drinking and feathered pillows for sleeping, like a guest upon a galleon.

I wasn't sure what game she played, but I wouldn't be deterred. Charlotte took her time as she lowered the dress to a puddle around her and delicately stepped from the garment.

"I hope you meet the devil in hell when you die," she declared, wrapping her arms around her torso. "And I hope it's soon."

I barked a laugh. *There was the saucy Charlotte I remembered, underneath this lady act.*

"Perhaps I will, *Miss Charlotte,* was it?"

I could play this game just as well as she could. I could *outplay* her.

"But not before you. I'll remind you I'm the devil on this ship." Roughly, I grabbed her by the hair, yanking her head back. "And I'm about to show you hell."

CHAPTER 6

CHARLOTTE

"YOU DON'T REMEMBER the way to a captain's cabin?" Colt taunted, grabbing my bicep and yanking me back too hard. Pulling me too close to his body.

"We did acquire a new ship in your absence, but I doubt you'd find a cabin in that direction on any vessel. *The Dark Blade* is gone, traded to another captain. Miss her?"

Every passing minute confirmed the unavoidable. I'd been on a ship for months, years perhaps. But in what capacity? As a prisoner? Crew? God forbid, as a ... *companion?*

That couldn't be. Women were considered bad luck upon ships. And the way I was being treated told me my consent wasn't entirely given, if at all. In some manner, I must have existed unwillingly aboard Colt's ship. Perhaps blackmailed? Maybe this cold-hearted captain knew my parents and threatened them. Maybe I'd agreed to stay aboard his ship to spare them pain, or death.

And I'd finally managed to escape… but had somehow lost my memories.

Whatever had happened, pretending I was too far removed from the experience, too above it all, seemed to be serving to cover the amnesia.

I planned on clinging to my act. My life might very well depend on it.

I'd started hopelessly, however, marching aft when instructed to Colt's cabin. Above the briny scent of the sea, I could smell him—curiously clean for a pirate, though tinged with something spicy, musky. I gulped. *Manly.*

"Have you forgotten your way around a ship?" he repeated, eyes narrowed with suspicion.

Towering monster. He must be six feet tall, or more. I had to look up to meet his eyes, when my height allowed me to meet some men with a level stare and to look down upon the shorter ones.

Throwing myself into the safety of my pretend-act, I declared with exaggerated haughtiness, "I am a lady." The night wind whipped loose strands of my hair about my face, and I tucked them behind my ears, trying to muster all the dignity I could, clad only in my chemise in front of at least two dozen swarthy men. "I've never been on a ship in my life. This one, or your old one. I'm afraid if you want me to do something you'll need to give precise instruction."

"You're in luck. I plan to do *precisely* that."

I shivered at the thinly veiled threat.

One side of Colt's lips turned up into a sardonic grin. "I see you remember some things, don't you?" Roughly, he turned me by shoulders to face the main mast. "You're familiar with the post used for whipping insolent crewmen, aren't you?"

My eyes rounded and I gulped.

"Ah, but a *lady* would never find herself bound for the lash. Would she?"

The emphasis Colt gave the statement told me he referenced something from my past—but what? His head, tilted back, forced his hooded eyes to peer further downward, lending him an even more arrogant look. I found his haughty manner unusual for a pirate—not that I'd come into contact with many of his kind. But the carriage and mannerisms of this particular captain were surprisingly measured, giving them an air of… if not civility, certainly intelligence.

Yes, cunning. I needed to be wary of what he saw with those dark eyes—and how he processed information in his dark mind.

With his large hand caging my arm, I had no choice but to follow the captain up a short flight of wooden stairs from the main deck onto a higher, smaller one. With quick, long strides Colt half-dragged me through a tight hallway until we reached a door at the end.

His private chambers.

Mrs. Penningham said he wouldn't rape me, I assured myself. But why else were we headed to his cabin?

Thrusting me inside, Colt slammed and locked the door behind him. I quickly took stock of the room as I spun around to face him. The far wall bore a series of paned windows and scarlet curtains. Elevated from the rest of the floor, a desk and chair sat before it. The wooden desk was littered with all kinds of books, maps, and documents. Almost in the center of the room stood a dining table large enough to seat six or eight. On the tabletop and jutting from sconces, candles glowed, long tapers freshly-lit.

On one side of the room a bed was built into the walls. It too bore deep red curtains, though they'd been tied back with gold, woven cords.

Keenly aware of my state of undress, I moved away from the bed, toward the large table near the room's center. One step backward.

Colt matched it with a step forward, boots thumping ominously against the floor.

I took another step, in reverse.

He took one more in my direction.

Seeing the fruitlessness of my retreat, I stopped, grabbing the table's edge to steady myself. Colt's eyes missed nothing. He looked down at me like game to be hunted and roasted. Or as if I'd already been ensnared and prepared and all that remained was to spear me with a fork and eat.

Mrs. Penningham said he wouldn't kill me. Said he wouldn't rape me.

What did he want with me? Why was I here? Who was I to this cruel captain?

His eyes were black, impossibly dark and enthralling to the point of sucking prey right into that molten pitch. *Black eyes don't exist,* my mind insisted. *They must be the darkest shade of brown.* Yet I couldn't discern the difference. Candlelight reflected menacingly off his pupils—indistinguishable from the irises themselves. His hair and clothing were equally as dark.

"Shall we pick up where we left off?"

I blinked. What did that mean?

Colt stepped forward again, now no more than two feet away.

"Or try something new, seeing as how much time has passed?"

Before I could respond, he invaded my personal space, grabbed the back of my head, and brought his lips to mine. Balling my hands into fists, I punched against his chest in a pathetic effort at stopping him. Colt's other arm snaked around my waist, locking my body to his, crushing my arms between us as he attacked my mouth.

I'd never been kissed before. Had I?

It wasn't quite a kiss. Not only because the tips of his fingers dug painfully into my cheeks, but because I didn't kiss him back.

My mind spun—he both felt free to kiss me yet implied he hadn't done so before. *What was my strange relationship to this man?*

It lasted only a few seconds. Abruptly, the one-sided kiss ended when Colt pulled back and blinked once as if *he* were the one startled. To my horror, instead of remaining in a state of ardor, the kiss had the opposite effect, and a look of even more menace grew upon his sinister features. It was as if he was not only mad at me for not kissing him back, he was mad at himself for doing so in the first place.

"I want the whole story of what happened that night. And I want every man out there to hear your cries."

My stomach lurched as he unbuckled his belt and folded it over in an unmistakable threat. "Don't hold back. I won't."

I could barely form words as the room swayed, all courage I'd summoned to board the ship quickly abandoning me.

"You mean to whip me?" I whispered, voice cracking.

Colt threw his head back, roaring with laughter.

"Believe me, I've half a mind to tie you to the mast and whip you as so begged. But I've got no mercy for you after what you've done."

Mercy? How could publicly whipping me be a mercy?

"You'll take my belt on your backside until I've licked every lie from those lips."

My heart galloped and an instant sheen of sweat broke out on my brow. He couldn't be serious.

Colt's eyes roved my body, blazing with rage. "Take off that slip before I tear it off."

I crossed my arms protectively against my chest. "You request tribute like a so-called gentleman pirate, but you're no gentleman!"

"And you think wearing ridiculous dresses and silky chemises makes you a lady?"

I scoffed. How *dare* he speak to me like that? My dress was anything but ridiculous. Daniel said it was the latest fashion in Paris. Mrs. Penningham said the pink beautifully complemented my honey curls and hazel eyes. *How dare he; this dirty, swarthy pirate?*

I jutted my chin. "My manners make me a lady. And furthermore, I am a–a *godly* woman."

I'd hoped that pronouncement would buy me some protection, but it amused Colt instead.

"Godly?" he mocked. Bright, white teeth flashed against his tanned skin when Colton grinned widely.

"You've been pretending to be something you're not since the day I met you. You've been a liar since day I let you live. Do your games ever stop?" He chuckled, darkly. I didn't know if he expected a reply as he glowered, but I had none to give.

"Well then, it's as I said. No whipping post for you, *lady*. You'll be punished in the manner befitting a woman. With my belt. On your rear."

A twinge in a region I'd never previously felt such a stirring, alarmed me. The rest of my body understood the danger it was in—especially my backside, which tingled with anticipation. But the area between my legs felt as if… for the first time in my life… that private region had been stroked, awoken.

The feeling frightened me as much as this man's leather belt. *No, no, not a man.* A pirate, a devil. Thinking of him as a man would be folly, lulling me into some false belief he'd have… what did he say? *Mercy.*

Colt the Cruel had no mercy. I didn't need the warning; his reputation proceeded him.

Before I could run, Colt's strong hands grabbed mine and held them together as he pushed me toward the bed. It seemed unreal; I was in a nightmare and I had to wake up.

"Let me go!" I cried and he laughed, he *laughed.*

"Keep it up, please. I want everyone on this ship to know you're being thrashed to tears."

Oh God, why? What had I ever done to him?

"Just save enough of your voice to tell me everything I want to know when we're done."

"Please, *sir,* don't," I babbled. "Please, unhand me."

"It's *captain* and you bloody well know it."

Roughly, Colt threw me onto the low bed and I felt his weight disappear. Before I could scramble, his tall frame covered mine as he brought my wrists together once more, this time binding them with rope while I wiggled. Somehow, Colt tethered the rope to a hitch beneath the bed, tying it securely.

"Stop, stop, please," I protested frantically, never having experienced such panic in my life. Tears threatened to spill and Colt hadn't even beaten me yet.

Bent, with my arms secured to the wall, I kneeled upon the cabin floor, torso draped over the bed's center.

"No, you can't!" I shrieked, when I felt the cool night air on my skin as Colt lifted my chemise up and out of the way. I had forgotten to be quiet; no longer cared.

I was bare from my waist to the tops of my white stockings.

CHAPTER 7

CHARLOTTE

B ARE. NO MAN had ever laid eyes on my naked backside. No woman or child, for that matter, had ever seen what Colt now freely eyed. Except Daniel, of course, as he'd discovered me washed upon the shore. But he'd been a gentleman and quickly averted his eyes before covering me with his waistcoat.

I felt the air behind me change, move. To my relief, Colt didn't lay a hand upon me—at least not yet. He seemed to be still, staring. Above my own panting, I could hear *his* hard breathing.

I pressed my already-closed legs even tighter together.

"Please. What are you doing?" I cried the stupid question. Colt already made his intent clear. I just couldn't believe it.

I could tell him the truth and stop this horror, I thought. *Tell him I have no memory of the past.*

But then I'd lose my chance at capturing him, as well as expose myself to be manipulated into whatever story he wanted to concoct. Who knew if he wouldn't take advantage of me? Lie to me about my past, knowing I couldn't tell the difference?

I heard the awful sound of a belt buckle jangling.

What had I ever done to deserve this? Surely God, in all his mercy, couldn't allow a good Christian woman to be abused by a criminal.

I must have muttered something to the effect—a prayer whispered in desperation—but I didn't even know I'd done it.

It was only the bark of Colt's laugh that jarred me.

"It's too soon for prayers. I suggest you save the begging for later. And pray only to the man who holds your fate in his hands. Me."

His smug statement did send an initial flash of fear through my belly… but anger quickly followed. Strengthening my resolve, I vowed, *beat me if you must, but I will not break. I will never break. I hate your kind and perhaps God has given me this chance to see all your necks in the noose.*

As if he sensed my courage, Colt wedged one boot between my knees and kicked my legs apart, making me gasp as the act revealed all of my feminine charms to his filthy gaze. Before I could snap my thighs shut, he growled, "Keep your legs spread or I'll call someone in to hold them apart. Do I make myself clear?"

I could only whimper as I struggled against the urge to close my legs. My muscles tensed, fighting instinct.

Dear God, this can't be happening. What could he see?

"Spread. Wide," Colt declared. "If you close your legs, I will call every crew member in here to watch as I belt you. Do I make myself clear? Answer me!"

Tears of fear and humiliation fell as I blinked. Shaking, I breathed, "Yes. Yes, you make yourself clear."

Something made the area between my legs feel warm… maybe it was the heat of this devil's gaze, but it felt as if it came from inside me as well, low in my belly and working shamefully downward.

The snap of a leather belt made me jump, but no pain followed. He'd only done it to taunt me.

It worked.

"Sir, captain, please," I begged.

I can stop this. Just tell him the truth. Whatever I was in the past, whatever made him feel he could do this to me, I do not remember.

Stubbornly, I folded my lips between my teeth.

"Your new lady act has you begging sweeter than you ever begged before. Excellent. I'm going to punish you harder than I ever punished you before."

My stomach dropped at his promise.

Colt leaned down, his warm breath against my ear. "Let's see what other sounds we can wring from your lips, shall we? Let's hear you scream, Miss Charlotte. Your screams will be a balm to my soul."

I shivered. He noticed.

Still against my ear, Colt whispered, "Scared? I'll give you one last chance. If you're ready to talk, I'll untie you. We can sit at the table and if I'm satisfied with what I hear, I'll reconsider your punishment. This is the last opportunity I'm going to give you. Think carefully. Once I start your belting, no prayers will make me stop."

A storm of emotions rose and clashed within me. Fear from his threat, from the imminent pain. Rage from him wielding superior power and strength over me. Fury at my helplessness under it. And still that strange *warmth* tingling in my lower half.

Colt's lips were close enough they almost brushed my ear. I noticed, with alarm, that new, tingly sensation was in my breasts, too.

All I had to do was submit to a child's punishment and this would all be over, I reasoned. I would win. I could continue my charade and use my time aboard this Godforsaken ship to learn their pirate ways and bring them down.

Bravely, I pursed my lips again.

Colt's breathy chuckle tickled my neck. "Think you've won?" he taunted, almost reading my mind. "I was hoping you'd defy me. For two years I've been fantasizing about striping your arse. You're giving me exactly what I want. And when I'm through with you, you'll be begging to tell me anything I ask."

I gulped as Colt rose.

The first blow of the belt came quickly and stung enough to make me reconsider everything. Like a branding iron, a line of fire erupted across the full center of my backside, making me yelp. The room melted away. Colt commanded my full attention as I braced for another lash.

It came, followed by a third so quickly the pain of the second hadn't even fully set in. I threw my head back, pulling desperately at my tied wrists.

Living up to his name, the fourth and fifth lashes landed cruelly on my thighs, wrapping around to my delicate inner-flesh and making me wail. Instinctively, I snapped my legs shut.

"Get those legs spread, now," Colt growled. "Or I'll tie them apart and call every man on this ship to watch."

Whimpering, I spread my legs wider than before. The act called to my attention something… sticky… between my thighs. For a horrified moment, I wondered if I'd wet myself. And then, with a flash of terror, I thought the blackhearted pirate had drawn blood. But neither of those substances felt quite right. There had been no urge to relieve myself and I didn't *feel* injured in the crevice between my legs. In fact, a sort of hungry ache began.

Another cruel blow struck and more tears welled.

Below, I was curiously inflamed. As if engorged and needing something or someone to touch the throbbing area to relieve the swelling.

Another blow struck where my rear met the tops of my thighs and I jumped as far as the restraints allowed. Instead of giving a moment for the pain to settle, Colt belted me once on each thigh again.

"Please, not there!" I cried. Frantic, I tried scrambling up onto the bed to avoid the punishing snap of leather, but Colt's strong hands found my back, pressing me into the mattress.

"Stay down, girl," he commanded. "Back into position. Legs wide."

Whimpering, I obeyed, offering Colt the area he wanted to punish. A maelstrom of confusing emotions raged within.

"You have the power, Charlotte," Colt said, low and controlled. "You can end your punishment any time you want. Just tell me the truth about that night and tell me where it is."

I don't know where it is! I thought, frantically. *I don't have the power.*

"Do you feel like a lady now?" he taunted. "On your knees with your slip around your waist?"

Smack—another blow landed high on my rear, crossing over previous marks.

"Might as well drop the act. It won't save you."

More tears streaked my cheeks. I prayed Colt's arm would miraculously tire before he bruised my rear black and blue, or worse—broke skin.

Crack, and I shrieked.

Yet I would have to break apart physically because I refused to drop my act. There was no other way to end this. In the battle of wills, we were at a stalemate. My backside paid the price until... until, what? He belted the flesh clear off my bones?

Colt wouldn't relent. God, this beast of a man wouldn't stop until he'd broken me.

Crack. I freely sobbed my agony to anyone within earshot.

Colt was too powerful. Too unyielding. Strapping me over his bed. Cruel, just like his name.

Another lash fell and the tip whipped in between my unprotected buttocks to sensitive, forbidden flesh within.

And yet, this wasn't the same cruelty doled out to insubordinate crew. This was a strange, intimate cruelty just for me. A woman.

Such a funny thought. Such a funny feeling at the thought.

A woman... *his* woman? But no, he wasn't familiar with me in that sense. Yet he must have abused me in an intimate manner before. Possibly even stolen a kiss or had been close to it.

What would it be like to kiss him back? To run my hands through his thick, dark head of hair? *What an absurd thought to have at a time like this.* Why would I imagine kissing a man who strapped me?

I pictured Colt's strong arms rising and falling. The muscles in his back rippling with the effort. All that power being used to punish me in a manner somewhere between wayward child and headstrong woman.

Too intimate. Too powerful.

Large hands to punish... or to please.

Smack—another fierce bite of leather against my bare, helpless skin. This time, after I cried, I groaned.

Moaned.

Panted.

My mind clouded with a pleasant fog and I realized my hips were canting, though I couldn't say how long they'd been doing it. My sex swelled further with that strange sensation of *need*. Something tantalizing built inside me, demanding I seek it, chase it. I ground my hips faster against the bed's edge.

It wasn't quite right, I needed something more. Harder. But my hands were tied and I'd have to make do because the feeling ordered me to heed its call, like a master possessing a servant. And I obeyed.

"Oh God, help me," I babbled half-consciously, terrified of moving forward in this diabolic possession, yet unable to retreat. The intensity grew to a crescendo and my hips bucked more frantically as I chased, as I needed... release... now —

— *Yes!* There it was. Indescribable bliss washed over me as I moaned and writhed a lewd dance against the mattress. My heart raced and an ocean roared in my ears so that I could see and hear nothing beyond the rapture.

In the midst of my madness, I had the bizarre thought.

It was as if I touched heaven. Colt led me to heaven... through hell.

When my breathing slowed, the realization that I'd just done something mortifying in front of the strange pirate captain gradually dawned on me. I didn't know why I cared. Fierce shame coursed through me, yet I feared Colt too much to snap my legs shut. I tried freeing my wrists but it did nothing other than earn me more scratches.

He'd stopped belting me. Since when? I searched my foggy brain but couldn't remember when I'd last felt the burn of a leather stroke.

Oh God, what had happened? Had he watched?

Dead silence behind me.

Colt wasn't moving. I couldn't even hear him breathing.

Inside, my thoughts ran in all directions, but outside, I felt limp, weak. The belting and… whatever had just happened had stolen all my energy.

CHAPTER 8

COLT

I'D SEEN MEN the size of mountains break down and beg for mercy. I'd seen knaves I'd thought bore no honor sacrifice themselves for the right cause. I'd seen unimaginable wonders deep inland that no one would believe back in England.

But nothing mystified me more than the wanton writhing of Charlotte, bent over my bed and grinding herself to release.

I snapped my dry mouth shut. The girl I knew before never...

I narrowed my eyes.

Had someone shown her pleasure? That skinny boy called Daniel?

Red threatened the edges of my vision.

But no, astoundingly, she'd *called for help* at the height of it. As if the poor thing couldn't understand what was happening. As if it were the first time.

Her first climax. Brought on by my belt.

Unless it too was an act?

"Please," she breathed, once her convulsions ceased, almost too low for me to hear. "No more."

Kneeling, I brought my face to her cunt and heard her shamed squeak above. My eyes widened. Soaked. *Like a whore,* came the enticing thought. *My whore.*

The erection I'd had since closing the door to my cabin now strained painfully against my breeches.

Was she playing me false somehow?

I moved up the bed, bringing my face to hers. Charlotte squeezed her eyes shut. Even in the dim light, I could see pleasure and mortification flush her face.

"Open your eyes," I ordered, soft, but firm. When she didn't move, I added, "Unless you want to repeat your punishment."

Her eyes flew open. Terrified, tear-filled. *Guileless.*

I stumbled backward as if I'd been struck.

If this was an act, it was her greatest yet. No. *No,* she'd climaxed against the edge of my bed. The evidence was plain. I ran a hand down my face. *Jesus.*

Charlotte didn't dare move. Her slip remained bunched at her hips. Her hair hung in disarray down her back. Her wet cunt spread before me, ready, inviting. A ploy?

Backing up, I palmed my erection, gritting my teeth. Nothing would stop me from shedding the cumbersome breeches and burying myself to the hilt in her sopping cunt right now.

What would she feel like? Taste like?

I grew lightheaded—the idea of lapping my tongue against her slick folds and hearing her moans actually made me dizzy.

Which was probably her intent. Bloody wench. Slippery little liar.

I adjusted my throbbing cock, refusing to even relieve the agony with my own hand. She'd hear it. Know what I was doing right behind her. Know I'd played right into her plan. *My, how she'd grown into a temptress these past two years.*

Damn the bitch. She could spend the night in the brig. She could spend every night there. I'd refuse to even acknowledge… whatever that lust-filled display was supposed to be. She thought to trick me? I'd simply refuse to even speak on it. By now, the crew certainly heard her punishment.

A rise of jealousy flared in my chest. *If they heard what she just did, I'll cut off all their ears. And their tongues, so they can never speak of it.*

Damn them all. And damn her too.

I ran my hand down my face again and withdrew my dirk from its scabbard, now laying upon the table. Reaching over, I sawed her ropes and yanked Charlotte to her feet. She was like jelly, wobbling and ready to collapse. I had no choice but to capture her, to hold her upright.

Charlotte lifted her head as she looked up at me, pink lips parted in shock.

Covering the twitch of my own lips at the urge to kiss her, I sneered, transforming my mouth into a look of scorn instead.

Charlotte drew in a breath as she blinked rapidly. Scared? Confused? I couldn't read it. It didn't matter; it was an act. My eyes flashed down to the golden locket. *But why did she still wear it?*

I watched as she worked to find strength in her knees. Briefly, I contemplated letting her fall, but couldn't make myself do it. I'd left my mark on her; she'd bear welts for days. Even if her little pleasure-taking at my expense had her sleeping soundly for a few hours, the pain in her backside would wake her soon enough, if not the discomfort of the brig itself.

I needed to deposit her there, quickly, and take care of my own needs.

Damned wench. I wouldn't be sleeping soundly either. Not since I found her after all this time, and certainly not after watching her half-naked writhing on my bed.

Did she think it would save her? Well, it had. This time. 'Twas but a stay. I'd resume punishing her the next night. And the next. Until she told me what happened to Maurice, the Crimson Eye, and all the rest of it. I wanted to know everything that had transpired up until now; until I saw her sashaying blithely in that Godforsaken tavern in that ridiculous dress.

"You'll sleep in the brig tonight," I told her, gruffly. To my satisfaction, her eyes rounded. She managed a wobbly step away from me. I could almost see her mind race with fearful possibilities. My cabin might be a threatening prospect but being thrust unprotected amongst the men she'd betrayed was a different level of hell altogether.

A smidge of guilt made me qualify, "I don't trust you on this ship and I don't trust the crew with you. Not all of them. I can't say one of them won't try to kill you in the night. I can't say you wouldn't deserve it. In his eyes anyway. But at least no one will *touch* you in there."

A bit of the spitfire returned as she declared, "You'll protect me from the molestation of your crew but not from murder? Some captain you are."

"You want to tell me what happened that night? I'll bring you above deck right now and you can explain to all of us how it transpired."

For a moment, she searched my face, and I thought she'd capitulate.

Stubborn as ever, she looked away in refusal.

CHAPTER 9

COLT

S HE SHOULD CONSIDER herself lucky I didn't remove the hammock before depositing her in *The Dread Night's* tiny prison. Although the floor might be more comfortable than that rough netting cutting into her sore flesh.

After her wanton performance, I expected Charlotte to comment on the bulge below my waist, but she failed to even *notice.* She never broke from her act, going so far as to feign disorientation through the ship's passages, as if she didn't know up from down.

I'd instruct the crew to humor her—I didn't plan on wasting any energy arguing with her to drop the charade. I planned on re-directing it into her punishments. If she thought clinging to her newly formed identity as a lady would save her, I'd simply raise my retribution until she broke. She wasn't vexing me; she was simply increasing my enjoyment.

Well. I adjusted my erection once more. *She was causing some agitation.*

"You can't mean to leave me here," she cried, as I opened the door to the metal cell.

As if you haven't been imprisoned in a similar brig many nights before.

"Oh, but I do," I said, stalking toward her and forcing her backwards.

"I think you might grow to prefer the brig," I took another step forward and through sheer intimidation, she retreated a step, placing herself in the tiny prison, "because when I release you, Miss Charlotte, it will only be to drag you back into my cabin and stripe you with my belt again."

I relished how the color drained from her face. It *had* to be real. How could she fake it? But then, she truly had always feared the belt, lady or no.

She backed further into the ship's prison. I gave her my cruelest smile, the one I saved for enemies before running my blade through their gut.

"There's so much flesh to mark, maybe we'll try new areas tomorrow. Maybe we'll try them all."

Closing the door, I locked her safely inside. Her hands flew to her neck, rubbing anxiously as her eyes darted about the small cell.

"Maybe we'll try the cat on you next time. See where each of her nine tails can do the most damage."

At those words, she wobbled as if she'd faint.

I, however, only caused myself greater discomfort as I imagined exactly that—Charlotte spread upon my bed, leather flicking her most tender regions—and marveled at the wonder of her getting wet at my hands, my discipline. It gave rise to a strange exultation in my chest.

Storming out of the hull, I found Conks outside the doorway, rubbing his gray whiskers in thought. A man of forty-five, he'd grayed by his thirties, as if his outside matched the maturity of a man beyond his years, the wisdom of the old soul within.

"Keep an eye on her," I ordered.

"Aye."

"Some of the crew will be angry. They'll try to get answers from her themselves."

"Aye."

"I don't want her…" I struggled to find the word. *Hurt? Mistreated?* Lies. I wanted that, and more. I just wanted it at my own hands. And not… permanent.

"I don't want her damaged," I said, as if she were stolen booty.

Maybe she was. Maybe she always was.

"I can't blame them for trying anything they can," I added, angrily.

"Can't really blame her, either," Conks intoned, hands in his pockets and rocking back on his heels.

I shot him a look. Couldn't I?

"Were she a man, I'd have put her to death already."

"She might prefer it to whatever you have planned." Another dark look from me and Conks added respectfully, "Captain."

I gnashed my teeth. My discomfort might have escaped Charlotte's notice but I knew it hadn't escaped Conks's. He'd grown soft for her. Many had. Many hadn't. Sorting out who felt what—what each man wanted to do with her—was going to be a problem.

Almost as much as sorting out what I wanted to bloody do with her.

Wring her neck. Flog her. Fuck her.

I shook the thought from my head, focusing on the dimly lit hallway. My ship. My command.

Conks had spent almost as much time with Charlotte as he did with Johnson; loved her almost as much.

"Just… watch her," I said, brushing past him down the hall.

"They're on your side," Conks called out, stopping me. I turned only my head, to listen. "Most of them," he added, ominously.

I grunted my reply and continued through the darkness.

I hadn't lost control of my men. *They are on my side.* But what side was I on?

Flog her. Fuck her.

Fuck *me*.

I stalked up to my cabin. I hadn't meant to kiss her. Perhaps I belted her harder for my own mistake, to prove I didn't mean it. If she wasn't a lying knave I might feel guilty about it.

Maybe that was her fucking plan?

Alone, I slammed the cabin door and fumbled at my lacings. I didn't even make it onto the bed. Standing with one arm braced high on the bed's wood frame—right above where she'd recently bent—I grasped my cock and pumped hard. I pictured Charlotte spread and moaning, dripping for me. With each pump of my fist, I hated her for it. I thought of punishing her harder; thought of her thanking me for it. I imagined, instead of her cries to the lord, she'd cried my name. Called for me, begged me to take her. I pictured sliding my cock into her tight, wet passage and taking my pleasure with her pain, muting that pain into her pleasure.

Groaning, head thrown back, my orgasm ripped through me faster than a boy at his first tumble. I shot ropes of seed onto the bedding, sullying it.

I wanted to drag Charlotte by the hair back to my cabin and bid her lick it up.

An idea for another night.

CHAPTER 10

CHARLOTTE

I BEGAN TO UNDERSTAND, and I was disgusted with myself.

My own body succumbed to pleasure in a way known only to men. And whores perhaps. But no Godly woman sought such bliss. A lady wasn't even capable. Was she?

And even if she was (which she *wasn't*) a beast of man like Colt couldn't stir such passion in a woman.

And if he had (which he *hadn't*) it wasn't because of his punishment.

No, no. There must exist some other explanation. An episode of some sort, brought on by pain and terror. The mind, in a desperate attempt to save itself, worked to find pleasure to escape the pain. Obviously.

But why did I *still* feel an ache between my legs?

Why did I have a troubling dream about Colt—the man I hated—relieving that ache with those long fingers?

CHAPTER 11

CHARLOTTE

REASON ROSE WITH the sun.

I despised the pirate captain more than ever. Naturally. I'd have my vengeance when we docked back in Carolina. Maybe I'd be lucky enough to see *him* lashed before they hanged him. *His strong back bare for my viewing. The corded muscles in his arms straining as he thrashed. His beautiful lips snarling, refusing to cry out.*

Those long legs… had a man ever possessed such long legs before?

I shook my head. What was I thinking about?

Ah, yes, whipping. The tables turning and Colt being under *my* control.

I meant our control—the townsfolk.

Yes, he'd be punished according to the law. I'd make sure I was the last thing those chilling, dark eyes saw before they dimmed forever.

A scrape sounded from my left and I bolted upright.

"Did you sleep well, Miss Charlotte?" the man asked,

coming into my room and carrying a cup of some kind. *Conks,* I'd heard him called.

"Very well, thank you," I lied, jutting my chin. He'd probably heard my screams, but I wasn't going to admit to anything unless I had to.

"Drink this," he said gently, sliding the glass through the bars of my cage.

I hesitated.

"It won't hurt you. It will help with the... discomfort," he explained.

My face reddened. So, he knew.

"It's not that," I protested, looking at my feet. "It's that I need to... relieve myself. I'm afraid if I drink anything more, I won't be able to wait any longer and there's no means to do what I need in this cage."

"Then we should leave you in there as a lesson," came the proclamation from the doorway.

Colt.

My face burned. *How long had he been listening?*

"You're vile," I spat. Turning to Conks, I lied haughtily, "Thank you, but I don't need anything to help. I'm not in any discomfort at all."

Colt, the smug bastard, laughed. "Perhaps you don't need to relieve yourself either?" He laughed harder at the panic rimming my eyes. Without turning to Conks, he said, "You heard the lady. She doesn't need your tonic. Leave us and take it with you when you go."

Colt watched me carefully, but I wouldn't allow him to see my disappointment. My backside smarted. I wanted that tonic. Once alone, I grasped the bars of the cell and fixed Colt with my angriest stare.

"You are truly vile," I swore.

"So you've said," Colt replied. Pacing, he mused, "I'll make you a deal. Tell me what happened that night and I'll release you. I'll give you the privacy you require to… take care of your needs."

I looked away. *I'd rather soil myself than give up my plans that easily.*

I heard Colt make a strange noise, between a sigh and a huff, before turning to leave.

"Wait!" I cried. "Please. Don't."

He stopped. My whole body ran hot with shame.

"Please. I have to… please don't make me. Here. Like this."

"What will you give me in return?" he asked.

I chewed my lip. "What do you want?"

"I want you to answer my questions."

Dammit. I couldn't do that convincingly; I was sure I'd trip up. Colt turned away again, as if to resume walking.

Maybe I could negotiate?

"Alright," I said, before he could disappear and leave me desperate. "One."

CHAPTER 12

COLT

WHY DID YOU *kill Maurice? Where is the Crimson Eye? What happened to the gold?* Pertinent questions to ask. Instead, like an utter fool, I demanded, "What were you thinking when you saw me in the tavern? *Us,*" I corrected, gruffly. "Saw me and the crew?"

Surprised as much as I was by the question, Charlotte blinked her wide, hazel eyes, then narrowed them, suspicious.

The question threw her. Fine. Good. Yes, that was my clever intention all along.

"Thinking?" she repeated. "I was… um… frightened?"

"Obvious," I dismissed, though it wasn't. For all I knew, feigning fear was a part of her plan. Maybe she wanted to get caught, to get back onto my ship for some reason. Except this was no longer the same ship… so maybe she wanted to speak with someone in my crew? Maybe she had worked with one of the men and was secretly coordinating… I shook my head. It didn't make any sense. None of this made sense. Coordinating what, after two years?

"I was," Charlotte searched the brig, as if the answer lay somewhere around her, "surprised to see you."

Again, it came out like a question. I frowned.

"You agreed to tell the truth for one question. Not to play the lady act. What exactly was going through that pretty little head of yours when you walked blithely into the tavern? Why not hide? Did you think to shock me?"

"I—yes." Charlotte lifted her chin. "I thought you'd be stunned to see me, but I didn't count on being stunned by you. You've changed."

I searched her face for the lie. I had cut my long hair. Allowed the stubble on my face to grow without scraping it for several days.

"You knew I'd take you, punish you," I insisted. "Why not run? Why play like you're a lady who's never been aboard a ship before?"

Charlotte shut down, I could see it as I watched her face smooth into indifference. "You said one question. May I please be released from this hold now?"

What game was this? I fisted my hands at my sides. I could break her. She knew it. I could torture her until she talked. So why did she willingly place herself in my hands? Why under the guise of a ladyship?

None of it made any sense. Every action of mine own felt like it played into her diabolical plan.

I needed to do what she wouldn't expect.

I smiled, baring teeth as I unlocked the cell door and stepped aside.

"My lady," I bowed with a flourish. "My ship is yours. During the day, you're free to roam as you will and do as you please."

Not missing my implication, she asked, "And the night?"

"At night I'll do *I* will and as *I* please. You'll return to my cabin. We'll have our *discussion* again. And when I'm through with you, I'll deposit you here, to sleep in your cell."

"You call beating a lady a discussion?" she said, snarling the accusation.

"No," I replied, stepping close so that she had to look up to meet my eyes. "Beating a lady is a despicable act. Last night involved neither a beating nor a lady."

The corners of her pretty mouth turned down, affronted.

"The journey to Nassau is several days. That's many evenings for us to *discuss* matters. The power to stop anytime is all yours, Miss Charlotte. Just say the word."

I held her gaze, almost afraid she'd fold and end the game I didn't want to admit I might enjoy playing.

"I don't know what you mean," she said, brushing past me.

A grin I shouldn't have allowed crept across my face.

CHAPTER 13

CHARLOTTE

I COULDN'T EXPLORE THE ship in a chemise. I wouldn't deign to ask Colt for something to wear. But the man who'd stood outside the brig, Conks… he seemed to at least respect a woman's dignity.

I found the old sailor near the doorway. Maybe he'd stood by to eavesdrop and spread gossip amongst the crew. Or could he have waited, ready to intervene on my behalf?

Were we friends in another life?

Before I could speak, Conks flourished the tonic I'd refused.

Blushing, I grasped it and said, "Thank you."

After gulping the bitter, medicinal concoction, I asked the kind crewman, "Could you help me find my dress or, at least, something else to wear?"

He stroked his graying whiskers and said, "Johnson's already got something set aside for you."

We found Johnson below deck, having sourced a pair of clean breeches and a blouse with frilled-trim. It wasn't clothing fit for a woman, but it was better than ambling about in nothing but my slip.

"No boots," the tall, skinny crewmate said. From his height and his voice, I recognized Johnson as being the eloquent man who'd announced Captain Colt back in our tavern. "I can't get you those without the captain's approval."

"This is more than enough, thank you," I replied, grateful. Although I didn't fancy exploring the ship barefoot, at least I had something to cover my body.

Not that it matters come moonrise, I thought, heart skipping a beat. *Colt will easily strip it all off again.*

Neither Johnson nor Conks spoke much, waiting with patient curiosity and filling the air with an anticipatory tension.

"I—it's been a long time since we've talked," I said, unsure how much of my supposed lady act I wanted to drop around these two men. But I needed to glean *some* information, otherwise I'd be lost, and that could leave Colt with a massive advantage if he ever saw through me.

"Aye, and I've so missed our chats," Johnson replied with a twinkle in his eye.

"Are you as angry with me as your captain, for my supposed crimes?" I tried.

What crimes, I wanted to ask. *What is it he thinks that I've done?*

"We're glad you're alive, first. And we're disappointed you ran off without saying goodbye or explaining your actions, second," Johnson said with a sad, kind smile. "You know we'd have understood. But we know you had your reasons. Just like we know you have your reasons for whatever it is you're doing right now."

We. He continually said *we*. Were Conks and Johnson…
together? In the Penningham's tavern, I'd heard stories of
such partnerships as common amongst pirates, but I hadn't
known any couples to speak openly in our small settlement.

Johnson had replied with genuine vulnerability and care.
I couldn't help but whisper, "I'm sorry to have let you down."

"'S'alright," Conks chimed in. "These things have a way of
working out, in the end. Though I dare say the captain's gonna
make your end pay for it, until you tell him the truth. I'll
keep a bottle of my special tonic on hand for the mornings."

I couldn't have turned any redder. The fact that Colt
planned to punish me, intimately, was horrid enough. Having
it whispered about by the crew was utterly humiliating.
Probably to Colt's delight.

I'd planned on probing for more information, but instead
I stammered, "I—uh, better get dressed now."

After being left alone and changing into the clothing
provided, I made my way above deck to take in the salt air. It
was a bright, beautiful day, with only hints of clouds dotting
the sky. Men bustled at their work stations or lazed about
chatting through breaks.

My appearance immediately drew attention and I could
see the mixed reaction in the crew's eyes. Some men regarded
me with suspicion and anger, some with relief and pity, and
others with small-but-welcoming smiles, half-hidden beneath
tipped hats.

Sometimes all possible reactions flitted across a single
man's face in rapid succession.

Robert the Red's unconcealed rage stood out amongst the
crew. *Redhands,* I'd heard him called. His gaze turned my
knees to jelly and I had the intrusive thought that he'd have

been better nicknamed Bloodhands, because he looked as if he wanted my blood upon his.

My throat caught. *What had I done? Could it be true?*

I backed away, hurrying to the emptiest part of the deck. The constant rocking of the ship didn't disturb me and *that* disturbed me. Some part of my brain clung to the idea that this was all a part of an elaborate ploy, that I'd never really been aboard a pirate's ship, let alone a member of the crew. But even I wasn't stubborn enough to deny it any longer.

The only way I could bear this knowledge was if I'd been a prisoner and Colt's treatment of me confirmed I *had,* in some manner.

Curious.

I didn't know what to do with myself throughout the day and spent hours staring at the sea as if it could give me answers. I watched the sun move across the sky with increasing dread. When my legs stiffened, I ambled about the ship, but whenever I saw Colt, I immediately scurried in the opposite direction. Clearly, the crew had been instructed not to engage with me because they watched my movements with accusing eyes but never dared to speak.

Midday, Conks brought me to the galley and introduced me to a polite but reserved crewman named Miguel. Responsible for preparing everyone's meals and for maintaining their rations of food and spirits, Miguel made me a meal of eggs and biscuits. The taciturn cook said nothing but joined me as I ate, and a warm feeling of security enveloped me. In my shrouded past, had we dined together many times before? The way his eyes darted to me and quickly looked away told me we'd meant *something* to one another. And if we weren't allies before, I wondered if I could gain his friendship in the present? If I could manage private access to the food stores, I could poison them and take down the entire crew in one swoop. I wouldn't have to report back to Daniel or send our townsmen into battle.

Of course, there was the obvious problem of not having access to any poison. Perhaps some could be acquired when we docked in Nassau.

After I'd eaten the last crumb from my plate, Miguel startled me by mumbling, "I know you had good reason."

"Pardon?" I whispered, staring into his deep brown eyes. "What do you mean?"

"For whatcha done," he muttered, looking at me with almost pleading eyes. "For stealing the gold and-"

Miguel quickly cut himself off and I stiffened, hearing someone enter the door at my back. I turned to see Conks had come to collect me.

Was I but a common thief? *No, it couldn't be true.*

Better than a common whore, argued a voice inside my head.

You are, said another voice. *Colt whipped the whore to a wailing release last night.*

I'd gone mad. Having no past for so long and being so close to answers, the space in my mind opened, filling with voices frantically searching for the truth.

"Thank you for a lovely meal," I told Miguel, and he nodded as Conks and I took our leave.

"I wanted to check on you but I'm actually in the middle of some work with Johnson. Will you be alright on your own for the rest of the day? I'll return at supper and we can eat in the galley."

I heard what Conks wasn't outright saying—that I was

to stay away from the crew. Either because Colt had ordered it or because perhaps Conks worried for my safety.

"Of course I'll be fine." I laid a gentle hand upon Conk's bicep and whispered, "But I was wondering about the supposed gold in question…"

Conks eyes flashed and I realized it was true. *Was I a common thief?*

Surely, I had a reason. Maybe it was my gold to begin with and I was only stealing it back. Maybe I needed it to escape this Godforsaken ship.

"I was just hoping that the absence of the gold… didn't affect you personally."

Conks's eyes clouded with sadness. "Are you asking if the captain took it out on me when you stole his bag o' bits? Nah. That was the least of his worries that morning."

I couldn't say why exactly that relaxed me, but it did. I didn't want to have hurt the kind man before me—although I'd apparently disappointed him, as Johnson said.

"I don't think the captain cares much about the gold, considering what else you stole."

I snapped to attention. *What else could there be?*

"But don't you worry, the crew don't know about that. 'Cept Robert and maybe one or two others. If they knew, I don't think you'd survive on *The Dread Night* very long. The captain wasn't planning on telling anyone until he had the profit to be shared. Too much could go wrong beforehand." Conks shrugged. "And it did, though never in the way he presumed."

My head swum. *No. I'm a lady, not a thief.*

"I reckon he'll wring a confession out of you one way or another before he ever lets you off this ship," Conks said. "So it would be in your best interest to tell the captain what he wants to know. The longer you wait, the harder you'll make it on yourself."

I blushed at the knowing look Conks gave me before taking his leave.

Alone once more, I explored below deck, surprised to find the ship much tidier than I'd expected. Storage was neatly arranged and labeled. Rations and supplies were tracked with precision. And despite the chore it must be to keep a ship clean from mud and mold, the cargo hold was spotless—save the area for livestock, understandably, which bore a distinctive odor that couldn't be easily masked.

As I explored, I was shocked to find several chickens and even a goat aboard. Perhaps my eggs had come fresh from the small coop.

"Caged like me," I whispered to the noisy little creatures.

Captain Colton Pearce ran a tight ship. I tried to reconcile the murderous pirate to the man with such immaculate and exacting standards for cleanliness and had difficulty. I tried to mesh both truths with the image of the devil who kissed me and whipped me and found it all just a pile of contradictions.

The rest of the day passed in a daze. I dined with Miguel, but Conks joined, making it impossible for me to try to probe for information. I could tell I was being contained, as the rest of the crew supped above deck. Their raucous laughter and songs carried down to the galley, filling me with a strange sense of longing or wistfulness I didn't understand.

Not to join them, I reasoned. *Simply to sing. I miss singing, especially for a crowd.*

Rum was served and with unsteady hands I drank all of it from my cup. Whatever was to befall me that evening, I considered it a blessed fortification. The only other thing I could do was renew my vows not to break, and to strengthen my resolve to bring down these vile pirates from within.

After we finished our meal of cod, cabbage, and a surprising array of fresh fruits, I had nothing left to do but wait with increasing fear. At dusk, I stood at the stern while the sun melted into the horizon.

Don't go, I begged. *Stay and light the sky. When you plunge this earth into darkness, my world will darken along with it.*

At the thought, the image of Colt's black eyes passed through my mind. Certainly, such a color for eyes did not exist. Unless some devilry had blackened them to match his soul.

Nonsense, Charlotte, I warned. *They're just a deep brown.*

I'd have to keep my wits about me to survive whatever brutal treatment the captain planned and to outmaneuver the monster. Those keen eyes seemed to glean more than other men saw.

Even before he'd had free view of all my private, womanly areas, I thought with shame and resentment.

I squeezed the railing until my knuckles turned white. For some reason, I squeezed my thighs together too. My heart raced and I could feel myself dampen with sweat in a very un-ladylike manner. I looked up to see the moon shining brighter, bolder.

Don't, I begged that glowing orb. *Hide yourself. Retreat and keep me safe.*

But the moon was as cold and unfeeling as the captain himself, whose ominous footsteps I now heard thudding behind me.

CHAPTER 14

COLT

I SAID NOT A word as I dragged Charlotte to my cabin. I wouldn't give her snake-tongue the opportunity to lie her way out of what she had coming.

I'd stayed away from her all day for the same reason.

Fuck. That was a half-truth. I'd stayed away from her because I needed to clear my head and examine what had happened the night before, to review the events as they unfolded and to look for clues.

I had reviewed the events repeatedly in the privacy of my cabin, as planned. With my hands around my cock.

Unplanned.

It may have made me quicker than I'd wanted when I slammed the door behind us and moved Charlotte deeper into my cabin. I could tell my haste frightened her as I tied her wrists, tighter than necessary, to a beam above her head.

Without preamble, I grabbed the leather crop from my drawers. Meant for the hides of horses, it would do wonders on Charlotte.

"Are you going to beat me into submission each night?" she cried. "Is that your diabolical plan, captain?" Although she'd spat it with defiance, her voice caught at the end.

"Are you ready to confess?" I asked, pausing.

Say no, came an irrational voice in my head.

I shook it away. Of course I wanted her to tell me the truth. Immediately.

Yet something in my chest relaxed when she refused, a tension ebbed and made room for excitement to flow in its place.

"Please, wait, wait," Charlotte babbled when I fisted the neck of her shirt.

Ignoring her, I tore down the middle of her garment and her breasts spilled forth. Heavy and round, nipples pert and pink. Charlotte tucked her head against her shoulder, hiding. Briefly, I debated cutting the remainder of the garment from her arms, but it hung limp on either side of her torso and wouldn't impede my strokes.

Of which, there'd be plenty. Breasts, nipples, tight little stomach. All begging to be marked.

I could touch her right now, I thought. She was helpless to stop me. My thumb and forefinger rubbed against each other, pantomiming rolling one of those hard nipples between their grasp. My tongue snaked along the back of my teeth, eager to lick, to suck, to bite.

My desire by her design, no doubt. I could see it in the way she arched ever-so-slightly, as if she didn't know she was doing it. Offering her breasts to me, to use as I saw fit. Her neck stretched, angling to the side. Like prey having given up, presenting its most vulnerable areas to the predator in submission.

I tilted my own head.

Or was it the opposite… Charlotte stretching to escape, to retreat?

The devil of a woman was always so hard to read.

Who cared what she thought or wanted? I glanced down, knowing what I desired.

I'd never seen her breasts after that day, that fateful day four years ago.

Breasts that weren't as tempting as now. She'd been a skinny thing, late to fill out. The woman struggling before me now had hips soft and round, breasts curved and swollen. Woman, all fucking woman.

Stepping back before I could do something foolish, I raised the riding crop and brought it down on the top of her breast with medium force, testing. I'd never whipped her there before and didn't know what would be too much or too little.

Charlotte threw her head back with a yelp as a little pink mark appeared.

"Noo…" she whined, so sweetly.

I shrugged. "We can stop whenever you like. Just tell me what happened."

Charlotte's reply was to turn her head to the other side, so I answered by applying my leather to her other breast.

Her squeal morphed into a groan.

A small part of me thought she'd start talking when I bared her breasts. A larger part thought it would be from the first kiss of the crop. Seeing as how neither had the necessary effect, I began whipping her in earnest—licks to the underside of her breasts, lighter slaps against her stomach, cruel snaps to the area nearest her nipples.

The stubborn wench didn't talk. She gritted her teeth and

determination, if not outright defiance, blazed in her eyes when she met my stare.

Eyes blazing right back, I tapped directly the tip of one nipple, letting her know where my next stroke would fall.

"No, please, no!" She wailed and jerked as far as the ropes would allow.

Charlotte squealed when the pain registered. Her face flushed with a sheen of sweat.

"Keep screaming. I'll have your screams or I'll have your confession. Both delight me."

"Nooo…" she pled, rocking her head back and forth as I aimed the leather at her other nipple.

I grinned and cocked one eyebrow. A question.

She clamped her lips. An answer.

I brought down the crop, hard.

Charlotte shrieked even louder this time, twisting and writhing in a most erotic dance of pain.

After pausing to see if she changed her mind, I shrugged and I resumed striking her vulnerable breasts, then moved on to her sides and low on her belly.

Charlotte panted and sweated… and so did I. The only difference was I controlled my labored breathing, my movements. Charlotte's motions were erratic, guided by the sting of the crop. *Guided by me.* I was so transfixed with a heady sense of power that for a few moments I didn't notice a change in her expression. When I took better stock of her face, she seemed in a daze of some kind, and I cursed myself for not paying better attention.

It was almost as if the blows didn't hurt her as much. I paused, brow furrowed. She seemed distanced from the crop, from even the ship.

"Charlotte? Charlotte, can you hear me?"

Her only reply was the lolling of her head to one side as she moaned softly.

I gently-but-firmly grabbed her chin, the pads of my fingertips digging into her flesh to hold her head straight. I expected the usual flash of annoyance or defiance, but she barely reacted to my manhandling, save the fluttering of her eyes. Charlotte allowed herself to be guided forward, but as soon as I released her, her head fell back to the side.

Her eyes were hooded as her head tilted back. Her breasts were high, full. *With desire?* I shook my head. Could she fake such a reaction? How?

Frowning, I studied her. She seemed far away, as if in a state of rapture. I looked down at the menacing implement in my hands. *From my crop?*

It couldn't be. Even though I'd had similar evidence from the night before, I couldn't believe it. It had to be an act, I thought, blinking. But why, to what end? If she was playing the lady, what lady would so wantonly grind herself to orgasm before the man standing above her, belt in hand?

None of this made any sense. Her games were always… I cursed under my breath, hating to admit it. Her games were always one step ahead of me. She was always one step ahead of me.

But this didn't feel like a game.

Testing, I touched the tip of the crop to her nipples, caressing gently.

Eyes still shut, Charlotte moaned softly and arched into the leather.

With the flick of my hand, I gave her one sharp smack directly beneath her nipple.

Throwing her head back, she cried out her pleasure.

I licked my lips. *Unmistakably,* that was pleasure. A rush of power and euphoria raced through my brain.

What had changed in the past two years? Red threatened the edges of my vision. Had some other man touched her? Taught her the ways of passion?

Charlotte-the-traitor I wanted to strip bare and punish before a tavern full of drunk men.

Charlotte-the-wanton stirred an almost painful desire to toss her limp body onto my bed. To make her cry out from my cock the same as she had from my crop.

I shook my head, equally entranced. I'd been so focused *I* barely noticed the cabin around me. I could have been standing above deck, off the ship entirely, or somewhere on a beach in the bright afternoon, and I wouldn't have noticed anything but Charlotte.

Another emotion swelled in my chest, something like protectiveness. Whatever was happening, I had stay in control, for her sake. And for my sake, I couldn't take her to bed.

She might gut me in my sleep.

I'd have never thought her capable but she'd proved willing to do many things I'd never before believed.

Charlotte hung from the beam, limp, head resting on one arm for support.

I could release her and restrain her to my bed.

Scratching my stubble, I questioned, *but was that a part of her plan?*

No, I'd already commanded it—she needed to sleep in the brig. But not half-naked. Fumbling through a trunk, I found my softest shirt. Charlotte didn't move. Whatever strangeness had seized her, it was as all-encompassing as the night before. I'd wager that if I dipped my hand inside her breeches, I'd find her dripping down her creamy thighs.

I adjusted the strain in my own breeches. *Who was being tortured again?*

The fantasy of applying ointment to her marks flashed through my mind but I dismissed it. She didn't deserve the relief and I couldn't handle rubbing my hands all over her breasts without throwing her onto the bed.

Damn her to hell.

Scratch that. I was the one probably headed in that direction.

I chuckled. *But what would be my hell exactly?* Because it looked a lot like this, right now. Charlotte, half naked, and me unable to touch her.

Watching another man touch her, came the infuriating thought.

I'd kill him, I vowed, even though Charlotte was the one I should want to murder.

Adjusting my waistcoat, I determined three things. One, I'd deposit Charlotte in the brig. Two, I'd find some rum above deck. And three, I'd drink until I passed out. A fine plan indeed.

When I cut her ropes, I braced and, sure enough, she collapsed into my arms.

"Charlotte, can you hear me?"

She moaned her reply through pink, parted lips.

"I'm going to put this shirt on you," I explained, guiding her to the bed. "Lift your arms."

Incapable of obeying even the slightest command, I had to hold each delicate arm aloft while I slid the garment over her battered torso. Her brow furrowed slightly in pain but smoothed once the garment lay flat.

My eyes flicked down to her breeches and I didn't like the access they blocked. Depositing Charlotte on the bed, I rummaged through my drawers until I found an old skirt that would fit.

Hers. I'd moved it from our old ship to this one. For a time, it had smelled like her. Until the salt of the sea faded the scent, as it did most things.

With Charlotte in a daze, I slid her breeches from her legs and buttoned her into the skirt, denying myself the glimpses between her legs that I desired, because I couldn't torture myself any more for the evening.

Realizing she couldn't walk, I scooped her up and carried her out of my cabin, careful not to smack her head against the doorframe or the walls of the ship's tight hallways. Throughout, Charlotte hovered in a strange state between sleep and wakefulness.

Conks was thankfully absent when I reached the brig. I didn't want his accusing eyes and couldn't explain what happened to Charlotte anyway. Using my foot, I slid the prison door wide.

Charlotte didn't stir, even as I maneuvered her into the hammock. Before I could change my mind, I stripped my waistcoat, balled it into a makeshift pillow, and wedged it beneath Charlotte's head. Her eyes had closed, leading me to believe she'd fallen asleep.

Until under her breath she murmured, *"Colt."*

Captivated, I brought my fingers to her face, tracing her cheekbone and the outline of her lips. She sighed, parting her mouth like an invitation.

Without thinking, I slipped my finger inside, probing deeply. Instantly, Charlotte sucked, her tongue laving my digit. She moaned as if I rewarded her with my penetration and it went straight to my cock. It was impossible not to imagine her hot, wet mouth around it.

Quickly, I withdrew my finger and though she didn't open her eyes, she gave a little squeal of protest. Backing away, I brought my finger to my own lips and sucked her saliva from it, picturing what it would be like to freely swipe my tongue inside that willing mouth.

I closed the cell and locked her in, frowning. That was twice now I'd resolved to punish her until she broke, and twice she'd thwarted me.

Although, she'd broken in another manner entirely; once in a way I'd never anticipated and another in which I couldn't explain.

Had she blossomed into a temptress in my absence? Was that her game? To beguile me? Break me with lust and longing?

Maybe I'd break her with lust and longing first.

Storming above deck, I joined Conks and Johnson at the table they'd dragged from the galley. Gentle waves rocked the ship and a light wind gave us fair speed.

"Rum," I ordered, and Johnson poured me a drink. From the corner of my eye, I caught a small nod he gave Conks.

"What you're doing to the girl ain't right," Conks said, spinning his cup.

"And you think a pleasant chat will get us the answers we need?" I countered.

"But why we all gotta play along with her game?" Sedge piped up with anger from across the table. "To learn the truth or so you have an excuse to see what's under her skirts?"

Before I could reply, Robert plopped down next to me, clapping me on the back too presumptuously. "Heard the bitch squeal, captain. Nice work. A few more nights under your hands and she'll be singing like a bird for us."

I grunted. Sharing a cup with my men had been a mistake. I didn't want their opinions.

I took another deep swig of rum. *But I needed them.*

Charlotte's game provided a distraction, an amusement. The trip to Nassau would take several more days and she wasn't going to escape again anytime soon. Once we docked, I'd get each of the men a turn to crack jenny's cup, on me. Maybe I could find a whore for myself while I was at it.

With honied hair and hazel eyes. Green by the light of the sun and brown by the moon. With an elegant neck to wring as I spent my seed inside her.

I scowled and drank deeper.

Charlotte thought I meant to beat her into submission? Then I'd unsettle her by devising more intimate punishments for her displeasure.

CHAPTER 15

CHARLOTTE

ONKS'S KIND FACE was the first thing to greet me as I awoke the next morning.

The unwelcome rush of memories was the second.

I thought Captain Colt would be a quickly-following third, but he didn't appear. Instead, I looked down in surprise to realize my clothing had been changed. I wore a man's shirt and a lady's skirt… though I bore no stockings beneath the skirt to cover my legs nor any apparel to guard my intimate regions.

I smoothed my hair into what few pins remained in an effort to maintain some dignity.

Hearing me stir, Conks entered the hull and this time, I gratefully accepted the tonic he proffered.

Drinking the contents, images of the night before flashed through my mind. Curiously, the later into the evening the memories progressed, the fuzzier they became. I recalled with clarity Colt stringing me to his ceiling and wielding that awful leather with precision upon my bare breasts. Each hit stung so dreadfully I'd slipped into a strange state of mind where they didn't smart as badly.

For my own protection, as I'd done before. Clearly.

I'd gone to a place where, instead, it began to feel almost… pleasurable.

Curiouser still, I'd next travelled to a world where I hardly felt anything at all or barely even registered my surroundings. As I tried to recall what transpired toward the evening's conclusion, it was as if a gray mist clouded my eyes, blurring out the picture of Colt's cabin.

Released from my cell by Conks, I was once again free to amble *The Dread Night* alone, and the first place I headed was the galley. I wanted to see if I could loosen Miguel's lips a little more, but when I arrived he grumbled something about being busy with his duties and politely—but quickly—escorted me out.

Someone had obviously instructed, or re-instructed him, not to speak to me about past events. Sighing, I instead headed above deck.

Low clouds hung in the sky and the seas were a bit choppy. Yet something about the crisp air and feisty waves stirred my soul. I made my way to the forecastle deck, wanting to feel the wind upon my cheeks. Crewmen whispered as I passed, but none dared approach. I wondered if the gray skies evoked a feeling of wistfulness in the men as well, because I heard a few begin a shanty that was quickly picked up by the rest of the crew as they worked. I didn't want to turn around and let them know I listened, but I couldn't help but tap my foot in time to the beat.

These men are murderers and thieves, I reminded myself. *Your goal is to learn more of their ways and to perhaps coordinate a capture with Daniel. They are the enemy.*

When the song repeated the chorus a final three times, it died down, and I heard footsteps behind me. I spun, expecting to see Colt, but it was Redhands. Nothing about Robert was actually red. His hair was brown, his eyes were blue, and his skin was as tanned as any sailor's. Robert was tall and well-built, though not as muscular as Colt.

Though he seemed higher-ranking than the other men, nothing about his approach signaled any intent to act according to station. Robert moved closer to me in a slow manner, clearly meant to intimidate while at the same time, making it difficult for me to outright claim he did anything wrong.

"You think I don't know?" he snarled between clenched teeth, then cocked a half-grin full of hate. "You always thought I didn't have as much power as the captain on this ship, just because I don't have the title."

Yet, came the unspoken promise to the end of that sentence. *I don't have the title yet.*

"I—no," I stammered, unsure what to say to appease him.

"Of course I know about the Crimson Eye," Robert said, cornering me against the ship's rail. "And I want to know what you did with it. Sell it, eh? Find yourself a nice buyer with that pretty little face?"

Crimson Eye? What in the world was that?

Robert slid his dirk from its sheath with slow, intentional malice. "What if I cut up that pretty little face of yours? How many slices of my blade would it take before you started talking?"

"I—I don't know what you're talking about," I cried, retreating into the safety of my act. "I know nothing of a Crimson Eye and I surely haven't taken it. Good day, sir,"

I declared, attempting to end the conversation and escape Robert's threats.

"Don't you dare dismiss me," he snarled, grabbing my bicep and shoving his blade beneath my throat.

My stomach barely had time to drop before Colt appeared, smacking Robert's arm away from my neck.

"Cut it out, Robert," Colt ordered. "You're the one who's supposed to punish any men who touch her, not break the rules I gave you to enforce."

"I'm done playing her game!" Robert spat, pointing angrily. "She flounces around our ship while taunting the knowledge?" Redhands tossed his head back, sneering. I realized his face might have been handsome but for the lines his continually hostile expression seemed to work into his flesh. "I've had enough. If she don't start talking by the time we leave Nassau, I'm whipping it out of her. Or I'm tellin' the men about the Eye and they'll gladly do it for me."

Colt held up a hand, "Robert, calm down-"

"I ain't calmin'," he cried. "And I ain't waitin' another two years."

Colt squared his shoulders and clenched his jaw, carefully considering Robert.

"As quartermaster it's my *duty* to challenge you on these matters. And this is the deal I can offer you, Colt," Robert said, low and even. "She confesses everything by the time we leave Nassau, or I'll tie her to the whipping mast and bloody her back."

My spine turned to ice at his words. I could tell from Colt's hard expression he took Robert's threat seriously.

No, not a threat. A promise.

"You know the crew will happily encourage it once they learn she stole their fortune and their future. Might want to whip you too at the point. Certainly won't support your being captain no more."

My heart beat furiously as I awaited Colt's reply. Surely he'd protect me?

"You're right," the captain agreed in a voice both dark and conceding. "It's a fair deal you've struck and I honor it."

Wait… no.

Colt stepped into Robert's personal space, intimidating him with his height. "But if you ever speak to me again in that manner, if your negotiations ever again turn to threats, I will tie you to the mast and whip you myself."

Robert paled.

"Have I also struck a fair deal you can honor? Say the word and I can provide a sample of my intentions right now."

"N–no, captain," Robert stammered, contrition and anger warring in his expression.

"Scurry along to your duties. And remember—until we leave Nassau, your job is to keep her from any who would do her harm," Colt said. "I'll get the truth from her before it comes to the lash."

Redhands sauntered off the forecastle deck with a self-satisfied spring in his step.

I had no way of knowing what Colt next planned. But I didn't believe he would seriously hurt me—cut me or lash the skin from my back. Would he?

I gulped and whispered, "You'd whip a lady, captain?"

Perhaps a ridiculous question, considering what he'd done to me the night before. I knew he was thinking about those events as well from the heat in his gaze. The memory brought a flush to my own cheeks. No, the mere proximity of Colt's body made a warmth spread all over my flesh. The recollection and the hunger in Colt's stare made my breasts heavy and full, as if he willed it with his eyes.

This man, this stranger, could picture my bare breasts at any time. My naked arse. My exposed cunt. For the rest of his life, and mine, we were connected in this intimate manner.

And yet I had seen nothing of his form.

Ridiculous of course. I was glad for it. Not having him remove his breeches meant he couldn't threaten me with the equipment beneath them.

Thick, stiff, and designed to bring such pleasure —

"You know I wouldn't," Colt interrupted my thoughts, dark eyes considering me. My brief relief turned to stomach-sinking fear when he added, "But Redhands would. Unlike the king's navy, a pirate ship is a democracy. As you're well aware. And you've given the entire crew just cause, especially if they learn what you've taken from them."

"Their Crimson Eye?" I asked, as innocently as possible.

"Their *future,*" Colt said, eyes narrowed. "Though they're not aware of it unless Robert tells them." He cocked his head. "But we're getting somewhere if you're willing to address your theft. I'm pleased you're finally starting to speak the truth. But if you don't finish speaking it by the time we leave port, there's nothing I can do to protect you."

"You could release me," I pointed out.

Colt's eyes widened ever-so-slightly with alarm and he grabbed my arm. "Don't think you can escape again. Nassau belongs to our kind. There's nowhere you can hide where I won't find you. No one you can ask for help who would oblige."

Something in my face made Colt declare, "If you run from me again, so help me God, Lady Charlotte. You won't be able to sit down for a week after I'm done with you. And you can spend the rest of your days with your ankles shackled. Do I make myself clear?"

Shockingly, his threat made me tingle between my legs. What was it about being the focus of Colt's attention that I found strangely exciting? Heat and hate warred within me. Emotions battled on Colt's face too, and I think they were a combination of dread and desire. The air between us crackled with something akin to the energy of the impending rain… of an impending storm between the two of us.

Gritting my teeth, I mocked, "Aye, captain."

Colt dropped my arm and I felt oddly… disappointed.

But then he cocked his one-sided grin and declared, "I'll see you this evening in my cabin." Colt spun on his heel, but before leaving, he looked over his shoulder and added, "*all* of you."

I shivered as Colt left me alone to consider my fate, and there was much to consider.

Had I truly stolen gold and a gem of some kind? What did a gem have to do with the crew's future? It must have been quite a large stone if finding a buyer was a problem, as Redhands suggested. *Perhaps I'd only stolen the gem in order to return it to its proper owner,* I reasoned.

Yet… where was it now? If I'd escaped this awful pirate ship with a key piece of their treasure, where had I stashed it? Had I been attacked and injured in my quest to return it?

More importantly, what was I going to do now? Redhands would never believe that I didn't know.

Balling my hands into fists, I stared at the choppy sea and fought the tears welling in my eyes.

I'd thought that if things turned out badly enough, I could confess the truth about my memory loss. It was the one hope I held onto, giving me some sense of comfort and safety.

But now… would the crew even believe me? Would Colt?

Why should he when I'd been lying to him the entire time?

No. Somehow, I needed to escape when we reached Nassau. I believed Colt when he vowed to punish me if he caught me.

If he caught me. And anyway, the promise of Colt's belt was better than the threat of Redhands's lash. I gripped the railing, dizzy from the thought.

He'd whip me until I died, I thought. *Because no matter what I said, I'd never be able to confess to that which I did not know.*

THAT EVENING, I PLANNED TO sup with Miguel once more, but he told me I'd be dining later with the captain, in his quarters. Conks and Johnson were already in the galley, making it impossible to have any candid conversation about my past with the quiet cook.

Instead of a meal, I was offered ale, and I drank it all quickly to steel my courage. It wasn't long before the spirit worked its soothing magic on my limbs. Meandering the ship, I once again heard the rest of the crew dining above, singing and laughing, and it evoked in me a feeling akin to wistfulness. I didn't know what to call the sensation; it wasn't quite a memory, but it was more than just a longing. When their voices rose in song, I felt a familiar yearning.

Troubling, indeed.

I made my way above deck and watched the men from a distance. After they finished eating, someone brought out a fiddle and they clapped and danced together. Had I another glass of ale, I might have joined them—counter to my very vow to bring down these corrupt men from within.

Well, maybe not all *the men are evil,* I reasoned. *They were subject to Colt's whims, same as I. It's really just the sinister captain I need to bring to justice. And Redhands,* I added.

Too quickly the sun set into the sea and a taunting moon shone above. All thoughts of revelry were wiped from my mind when Colt came to collect me. Even in the moonlight, I could see the lust shining in his eyes, making me blush.

What is he going to do to me now?

Like the previous evenings, Colt marched me to his cabin. Each time that door slammed, my fate was sealed. I knew within these walls whatever happened would be whatever he decreed. No one would come to my aid, and I couldn't overpower Colt.

He knew it too. As soon as I turned to face him that strange sensation ran between us, linking us, quickening my breath, and his.

Unlike other evenings, the table had been laden with a meal I could scarcely examine without feeling like I might be sick. *Who could eat under threat of Colt the Cruel?*

The captain strode leisurely to the table and sat, eying me with expectation. I did not move. He could make me do all sorts of sinful, wretched things, but I refused to turn around and dine at his table with false civility.

Colt raised his eyebrows and I didn't like the satisfaction gleaming on his face. It felt like the drop of some handkerchief, calling a game to begin. A game in which I was an unwilling participant.

"Lift your skirts and sit down," Colt drummed his fingers against the tabletop, casually, while my face heated with fury. "Legs spread. Do not close them."

I wanted to scream at how easily he'd said such horrific things.

"No."

"You can spread your legs and bare your cunt of your own free will or I will belt your cunt until it hurts too much to close your thighs." Colt leaned back, languid, expectant. I wanted to throttle him yet it didn't stop the throb between my legs.

"How is it my free will if you threaten me otherwise?" I spat, hands balled into fists. I was doing that so much lately that I was probably digging half-moon dents from my fingernails permanently into my flesh.

Colt flashed a half-smirk. "Fair point. I stand corrected. But the choice remains. You can bare your cunt while we dine, free of pain, or I can bare it for you, throbbing from my lesson."

Tears of humiliation pricked my eyes. I clapped my hands over my ears in an almost laughable manner, but I couldn't help myself. "Stop saying that word!"

Colt tilted his head and stood slowly. Such a slow rise made quick work of racing my pulse. It was better when he sat. Safer.

"What word is that?" Grabbing my waist too fast for me to react, Colt pressed my body against his. Lowering his mouth to my ear, he whispered, "Cunt?"

I shivered.

"Your bare *cunt,* Lady Charlotte?"

His breath warmed my neck as Colt continued, "I suggest you get used to hearing the word. I'm about to do much more than say it. I'm about to see it."

That hot feeling rose in my chest again as Colt drew the tip of his nose along my neck, *inhaling.* Me? Soft lips and prickly stubble rubbed my skin as he said, "You're going to reveal that cunt to me. At my command. For my pleasure."

My hands hung limp with indecision—slap him… or curl my fingers around those biceps and plead for him to move his hands lower, to relieve the ache in my…

No.

What was wrong with me?

Abruptly, Colt released me, making me angrier for some reason. He returned to his chair, leisurely slung one arm over the back, and cocked a brow.

"I'm waiting."

Scowling, I stormed to one of the chairs and plopped down.

"Back up," Colt commanded, lifting his chin. "Stand, raise your skirts, then you may sit."

If I could have burned him to char with my stare, I would have. Jaw clenched, I rose, bunched my skirts at my waist, and re-sat.

Colt and I held each other's gaze, knowing what was to come next. The tension permeated the air like the moment before a curtain's rise on opening night. Me, the player behind the stage, preparing to give a good show. Colt, the patron, demanding to be entertained.

Odd that a power raced through my veins at that moment. Was I helpless to Colt's commands or was he helpless to my charms? Part of me wanted to turn my head away in shame as I spread my legs. But another part of me couldn't tear my gaze from the thrall on Colt's face. His dark, hungry eyes slid downward to my open sex. I knew better than to obey in halves and I widened my legs to either side of the chair, causing the lewd spreading of my folds.

"Don't move," he ordered, drinking his wine, never taking his eyes off me. Well—my nether regions, specifically. After a few moments, Colt occasionally shifted his eyes up to my face, as if taking stock… as if reassuring himself of something and, once satisfied, he lowered his gaze back where he desired.

Agonizing minutes passed. Or were they seconds? Hours? Who knew? I was too acutely focused of the feel of Colt's black eyes on my… cunt… to feel the passing of time.

His husky voice broke the silence. "You're dripping onto the chair, Lady Charlotte."

I felt the blush I knew he wanted.

"While an unfortunate lady might find herself subjected to unspeakable horrors at the hands of a captor, would such a lady soil the chair with her own lust?"

Waves of shame hit me so hard they dizzied me. I didn't know if he expected an answer but I had none. My mouth had gone completely dry. Every part of my body felt hot, feverish. My face, my neck, my breasts, and especially the region below my waist. And he hadn't even touched me.

Colt placed his wine back upon the table, grinning saucily. He picked up a piece of saltbeef and took a bite.

"Go on," he commanded. "Eat. You're free to enjoy as much as you like."

You know damn well I can hardly eat a bite like this, I thought, narrowing my eyes. But I wouldn't be defeated.

Meeting his challenge, I grabbed my own saltbeef and took a large bite.

Unfortunately, the meat was tougher than I expected and I bit off more than I could chew, literally.

The next thing I knew I coughed and wheezed as my throat was robbed of air.

I can't breathe, I can't breathe.

Gripped by panic, I wasn't even embarrassed when Colt's arms wrapped around my waist, squeezing.

Oh dear God, I can't breathe.

His strong hands smacked my back in an attempt to dislodge the meat.

I can't die like this, I thought, wildly. Tears welled. *Choking on saltbeef at a pirate captain's table.*

On a particularly rough cough, the meat finally shot from my open mouth, landing on the table in a vulgar display. Relieved tears spilled down my cheeks and I took great, greedy gulps of air. When I refocused, Colt was kneeling before me. He brushed my hair from my face and gently grabbed it, studying me.

"You turned purple," he declared, brow furrowed. "Jesus, don't scare me like that, Charlie. Our kind meets our doom at the end of a sword, not a rough bit o' bull." Something strange crossed his face, setting his mouth into a line. "Though I suppose you were never truly our kind."

I didn't pay much attention to that last part.

Charlie?

I blinked. He'd never called me that before.

CHAPTER 16
COLT

ALONE IN MY cabin, I ran a hand down my face. I had underestimated Robert's wrath and put Charlotte in severe danger because of it.

What choice did I have?

The crew would have noticed her soon enough in that cramped tavern. And I couldn't let her go. My fingers twitched as if I could grasp her at that moment. *Couldn't.*

No, it was better to take her under my protection. But even I couldn't shield her forever against a majority vote to lash the truth from her.

I tossed back a swig of the reserve rum I kept in my cabin, then poured and drank another.

I needed to convince Charlotte to tell the truth, not just for me but to save herself. Yet I had no wits about me when she was in my presence—never had.

I snorted to myself as I thought, *maybe it's better to simply allow her plan to unfold. Clearly, she has one. And it seems to involve allowing me to do as I please to her body.*

I laughed, spurred by lewd imaginings and rum. Letting Charlotte win didn't feel like losing.

Not if it ended with my cock sheathed inside her wet and willing cunt.

CHAPTER 17

CHARLOTTE

I COULD NOT CONFESS to that which I did not know. I'd tossed and turned in the brig's hammock all night, formulating a plan.

I had two hopes for escaping the lash and it would be best to employ both, I reasoned. One, I needed to learn more about the events of that fateful evening so that I could somehow begin to piece together the truth, and two, I needed to escape once we docked in Nassau.

There wasn't much I could do to prepare for the latter until we reached port. But if I could speak with Miguel privately, I thought, I could begin uncovering information about my past.

Figuring out a way to bring down Colt's piracy from the inside would need to play second fiddle to ensuring my own safety. I came first, after all, and there wasn't much I could do to tear him down if they'd already torn the skin from my back.

A terrible shiver ran through me at the thought.

Focusing on my plan, I spent the morning above deck but feigned lightheadedness from the sun by midday. Retreating to the shade below, I took my first opportunity to slip into the galley unnoticed.

Miguel was arranging pickled vegetables when I arrived and looked up with alarm, but shortly thereafter a warmth softened his gaze.

I knew it. We'd meant something to each other in the past; been friends perhaps. He was a weak link on which I could apply pressure to snap, but only because he cared for me.

I wish the same could be said for Captain Colt, I thought wryly.

"Miguel," I greeted him smiling, helping myself to an open chair. I wanted to work quickly in case Conks came sniffing about and I wanted to position myself below Miguel, to look up at him with the best doe eyes I could manage. I placed my hands demurely on my lap.

Miguel roared with laughter. It was a side of him I hadn't seen and I jumped at the sound. For the first time, I noticed he had the most adorable dimples if he smiled widely enough.

"I've spent too many nights watching over you not to know your tricks, Charlotte."

My mouth dropped, affronted, but it only made him laugh harder.

Miguel set aside the vegetables and took a seat across from me, offering the bashful smile I remembered from our first meeting. "I'm sorry to speak so bluntly and I didn't mean to give offense. I just want you to know you don't need to put on your lady act—or any other—here with me."

Relaxing into my chair, I nodded. "Thank you for granting me the permission to speak freely but I assure you, I am a lady."

Miguel shrugged. "If you say so."

"Only," I smoothed a stray hair behind my ear, "I was

hoping to get your version of the events that happened—that Captain Colt *believes* happened on this ship two years ago."

"Not this ship," Miguel corrected. "You know that. We traded *The Dark Blade* for *The Dread Night.*"

"Right. Of course. I meant, the events that happened two years ago on that ship."

Miguel shifted uncomfortably, looking over his shoulder as if someone could be standing by the plate of pickled peppers and onions.

"I can't–can't discuss that with you."

I folded my arms. "Why not? I have every right to know what it is you believe when the subject matter is *me.*"

When those beliefs affect my backside at Colt's whim, I thought. *When threat of the lash looms.*

Miguel worked his jaw, falling silent again for a while. Finally, he said, "Well, to be honest, it's you I've been wanting to ask questions of. I can reckon why you stole the gold." Miguel's warm brown eyes held mine. "You wanted out, you always wanted out." He ducked his head and whispered, "But the Eye?"

I blinked, startled.

"I know about the Crimson Eye," he confirmed in a whisper. "But don't worry, only a few of us do. If word spreads though, not even the captain can protect you from the crew. You stole from us all when you swiped it."

I wouldn't do that, I insisted to myself. *And if I had, it would only have been to return it to its owner.*

Miguel's voice turned grave and his whisper was so low I had to strain to hear him. "And what you did to Maurice," he said. "I don't blame you for hating him. He was a bloody bastard, alright. And maybe he tried to stop you from leaving. But I'm sure to Colt that didn't justify you killing him."

My heart beat furiously fast and sweat broke out on my brow.

Killing? I thought with alarm. *What did he mean—killing? Surely, he was mistaken.*

"I–I didn't… wouldn't…" I fumbled. "If it had happened—which it didn't—it would have been self-defense."

Miguel shook his head sadly. "Maurice would never try to hurt you if that's what you're implying. He was as mean as they come, sure, but Colt was like a son to him and you were too precious to Colt."

"Correct," came a voice from the door.

Oh no.

My stomach lurched as I turned to face Colt, pushing the galley door wide and stepping inside the small room. My mouth ran dry and I lost the ability to speak. I was sure I'd turned white as a ghost.

Miguel jumped to his feet. I quickly followed, making a pathetic attempt at a defensive stance.

"Now, captain," Miguel began.

"Leave us," Colt commanded Miguel without looking. "I'll deal with your transgression later."

Miguel bent his head. Sparing me one apologetic look, he departed.

Don't go, I thought. *I need your protection.*

Scratch that. Colt didn't care about having an audience. I gulped. *Maybe it was better Miguel had left.*

"You cannot punish him so harshly for my wrongdoings," I protested, using anger to cover my fear. "He was only trying to help me."

"Oh, I'm not. I'll dock his wages for the week," Colt shrugged. "But the real punishment for him will be to hear your cries." Colt stalked toward me. "The real punishment is all for you Lady Charlotte."

Colt grabbed my arm.

"What are you-"

My words died in my throat as Colt slammed me down over the galley table. While I flailed and struggled to rise, Colt's firm hand on my back kept me bent. As he raised my skirts, I warred with wanting to scream and protest and not wanting to announce my plight to the crew.

Feeling the cool air on my naked backside, I knew it was pointless.

"Stop!" I cried, head pressed against the smooth wooden table. No matter how hard I struggled, I couldn't rise.

Colt laid a resounding smack on my rear. And then another.

"Settle down. Keep fighting me and this will continue longer than I'd originally intended."

Gritting my teeth, I huffed through my nose as I determined to endure.

"That's a good girl," Colt mocked, boldly running his finger down the crevice between my bottom and making me shudder before he laid another hard smack on my rear.

I yelped, but he did it again—this time smacking me several times where my arse met my thighs, then letting his fingertips gently graze the lips of my sex. The bewildering onslaught of pain and pleasure continued—I'd suffer several harsh blows, only to be plunged into a state of confused desire when Colt would pause and touch me intimately. Before I had time to do more than sigh at the sensation, he'd resume his discipline. The strength of his blows increased, leaving me panting, turning my rear red, I was sure. Colt's caresses were never enough; he never even inserted a finger inside me. But they kept my head spinning, kept me wanting more. It almost was a reward, like he spoke to me.

Take a few more spanks, Charlotte. There now, I know it hurts. But look at what a good girl you've been. You can have the brush of my fingers against your swollen pussy lips. Such a good girl. Doesn't that feel nice?

The only thing more humiliating than arching my back to give Colt better access was the fact that he ignored it, choosing only to grace me with the barest of caresses.

Colt ended my spanking with his hardest blows yet, once again on the sensitive area where I sat down.

It wasn't my cries that had alerted the crew, I knew. I was able to keep them to muted whimpers throughout the spanking. It was the loud slap of Colt's palm against my skin. Any passerby would have heard it and known what he was doing.

I was mortified.

Released, I sprang upright. Tears welled in my eyes, though not as much from the pain as they were from the frustration at being helpless. Being punished. Being molested. *Liking it.* I didn't know what to do with my rage and excitement but it needed release.

"You shame me!" I shouted at Colt.

He was taken aback. Perhaps he'd expected contrition. Perhaps I should have shown it, given recent events.

"I shame you?" Dangerously low, he snarled the words from clenched teeth. "I shame you?" Louder now. Colt slammed his fist on the wooden table. "And how about how you shamed *me?*"

I watched the skin on his knuckles stretch and whiten as

his fist tightened. "You steal from me, you murder Maurice, and you escape in the middle of the night—right under my nose to make a fool of me for all the crew to see?" Colt threw his head back, laughing.

Murder. There it was again. I would never do that. There must *be a misunderstanding.*

Wary, I stepped backwards. My head spun to make sense of his words but I couldn't concentrate with the impending threat.

"I shame you?" Colt repeated, voice dripping with sarcasm. I squealed as he closed the distance between us and grabbed my arm hard enough to hurt. "Lady Charlotte, I haven't even begun to shame you yet."

"Wait, stop!" I shouted, as Colt kicked the galley door and dragged me through the narrow hall and back to his cabin. I had the feeling he would have thrown me over his shoulder, had the ceiling permitted room. Stumbling after him, I was forced to scurry or fall, and by his painful yank I knew he wouldn't hesitate to drag me the rest of the way.

"Colt, stop, please!" I cried. He'd never been so rough with me before. Even the first time when his anger practically exuded from his skin and shot right out from his dark eyes, he didn't manhandle me with such violence.

Had I truly done something so horrible as to warrant this treatment? I couldn't have murdered anyone. No, there must be a mistake or a reasonable explanation.

Colt slammed the door behind us and wasted no time forcing me onto the bed. Once again, I didn't want to scream and announce my predicament to the entire ship, but I couldn't help my pleading.

"Just stop for a moment, please!"

Colt ignored me. He was like a beast in those moments, incapable of reason. Colt grabbed rope, and, using his superior size and strength, pinned me to the bed. I thought I couldn't be any more panicked than when he tied my wrists to the posts, but of course he didn't stop there.

Ignoring my protests, Colt shoved my skirt to my waist, baring me.

But that wasn't the worst of it.

While I thrashed on the bed, he found *more* rope. Bloody rope was one thing this ship was never short of.

Though this surely wasn't its intended use.

Sheer terror washed over me as Colt seized one of my thighs and wrenched it wide. Encircling my tender flesh with the course rope, he spread me, tying the rope to the same post restraining my arms. Colt yanked my left thigh wide and repeated the humiliating process.

I squeezed my eyes shut while Colt inserted himself between my legs, pinned wide like a butterfly on a board. Nothing was hidden from his view; no ladylike modesty remained. *Staring.* I could *feel* his hot gaze on my sex, searing me like a brand in my most intimate folds.

He'd succeeded; shamed me as he said he would, and with only a glare. What was his fascination with what lay between my legs? Agonizing seconds crawled by. I couldn't stop myself from sniveling and I didn't care. *You won, see? Brought me low, shamed me. Now please, let me up.*

Why wasn't he letting me up?

I didn't understand.

I didn't know what was coming.

This wasn't the shame at all. This was just the maneuvering to get me in the position to shame me.

"Lady Charlotte, in all the time you were hiding from me, has a man touched you here?"

Oh God. I shook my head rapidly, eyes still squeezed shut. I knew what he meant.

"You're so wet." His whisper had a curious tone. Something like awe. "I can't tell if it's because you know what's coming, know how good it's going to feel, and you're panting like a bitch in heat for release… or if it's because you've been starved for an eternity and you're soaked with longing."

I wasn't… my body didn't do such whorish things.

"I'd make you answer the question, but then you'd just lie, wouldn't you?"

Me? You're the liar.

Colt's fingers traced my mouth. "These lips lie." His hand slid down my stomach, reaching the curls at the top of my mound. "But these lips don't."

At those words, his fingers traced my slit up and down, making me gasp and shudder. I couldn't turn any redder; it wasn't possible.

"Shall we see what truths I can wrest from your cunt?"

The terrors he might inflict upon my most sensitive regions were unthinkable. Would he whip me there? Pinch me? Smack me?

Rape me?

I shook my head back and forth rapidly. "No, please. You won't achieve your goal in this manner," I swore. "Use your body to hurt me all you like, but I will not break."

Why did my voice sound husky?

Even huskier, Colt rasped, "I'm not going to use my body to bring you pain. I'm going to use it to bring you pleasure. Although that might pain you more."

Colt thrust his finger inside me and my mind nearly snapped from the deliciousness. I flung my head back and cried out. My legs jolted in response. *Jesus Christ.*

Colt pushed his finger in and out, enthralling me in totality. It was like some kind of magic, a masculine power of bewitchment. It made my hips move at the command. My body certainly wasn't under my control any longer. It responded to *his.*

Then he inserted *two* fingers inside me and I groaned. It shamed me further; my own actions shamed me worse than if I'd been forced to simply be victim to some depraved act. I thought I'd lose my mind from the insistent pleasure of those two fingers violating me, and then Colt did something that had me convulsing.

He swiped his thumb over the bundle of nerves at the top of my opening. I didn't even know what to call the sounds tearing from my throat as he continued to circle it.

Something built inside me and I couldn't stop it. I didn't want to; it needed release. The sensation was similar to how I'd felt that first night when Colt bent me over the bed, and yet it was entirely different. This time, it wasn't me doing it. This time, my mind wasn't in that strange, detached state. This time it was shared, and immeasurably more powerful.

I felt like a lion behind a cage, roaring for release. I imagined Colt the master on the other side, whip in one hand, cage key in the other. He cracked the whip and it was as if something inside me roared, *let me out.*

Oh God, let me out.

It built inside me, a crescendo, the bliss just beyond my reach. *Yes and yes.* It was as if Colt came closer, bringing his hand to the lock, to freedom.

Yes, please, now, I need it —

— abruptly, he pulled his hand away.

The effect was horrific; the Godsent pressure suddenly gone. My hips bucked, seeking, begging.

I need.

His voice was another crack of the whip as he whispered into my ear, "Down girl. You haven't earned it."

Humiliated and desperate, I sobbed. Just minutes before, I cried for wanting him to stop. Now I cried because he wouldn't continue.

I had thought Colt and his ship were my cage and that only I could free myself, but I had it backwards.

I prowled in a cage of my own making and only Colt could free me.

For a few minutes, he let me cry tears of shame and desire. Colt brought me so low I couldn't make myself stop, even though he watched with such condensation it burned.

When I finally calmed down, Colt neared and I mistakenly thought he'd untie me. Instead, he brought his fingers back between my legs and helplessly bound, I was unable to stop his assault. I didn't even want to. I rocked, meeting his thrusts, wiggling my hips as he rubbed the spot that gave me the most pleasure.

"Are you ashamed?" he asked, voice rough. "Are you ashamed at what I'm doing to you Charlotte? Ashamed at how you like it?"

I nodded, still bucking.

"Only a husband should see you like this, isn't that right? And never quite like *this*. He'd approach with the candles low and only to make blessed babies. He'd never string up his lady wife and spread her wide for his viewing pleasure.

He'd never stick his fingers in her cunt to make her pant like an animal, would he?"

"No…" I whined, tossing my head. His filthy words mortified me but they made me hotter too. I think he knew it.

Colt watched my movements and the pleasure flit across my face. When I came close to a pinnacle the second time, he stopped again.

"Please," I begged, as his fingers disappeared. He sat back, leaving me whimpering. Each time he touched me the tether I had to reality, to the material world, snapped. My body shot up in an arc while my mind and spirit flew right up out of it. When Colt released me, I'd slowly sink back to Earth, to the rocking of the ship and smell of salt air. After a minute, my heart rate and breathing would slow.

I let my head fall to the side, eyes fluttering shut, and I felt the dip in the bed as Colt neared me a third time.

"No, no more, please," I begged, tugging at the ropes binding me too tightly. I couldn't stop Colt's fingers seeking their goal—my unprotected sex. He slipped inside easily for another round of torment.

I didn't try to fight him; knew it was pointless. He'd use my body as he saw fit. Fighting him only wasted my energy. He'd have his way, in the end.

"Are you ashamed at your whorish writhing, Lady Charlotte?" he asked again.

I nodded.

"Say it!"

"Yes! Yes, I'm ashamed!" I'd hoped he might let me have satisfaction if I said what he wanted. I needed completion so badly, my legs shook. But I knew no amount of begging would sway Colt's mind.

"As I've been ever since you played me a fool. Tell me the truth of that night and I'll let you come so hard you might pass out," Colt tempted, stroking my wet folds.

I could only whine. I heard Colt's low chuckle of disbelief, then he shoved two fingers deep inside me and curled them, making me wail and beginning the torture again.

I didn't argue when he left me wanting the third time. Or the fourth, and final. I no longer struggled when he untied me. I could barely move my sore arms; they fell to the bed. Desperate, I made an attempt to move them between my legs to finish the job myself, but Colt grabbed my wrists.

"Uh-uh," he tsked, placing my arms away from my throbbing cunt and chuckling when I whimpered.

He'd broken me again, in an entirely different manner than before. Weak, exhausted, and completely unsatisfied, I fell asleep in Colt's bed.

CHAPTER 18

COLT

I WAS THE WORST inquisitor in history.

So bloody bewitched by Charlotte's bare cunt, I'd neglected to truly press the main point of her humiliation—to make her confess. Not to her shame, not to liking it, but to the truth of that night. She refused me but once and I let it go.

At least I'd succeeded in forcing her to succumb to lust. But I'd missed the point entirely and was left feeling more enthralled than ever.

I dropped my head into my hands.

Who had won this round?

Charlotte's shoulders rose and fell gently as she breathed in sleep, beside me. I couldn't make myself seize those shoulders, to shake her awake and demand to know the truth. Funny how such a lying vixen could look so innocent in slumber. Her long legs splayed, free from her skirts. Her full breasts pushed at the thin cloth of her shirt. Her hair tumbled in all directions. Plump, pink lips parted to breathe—an echo of other plump lips, gently parted. She looked as if she was begging to be ravished. A Goddess, a temptress, a siren of the sea washed ashore.

A far cry from the half-starved girl I once knew.

What had I done to deserve such torment?

Nevermind. I knew.

It didn't stop me from hurrying to the laces on my breeches, eyes pinned to Charlotte's sleeping form. Standing above her, I moaned as I grasped my throbbing cock and pumped. If I'd had to wager, I didn't believe I would receive much resistance if I yanked her shirt out of my way and buried myself inside her. I'd tell her there was nothing to be ashamed of. I'd make her enjoy it.

I groaned at the fantasy, pumping faster.

Why should it be a fantasy? I had every right to take her after what she'd done. I could force my way into her wet sheath and spill my seed into her ready womb.

My right, I repeated in my head as I neared my release. *My Charlotte. My cunt. Mine, mine.*

I came into my waiting hand like a boy ashamed at his actions. Instant rage rose within me as I realized I was hiding it from *her.*

Why should I care? She was mine to mark.

Running my semen-covered hands up her legs, I coated her soft skin. *Would she realize it on the morn,* I wondered, *or would the stickiness just blend with the ever-present salt air aboard a ship at sea?*

Charlotte did not stir. Her breathing was even and her face relaxed, oblivious to my soiling her pristine skin.

With the final drops, I brought my fingers to her lips and traced them, leaving another coating of my seed around her mouth. When she still didn't awaken, I dared further, inserting my thumb and depositing a dollop on her soft tongue.

Mine.

CHAPTER 19

CHARLOTTE

I AWOKE ALONE IN Colt's cabin. Bolting upright in the bed, I quickly scanned the room to ensure I was, in fact, left to my own devices.

My heart leapt at finding the room to be utterly empty and I crept from the bed, rubbing my curiously sticky lips with the back of my hand.

Where was Colt? Had he slept beside me or taken a chair or perhaps he'd gone to drink with his men without returning to his cabin at all?

What I most needed was to find something that would help me learn the truth of my past, but second best would be access to the ship's schedule, if they kept one. A man as fastidious as Colt must have some general plans noting where *The Dread Night* intended to dock after my "check in" back with Mrs. Penningham. I suspected they'd sail north to Charles Town to restock supplies our small outpost lacked. If I could confirm and get word to Daniel, I could convey what I'd learned: how many men aboard, how they fought, who to fear. We could quickly work between our settlements to set up an immediate ambush.

At the very least, I could copy any schedule I might find and relay it to those in larger settlements with more men and arms at their disposal. They might have time to prepare a defense or to set a trap, thus ending the piracy of Colt the Cruel once and for all.

I smiled to myself at the same time my foot hit a squeaky floorboard and I froze. The sound echoed throughout the cabin and sure enough, the door swung wide, revealing a grinning Conks in the doorway.

"Glad to see you're up and about," he announced.

There was no point in pretending he didn't know what I was up to.

"I'm famished," I grumbled, smoothing my skirts and acting indifferent. "I'm going to get breakfast with Miguel."

"I'll join you," Conks said, patting his stomach.

THE HOURS PASSED uneventfully. Still unallowed to socialize with most of the crew, I spent half the day reading one of the captain's books and the other half helping Miguel pluck a recently-slaughtered chicken. Conks kept a watchful eye and regaled us throughout with stories of his pirating youth.

I'd initially wanted to balk at the request to touch the dead bird, but curiosity got the better of me. Though I'd never handled a chicken in such a state at the tavern, the lowly act of plucking fowl felt oddly familiar. Almost... therapeutic.

After I resolved to at least observe the crew from a distance, if not converse directly, I headed above deck to enjoy a pleasant day at sea.

The men were practicing with both wooden and metal swords, as well as grappling on the quarterdeck. For an hour, I watched them. Conks and Johnson wouldn't put up much of a fight when it came to battle. Their hearts might be in it, but they hadn't developed superior fighting skills. As they whispered in each other's ears or caressed overlong, I understood now they were in a relationship of some kind. Though that knowledge could be leveraged against them when it came to a fight, the idea saddened me.

Robert the Red and Sedge, a man with a shaved head, presented the biggest problem (aside from the captain himself.) Sedge, slight and serious, didn't look like much of a fighter, but I'd never seen a man move so quickly or wield a cutlass with such prowess before.

Useful information to convey to Daniel, at least.

I wondered if I could convince Daniel and the rest of our town to spare Conks… and Johnson… and Miguel. Conks, with his tonics, had been kind to me. And an eloquent man like Johnson certainly wasn't cut out for the pirate life. And Miguel was just the sweetest. Colt, however, needed to be lashed and hanged for what he'd done to me. For violating a woman, he should have his eyes gouged. For touching a lady, he should have his hands sliced from his body. *Those talented hands… rough and big and capable of unimaginable pleasure… I bet he could fit an entire breast in one of those large hands…*

My thoughts were interrupted by a shout from a man halfway up the ratlines.

"Captain!" he called down. "Cork in the tub!"

What did that mean?

"Sails!" someone shouted, answering the question.

Colt snapped to attention. "Colors?"

"She's a… small merchant ship from the looks of it," the watch guard shouted. "Local traders. Doesn't look to be threatening. Coming up fast with the wind though. She's gonna reach us."

Colt raced onto the afterdeck and I quickly followed. "If she's no threat why is she coming so hard for us?" he asked.

The rest of the crew quickly filled the deck and Colt swiped a spyglass from a nearby man to see for himself.

"They're either looking for help or to make a trade," James offered. "Could be good for us."

Colt didn't reply and everyone waited tensely while he examined the other ship. Slowly, he lowered the spyglass and brought his fingers to his lips, rubbing as he stared.

"She's fast, alright… small for a merchant ship though… can't be supporting too many men…"

"I think I see a white flag," a crewman on the ratlines shouted. "They must be needin' something."

"If we can't outrun 'er anyway, might as well see what they're offering," someone else chimed in.

Colt withdrew a long breath, then turned his hard gaze to the assembled shipmates.

"The only thing that ship is offering is death," he proclaimed, pointing. "It's a trap."

Murmurs ran through the crew. I gulped.

"That's a masquerade ship. They might not have large numbers, but they've got speed and they're planning on using stealth," Colt explained, storming off the afterdeck and forcing us all to stumble as we followed. "They're going to try to board us under the guise of needing assistance or wanting to trade. But once we allow them onto deck, they'll turn and attack."

"So let's give 'em a fight!" Robert roared. "Johnson, turn her 'round! Conks, ready the cannons!"

Men instantly sprang into action, hands on the hilt of pistols and racing to what I assumed to be battle stations while my heart galloped in my chest.

Colt's eyes quickly flicked to me and he commanded, "No!"

The crew halted.

"If we start blowing holes in each other's ships we're both going to come out the worser," he declared. "We play along. They don't know that we know. We'll hide half our men. Those above deck, act the part. We'll allow them *all* aboard and keep our weapons at the ready."

My heart continued its thunderous beat. *Were we really going to allow the enemy aboard? Willingly?* Dazed, I watched the crew split, the men dividing by half and then again, to take secreted positions below deck.

"Rum!" Colt ordered the remainders. "Break out the rum, quickly! Drink it, spill it, show it!"

The crew hurried to obey.

"Smile like idiots, men! Let them think us merchant fools amidst a celebration. And when I give the signal, *we'll* attack *them.*"

The crew cheered. I gulped again.

"They're gaining!" came the shout.

"Conceal your weapons," Colt ordered. "Wait for my signal. Charlotte!"

Colt turned to me, grasping my biceps. "Go to my cabin. Stay there no matter what you hear from above. Do you understand me?"

Nodding vigorously, I clutched my skirts and ran below deck and into the relative safety of Colt's quarters. A strange sense of déjà vu fluttered in the corners of my mind, as if I'd hidden here another time. I locked Colt's door and backed away, shaking. Determined to protect myself, I grabbed the heaviest candlestick holder I could find and held it aloft, bracing for an attack I imagined might come any second, before realizing I wasted my energy and let my arm slacken. Gripping the chairback, I waited, imagining the game of pretending above deck as each crew attempted to fool the other.

I heard the first shouts from above and a split-second later, pistols fired. I covered my mouth, straining my ears to hear every sword clash, every battle cry, every thud that might indicate a fallen man.

Colt, I thought, and it was as if my heart beat his name in time. *Did I care? Didn't I want him dead?*

Then why did my heart pound in fear for him in particular?

My stomach flipped when I heard fast-approaching footsteps and my mouth ran dry as the door handle jangled—then stopped. Nothing but my frightened breaths filled the quiet air for a moment. Then, a shot rang out and I jumped, knowing whoever was on the other side had blown the handle clear off the door.

I heard a kick and then a man burst into the room. He bore long, black hair to match his long black beard, nearly trailing to his chest. His grin resembled a snarl. He was too large to dream of fighting and winning.

That didn't mean I wouldn't try.

Having spent his shot on the doorhandle and seeing he only faced one unarmed girl, the intimidating man re-holstered his pistol, eyes never leaving me. He wasn't as tall as Colt, but he was wider, muscle cording his sizable neck.

Lowering my head and narrowing my eyes, I gave my attacker the deadliest stare I could manage above my fear. His own eyes twinkled with malice. Through simple body language everything was communicated in seconds. He intended to defile me, hurt me, perhaps kill me after. I intended to fight him with everything at my disposal.

Sadly, that was merely a candlestick holder and grit, but I tightened my grip on my weapon and braced.

When the man advanced, I swung, but he easily blocked my blow with his own. Hard muscle crashed against my soft arm, feeling as if he could have cracked my bone without much more effort. I whimpered and dropped the makeshift weapon as the man grabbed my wrists and yanked me tight against his body.

I did the only thing I could do—raked my nails down his cheek, drawing blood.

"You bitch!" He snarled, releasing me only to raise his hand and smack me across the face so hard I saw stars.

I was too disoriented to fight much when he shoved me to the floor and pinned me with his massive weight. My nose was assaulted with the smell of ale and body odor. I screamed for all I was worth as he forced himself between my kicking legs. Large, hairy hands clutched my skirts, raising and bunching them at my waist. With Colt's neglect on providing anything beneath those skirts, I was left with nothing left to protect me from the man's attack. He shoved both my wrists into one of his large hands, using the other to fumble with his breeches.

That disgusting hand brushed close to my intimate regions, as if ascertaining their location. Then he returned to grasping his cock, ready to rape.

This is it, I cried, tears spilling over my cheeks. *It's over. I can't fight him off.*

Squeezing my eyes shut, I prayed to God to save me.

But it wasn't God who answered my prayer. It was the devil.

I heard a door slam wide, causing my attacker to turn his head. He had no time to fight as Colt was upon him, jabbing his dirk into the man's neck. The man howled as Colt shoved him off me. Despite the blade grotesquely sticking out of his muscled flesh, my attacker found the strength to stand and face Colt, now weaponless.

What had happened to his pistol, his cutlass?

The bearded man withdrew his own sword and swiped at Colt, who was forced to jump back. I didn't think—panicking, I threw myself onto my attacker's back, trying to keep him from the captain.

In a flash, he bucked me from his massive back and threw me aside. My head slammed into Colt's desk and, crying out, I fell to my hands and knees.

Momentarily distracted, my attacker was left vulnerable to Colt's attack, and the captain managed to pull his dirk from the man's thick, corded neck, and plunge it into his flesh once more.

This time, he struck a vital artery.

The man fell to the floor in a lifeless heap.

I managed to sit upright and rubbed my head as Colt knelt beside me.

"Are you hurt?" he cried, grabbing my biceps. His terrified eyes searched my face.

"I'm fine," I whispered. "It's you I'm worried about."

Wait. I didn't mean *worried.* Did I?

As if he'd been holding onto his last strength until then, Colt collapsed at my words.

"You *are* hurt," I declared, wide-eyed as I took in the gaping wound on Colt's arm.

"Captain!" Johnson called, bursting into the cabin. His clothing was askew and blood-splattered, but a quick glance told me it wasn't his own blood. Despite being unusually disheveled, he seemed unharmed. He flashed a wide, white-toothed grin.

"The day is won."

Relief flooded me as I realized I could hear the cheers from above. I'd been so caught up in Colt I hadn't noticed.

Johnson's eyes widened. "You're injured," he declared. "I'll fetch Miguel."

Johnson quickly disappeared before Colt or I even had a chance to say anything.

"Is he your cook *and* your surgeon?" I asked, with the hint of a joking tone as I tried to distract Colt.

He saved me, I told myself. *I only care because he saved me.*

Although I'd never have been in danger if he hadn't abducted me in the first place, I argued.

Colt cocked a sloppy grin as if *he* tried to soothe *me.*

"He's good with his hands," Colt replied, lifting one shoulder in an attempt at a shrug. "He and Conks both."

Johnson and Miguel arrived moments later.

"Casualties?" Colt immediately asked, as Miguel examined the bleeding gash on his arm.

"All souls accounted for," Johnson replied.

"Injuries?" the captain asked.

"Several," the gray-haired man admitted. "None to be fatal."

"Prisoners?" Colt asked.

Johnson paused. He shook his head. "Redhands and Sedge slew them all."

Colt's eyes fluttered shut. He sighed. "Perhaps it's for the best. Is the crew seizing-"

Johnson laid a protective hand on his captain's head. The move touched me. Whatever Colt was to me, he was something else to his crew.

"It's all under control. Conks is taking stock of the booty as Redhands and Sedge unload her supplies. They'll sail her to Nassau alongside us. She'll fetch a nice price in port."

Colt nodded, letting his head tilt back, relaxed.

Johnson stood. "I'll come back and check on you after Miguel patches you up. Rest. You've earned it."

"Wait," Colt protested. "She saved my life."

I froze. *Me?*

"If Charlotte hadn't bought time by attacking this man, by jumping on his back like a rabid dog, I wouldn't have had the opportunity to slay him. Let the men know. I owe my life to Charlotte," he said, gravely, holding Johnson's eyes. "They owe their captain's life to her."

Johnson nodded sagely before departing.

"A rabid dog?" I asked, alarmed.

Colt laughed, then stopped when it pained his ribs. "Like a little terrier, climbing onto his back. All bark and no bite. It wasn't funny at the time, but now..."

"Glad I amuse you," I snapped.

"It was good to see a glimpse of the old Charlie," Colt whispered, staring deeply.

Who was this Charlie? A girl with a boy's name, who lied and thieved and attacked men and possibly murdered them? No, I refused to believe it of myself.

Miguel pointedly cleared his throat. He withdrew supplies from a bag he carried, and I determined to make myself useful. Kneeling, I brought Colt's head gently into my lap and he winced at the movement.

To my surprise, Miguel handed me a bottle of rum and I looked up at him quizzically. *Now is not the time for drinking.*

"Pour it where he's injured," Miguel instructed, lifting his chin toward Colt's bleeding arm.

My mouth dropped. "No."

"It will help. I swear it."

"You want me to infect his injury with spirits?"

Miguel shook his head. "It will heal, not harm. I don't know how it works, but it does. We've been using rum on the injured for years now."

I blinked as Colt nodded his agreement. *Perhaps a pirate's soul was so black, the devil's drink soothed it.*

"Wait," Colt said, taking the bottle from my hands. He brought it to his lips and drank deeply, closing his eyes in relief.

Handing the bottle back to me, he said, "Okay. Now."

After a moment's hesitation, I tipped the bottle above the wound, letting the rum spill forth. Colt hissed, baring his sharp canines. I turned my own head in sympathy.

Finished, Miguel set about dressing the wound. Colt filled his surgeon-cook in on what happened and crew came to remove the dead man's body from the cabin, even swabbing up the mess after they'd carried out my attacker's lifeless form. I wondered if they'd toss him overboard, without a proper burial or even a funeral.

I didn't care. Which shocked me, a little.

Miguel had a funny gleam in his eyes when he packed up his supplies and I realized I'd been unconsciously stroking Colt's hair and his sweaty brow. I immediately removed my hand.

"Well then," Miguel announced. "I'll leave you two alone. We've got it all under control, captain. It's as Johnson said. You need to stay down here and… rest."

With the same twinkle in his eye, Miguel departed.

Alone, I felt even more self-conscious with Colt's head in my lap.

"How is your arm?" I asked, attempting to keep the conversation on safe topics, such as injuries.

"Had I arrived seconds later, you'd have lost your virtue," Colt declared, ignoring my question. *Did he seem remorseful?*

"You're the one who's kept me from breeches or undergarments," I chided. "The man had ready access to violate me."

"When we reach the next port, I'll have a chastity belt made." Colt lifted half his mouth into a small grin. It was frustratingly charming.

"Excellent idea," I agreed. "It will keep out nasty pirates like yourself."

"Oh no, Lady Charlotte. I intend to keep the only key."

"If you weren't injured I'd smack you."

"If I wasn't injured, I'd see to it such a move was repaid in kind. Elsewhere on your lovely body, of course."

I rolled my eyes and looked away to hide my blushes. Why did the idea of being locked up for Colt's use make me tingle in parts of my body a lady shouldn't acknowledge? By God, Colt *more* than acknowledged them—he examined them, played with them, aroused them.

For a moment, all was still and silent. I listened to the waves against the ship and watched the candlelight fluttering on the cabin walls. *Had I missed someone preparing the captain's quarters while cleaning up the body?* Colt seemed deep in thought and I felt like he could see through to my own mind. It made me want to try to empty my brain so that he could not uncover any hidden desires there.

"Lay with me tonight," Colt whispered, breaking the silence. "Just beside me, nothing more. Not because I'm tying you down or forcing you."

I froze—everywhere except my heart, which seemed to hammer in defiance of my stillness.

"Stay with me because you want to," Colt implored, voice low.

How could a man so cruel look at me with such unguarded hope in his eyes? How did it work such magic to disarm me?

CHAPTER 20

COLT

"I WON'T TOUCH YOU. I can't…" I broke off in an annoyed chuckle. "Do much in this state anyway."

Holding Charlotte's gaze I said, "Stay with me, lay with me. That's all."

Her pupils had blown wide, perhaps with fear or arousal. But she'd moved away from me, as if the answer would be no.

Fuck that. No. I clenched my jaw to stop myself from clenching her arm. What had she reduced me to? What did I care whether she *wanted* to do something or not? Maybe I did care, once. But that was a long time ago. Right?

I lifted her chin with my thumb and forefinger. If she couldn't hide from me, maybe she wouldn't hide from herself either.

"Just stay this night, in my bed, beside me. Not because you're my prisoner, not because I'm forcing you. Because you want to."

I heard her breath, short and fast. I was so intent on her eyes, I wasn't even distracted by her breasts, rising and falling above me. Well, barely. Her eyelids fluttered closed, pained. I braced for rejection.

When she spoke, her voice was so soft I strained to hear her.

"What if what I want is for you to… force me to?"

Charlotte averted her eyes, seemingly alarmed with herself.

A sense of power tore through my chest, swelling with pride and possessiveness.

Easily done, my lady. So easily.

Well, it would have been easier if I'd remained uninjured. I stood, struggling a bit.

"Don't," Charlotte protested weakly, standing to match me. "You'll hurt yourself."

I grabbed her. She gasped but she *yielded,* limp in my arms, moaning as I escorted her to the bed.

That was all it took—I exerted my power over her and she moaned. Her arousal didn't even require I strip her, caress her, kiss her. The thrill it sent to my mind as she succumbed was intoxicating. The nearest I'd felt was the delight of victory in claiming another man's ship, the crew on their knees… but such triumph didn't stir my cock, certainly not to harden as painfully as when Charlotte submitted to my will. Unbelievably, this headstrong little girl captivated me more than a victory over the king's navy.

"Careful," she whispered as I laid her down, "you'll hurt yourself."

"Let me worry about me," I told her. "Stay where I've put you." I kissed her forehead and threatened, "Or I'll be forced to hurt *you.*"

She blushed so prettily as she looked down and bit her lip.

"What will we do, captain?" she whispered. "If you hold true to your word and don't molest me this evening, how shall we pass the time?"

"I could read to you," I suggested.

"I have to confess, I'm surprised a brute like you can read. I didn't imagine a pirate captain to sail with such a wonderfully curated selection of books."

I laughed so hard it pained my ribs where I'd suffered a blow during the battle.

"How else would I have taught wayward girls such as yourself?"

The crease in Charlotte's brow told me something was off. Maybe I'd struck a nerve. She'd come so far from those days, perhaps she didn't want to be reminded of them.

"I think it's better I should read to you," Charlotte said finally. "You can't use your arm well enough to hold up a book."

I snorted. "It's fine." But I allowed her to scurry off the bed and select a tome from my small library. She was right—I'd selected those books carefully, but they were ever-changing. One, because I hungered for new knowledge and two, because the salt air inevitably soiled any volume kept too long at sea.

I folded one arm beneath my head and arranged myself as comfortably as I could. When Charlotte returned to the bed, her swaying necklace caught my eye.

"Why do you still wear the locket?" I asked. "Did you keep it all this time and put it on only when you saw we were coming? Or have you always worn it?" My voice trailed off in disbelief.

Charlotte paused, stroking the gold oval, then quietly confessed, "I've never taken it off. I always wear it."

"Why?" I whispered, still disbelieving.

Don't hope, don't you dare, I cautioned.

"To remind me," came her cryptic reply.

To remind you of your hate, I thought, *and to strengthen your daily resolve for revenge.*

Yet that foolish, hopeful voice in me wondered if maybe some part of Charlotte wanted to be reminded of something else.

That night.

Charlotte opened the book and began reading but I couldn't even hear the words. Having her willingly in my bed, having her open a bit to the past, distracted me to the point that I was incapable of listening.

She'd only made it a page or two before I grabbed her hand to stop her.

"Why did you kill Maurice?" I asked, practically begging. "The truth."

"I wouldn't-" she protested, then stopped and lifted her chin. "He deserved it."

I studied her face. "That wasn't for you to decide."

"Whose decision was it? Yours?"

"Yes."

"Why? Because you're the captain?"

I tried to meet her eyes, but she refused.

"You know why," I said.

CHAPTER 21

CHARLOTTE

I HADN'T WANTED TO sleep next to him, hadn't wanted him to force me. That was the trauma talking. *Right?*

I told myself these obvious lies as I awoke in Colt's arms. Well, his good arm, at least, was draped protectively across my torso. Thankfully, I'd faced away from him as I'd slumbered and didn't want to turn around yet because I knew very well the condition in which most men awoke in the-

"Take off all your clothes," Colt whispered into my ear. "I want to examine you for injuries."

I blinked. How did he know I'd awoken?

"Whatever happened to good morning?" I huffed.

I could practically hear his lazy grin behind me. "It is for me. Is it for you?"

"Asks the man who beats and molests me at every given chance. *Do you care?*"

Colt barked a laugh. "I'm checking to make sure you're okay, aren't I?"

I drew the neck of my shirt tighter around me, hesitant.

"You're injured," I pointed out.

"I'm fine."

"You said you wouldn't touch me."

"That was during the night. It's morning now."

"I'm *fine.*"

"I need to make sure. As a captain I'm nothing if not thorough."

Yes, I thought. *I've heard the crew grumble about it often enough.* Colt's fastidiousness didn't match my image of a vulgar pirate captain.

I huffed again and yanked my shirt from the waistband of my skirts, wanting to get it over with quickly. Colt grabbed my wrist.

"No. Stand. Let me see you undress."

Grumbling, I shuffled off the bed and tuned to face him, still pouting.

Dear god, he looked handsome in the morning. His hair had tousled about in an appealing, carefree manner. His beard had grown into a deeper stubble. He was so very different from the men in our settlement, and yet an enigma, both more and less refined.

At the warning of Colt's raised eyebrows, I removed my shirt, bunched it into a ball, and threw it at his chest. He caught it with his good arm, laughing. Since I couldn't outright disobey, I resolved to follow his orders in the most rebellious way I could. He wanted a show, I'd deny him. Repeating the process, I quickly stripped my skirt and threw it at Colt, who once again caught it while laughing.

"Glad to see you're feeling better," I quipped in a voice to show I was not at all glad.

"I am. Now let's see how you… feel." Colt dipped his head in the direction of the bed, commanding my return.

Submissively, I laid down beside Colt. He rose on his good elbow to *examine* me. At first, Colt watched my face carefully, almost as if he hesitated. Then his hands roved by body and my breasts responded by swelling and rising to meet him, nipples hardening as if screaming that they longed for his touch, and with his keen gaze he missed none of it. I couldn't help but feel a sense of gratification from the persistent way Colt seemed unable to refrain from touching me for very long. His fingertips grazed my skin, reverent, almost worshipful.

Colt bent down and planted searing kisses on my flesh. I didn't know what was between us, but I didn't want him to stop. His mouth moved lower, tantalizingly close to the top of my mound. My breathing quickened in anticipation of the unknown.

"Is this okay?" Colt asked between kisses.

Why was he asking? Colt never requested permission. Did it have anything to do with yesterday's attack?

Did it mean the power to stop him was mine?

At my pause, Colt halted, making me whimper. Staring at me with concern in his black eyes, I realized he'd misread my silence. I realized he intended to put his mouth on me. And I realized my cunt was throbbing for it.

I was at a crossroads and one word would select my direction. His direction.

I was weak—Colt made me weak. Or was it strength to admit what I wanted?

Oh God. I was neither strong enough to speak the words nor strong enough to deny them.

I snuck glances at Colt's face as I let my legs fall slightly open—the only indication of my desires I could give.

Grasping one thigh, Colt spread my legs wider and I jumped a little as he inserted himself between them. My heart slammed against my ribcage as I wondered what exactly he'd do and how it would feel. He leaned his head down and the rough scrape of his beard against my sensitive, inner thighs made my eyelids flutter. I chanced a look at Colt and found him grinning with satisfaction.

"Lady Charlotte, do you realize you've soaked the bed?"

I nearly choked.

"You're so wet, it's dripping onto my linens."

To prove his point, Colt ran his fingers through my folds, smearing my wetness, coaxing guttural moans from me. Spreading me wide, Colt flicked his tongue against my clit and I screamed at the astounding pleasure.

"I don't think I've ever seen such a reaction from you, Lady Charlotte," Colt teased. "Is this the way to force you to reveal your secrets?"

Punctuating the question, he took my aching bud in his mouth and sucked. My legs fell wide and I melted into the bed with animalistic moans. My hands shook as I attempted to restrain them from grabbing Colt's head and pressing him closer.

He pulled back and I whined.

"Tell me what I want to know, Charlotte," he urged, lazily running a finger up and down my slit. His breath teased at the pleasure his mouth could bring. So close, but he denied me.

"Tell me everything."

I needed him to continue, but I had nothing about the past to reveal.

"I… can't," I protested. "It's too much."

What you are doing is too much. And not enough.

"Then we'll start easy," Colt advised. "Start at the beginning. Tell me, were you planning to escape for months or was it a spur-of-the-moment decision? What happened that night, Charlotte?"

I thrashed my head side to side. I didn't know what to say. I couldn't handle it if he tortured me with his mouth the way he had with his fingers, bringing me closer but never allowing satisfaction. In my lust-filled haze, I thought I might actually die.

"Tell me what happened, Charlotte," Colt softly implored. "Why did you leave?"

Colt's tongue ran the length of my slit, then he stopped again. I wailed and broke.

"I had no plan!" I shouted, looking down at him with unrestrained longing. Colt searched my face wildly and asked, "What changed? What made you do it?"

"I—I… don't know." *What could I possibly say that would sound plausible?*

Colt's tongue found my favorite spot once more, licking and sucking lewdly, sending me into bliss.

"Please, don't stop," I begged. I couldn't help it when my fingers wove into his hair—a plea to continue.

"Tell me what made you leave," Colt demanded between licks, his breath caressing my too-sensitive opening.

Desperate for him to continue, I cried, "You know very well! Don't make me say it."

"Because of… what I'd done? Or because of what happened between us that night?"

What had you done to me in the past?

"Both," I moaned, unsure which was the better option.

I felt Colt's warm breath on my sex once more as he sighed, sadly. "I'm sorry for everything, Charlotte." He nuzzled my wet cunt with his nose, lewdly inhaling, and I shivered. "I'm so sorry. Let me show you how sorry I am."

Without restraint, Colt dove into my sex, lapping and sucking. He slid two fingers inside me as delicious accompaniment to the ministrations with his tongue.

I cried like the whore I was. *Colt's whore.*

I didn't want to think about how many women he might have brought to pleasure like this, it made me insane with jealousy.

When my thrashing increased, his tongue-lashing matched my pace, driving me higher. I bucked frantically in his mouth. I prayed to the Lord Colt wouldn't stop, though I didn't think the Lord answered a harlot's prayers, and certainly not in askance of sin.

With no other option, I prayed to Colt.

"Please, don't stop. I'm begging you. Don't stop."

The god before me listened to my prayers. He kept going until I broke against his lips, coming apart with frenzied cries as if I spoke in tongues. Perhaps I did. *This is no god,* I reminded myself. The devil had me in his mouth. So what demonic spirits had seized my wanton soul in such a wicked state?

I'd never known pleasure could be like this. A fear, matching the joy in size, crept into my heart. As I came down from the heights of bliss, that fear spread throughout my limbs, causing a fight or flight response.

I couldn't fall for a man like Colt; couldn't allow him these trespasses upon my body. I couldn't take down all his shipmates on my own, either. Not without poison, at least. Which meant I had to flee. Because I was in danger of losing worse than the flesh from my back or even my life.

I might lose my soul. To the devil between my legs.

What happened in our past that makes you sorry now?

Perhaps Colt had done these wicked things to me—or at least attempted to—throughout my time on his ship. I must not have been responsive then. At least, not to this extent. And he was sorry for his attempts, I reasoned, because they were likely forceful. Maybe, one night, they'd gone too far.

Who knows how much further we'd go if I continued on this path?

Nassau, I vowed. *When we dock, I'll find escape.*

CHAPTER 22

CHARLOTTE

"LAND AHEAD!" CAME the shout from one of the watch crew. I hurried to the railing but as we sailed closer, I couldn't see the comfort of civilization anywhere. Where were all the buildings, the people? Nothing met my gaze but pristine beaches and swaying palms under a cloudless sky.

I heard Colt approach behind me. "Captain," I said, both dismayed and alarmed, "where is the town?"

"About five miles north and around that bend," Colt replied.

At my quizzical look, he explained, "We drop anchor here first. Wash up in the cove. Sober up, if needed, as the men ready for the first roaring night at port. Conks gives the crew a last-minute talking to, we take a secondary count of our stores-" Colt frowned and scrubbed a hand down his face. "Now you've got me talking as if your act is real. You know all this, Charlotte. Let's resume your little game when I don't have my hands full," he said, giving me a chiding look and quickly departing to manage the men.

I remained aboard for most of the day, while the crew took turns in the jolly boat, rowing out to bathe in a secluded cove. Returning to deck they stripped again and hung wet, recently washed clothing out to dry.

I couldn't imagine this practice to be common amongst pirates. It was as if Colt wanted to make a good impression upon docking.

He's a fastidious captain indeed.

Sometime in the late afternoon, Colt took my arm and announced, "It's our turn."

"Turn for what?" I asked.

He cocked that devilish, one-sided grin. "To bathe, my lady."

I gulped but had no choice but to follow Colt down the ladder and into the awaiting jolly boat. When I reached the last few steps, he clasped my waist, lifted and deposited me on a bench. Wincing at the pain in his arm, he asked Conks and Johnson to come along to assist in the rowing, yet the captain stubbornly tried helping with his good arm. I sat playing with my skirt and trying not to steal glances at Colt's muscles as they moved in his arms with the rhythm of his strokes.

"Why the cleansing ritual?" I asked, as we headed toward the cove. "Why not storm the town dirty and bloody and strike fear into the hearts of everyone who crosses your path?"

"Are we back to your game, Charlotte?" Colt asked, raising his eyebrows.

I didn't answer and he shrugged.

"Men at sea forget themselves, forget they're even men. I've found that taking a day to remind them helps bridge the gap between the wilds of these waters and the customs of town. Long ago, when we docked, their energies spiked too high. Fights broke out, theft ran rampant, women were not treated in a civilized manner. Maurice wasn't a help in-" Colt cut himself off at the mention of the man I supposedly murdered.

I didn't do it, I wanted to shout.

There was a tense pause between us before he concluded, "Such behavior threatened our welcome in certain establishments. As you're well aware, my crew has enough of a reputation that we don't need theatrics of any kind to intimidate anyone into compliance."

Yes, I thought wryly, *I'm not only aware as your reputation preceded you, I'm familiar with your intimidation first-hand.*

"You didn't feel the need to bathe before raiding our settlement," I pointed out.

"That's because it was a raid," Colt said, as if I tested his patience. "Didn't know if we'd only bloody ourselves further in the process."

"But in the pirate capital of the world your band of sailing heathens act as civilized men?" I scoffed. "What is it, honor amongst thieves?"

"Flawed as it may be, you've always known I find more honor in our democratic world of *heathens* than in that oppressive one of kingly privilege you're so determined to defend."

Conks and Johnson, who'd been politely trying to pretend they weren't listening up until this point, nodded their heads in agreement.

I could tell from Colt's tone I'd struck a nerve. Head bent, I must have looked shocked or chastised at his temper, because Colt softened and amended, "I concede your point that merchant ships do not feel very honored to have their cargo plundered at the hands of my men. But there's honor *between* pirates."

ONCE WE REACHED THE SHORE, Conks and Johnson rowed back while Colt took my hand and led me to the edges of the rocky cove where the men before us had bathed. I'd imagined they simply dipped in the sea and called it cleaning, but I was surprised to find rough wedges of soap and scrubbing brushes scattered about the rocks.

Colt wasted no time in stripping his clothing and jumping into the turquoise water so quickly I didn't even get a look at his manhood.

Not that I was trying.

Grinning, his head appeared above the surface.

"Your turn, Lady Charlotte," he commanded.

I clutched the neck of my shirt. It was one thing to be naked in the seclusion of the captain's cabin, it was another matter entirely under the open sky.

"I'll stay in the water," Colt said. "Take off your clothes. Now."

"I can't," I protested, glancing over my shoulder. The cove was hidden from view of *The Dread Night*, and no one seemed likely to happen upon the beach, but that didn't make it right. "Not here."

"I can come up there and do it for you."

"No."

"It's safe," Colt teased. "Sharks tend to stay by the reef out there."

My eyes bulged and he laughed. I couldn't tell if he was joking or not—cruelty was Colt's currency after all, paving his way forward in this new world. Or repaying in merciless doses those who defied him.

So why hadn't he simply threatened my life to learn the truth?

Because it's crueler this way, I argued. *To drag it out.*

Colt tilted his head, eyebrows raised—a command. Impossibly, with rivulets of water dripping from his thick, dark hair and down his strong, bare chest, he was even more handsome. Too handsome to trust myself near.

"Strip, Charlotte," Colt said, his tone alone a warning.

Reluctantly and as slowly as possible, I removed my recently-acquired boots, skirt, and shirt before the setting sun. Standing as bare as the day I was born, I crossed my arms over my chest and made no further move. The water looked shallow enough to stand, but I didn't want to get into it naked, and not with Colt especially.

"Now jump. Jump or I'll belt you," Colt said. He thought a moment, then corrected, "I'll get your bottom wet and *then* I'll belt it and it will hurt a lot worse."

I groaned, knowing that option only pleased him more.

When he made a move toward the rocks, I jumped —

— and screamed as I hit the water.

It *wasn't* shallow; I had misjudged. My feet scrambled, toes just scraping the seabed if I sunk a bit, but not enough for me to keep my head above water. Thrashing and shouting, I felt Colt's solid arms wrap around me.

"What are you doing?" he cried, brow knit with confusion.

"I thought it was shallow," I sputtered, coughing up water. "I can't swim."

"You can't-" He froze and then threw his head back, laughing heartily. "No, a lady wouldn't know how to swim, would she?" Colt pulled me close. "Hold onto me."

I already was. My hands loosely clutched his shoulders, but at the offer I held on tighter. Curiously though, my legs kicked languidly, as if muscle memory took hold. As if they *did* know the sea.

It was probably true. How could I still cling to foolish hope when so much evidence to the contrary existed? *I'd been aboard a pirate ship, and thus, it was likely I had known how to swim.*

But certainly never like this. Naked. With Colt.

"No, tighter," he said, voice low and husky. "Wrap your arms and legs around me. I want those wet breasts pressed against my chest."

I snapped my eyes up to his, shaking my head.

"Do it or I'll let you drown."

Gritting my teeth, I kicked my legs up around his waist and encircled his neck with my arms. But it wasn't enough. Colt pressed me firmly against him and I squealed. I could *feel* his sizable hardness beneath my rear.

Too big. Too long. Lurking beneath the water like a bloody sea monster. My breath quickened at my own dirty imagination.

"Do you know what I'm picturing, Lady Charlotte?" he teased in my ear. "Your cunt. I can picture it any time I want. It's spread wide open right now, isn't it? Unprotected. At my mercy."

His words made me whimper. *Monster was accurate.*

"Hold on tight. If you let go, all I have to do is bob you down… just a little… and slide you right onto my cock."

Retreating into the safety of manners, I spat, "Your speech is filthy. Unbefitting a captain."

Colt grinned. "Befitting a pirate captain, I'd say. And how would you know? How many of those have you met in your pampered life, *my lady?*"

"One too many," I countered.

Colt barked a laugh, sharp white canines poking out.

"Kiss me," he commanded suddenly, and my heart skipped a beat. After my first night on the ship, he'd never ordered me to kiss him. He'd forced unimaginably lewd activities on me, but never a kiss.

I pulled my head back in refusal.

Colt immediately loosened his hold around my waist—a threat to let me drown. I instantly clung to him harder.

"Shall I peel your arms from around my neck?" he taunted. "I'll do it unless you kiss me."

"The only way you can ever inspire a lady to kiss you is by threatening her life," I snapped.

Colt slowly tilted his head to the side as he gazed at me with those impossibly black eyes. The act, though minor, held such menace. It was animalistic, predatory.

"Now that's not true at all. I know another method to *inspire* your kiss. Shall I try that, instead?"

In case I had any doubt as to his intent, Colt's hands shifted, cupping my bottom and squeezing. He raised one arrogant brow at my accompanying squeak.

Quickly, before his hands progressed, I turned my face to his and relaxed my mouth, preparing for him devour to it.

Better my mouth than… other places. Even if those places were oddly screaming for attention. *His.*

Colt the Cruel. It was far crueler to make me participate in my own shaming at his hands.

His eyes lowered as he brought his lips to mine, tongue sweeping boldly inside my passive mouth. Colt's fingers tightened on the flesh of my rear, but all I could do was squeak again, a sound swallowed by his kiss.

Why did shame taste so sweet?

Against my will, my tongue moved, and I couldn't help but arch into his strong chest to relieve some of the ache in my breasts. I didn't want Colt to feel what I'd done, but I knew he had when his hips jerked upwards in response. My reaction was to buck forward to escape the pressure of his rod against my rear—I *swore* it was in avoidance—but it had the unwanted effect of grinding my sex against the flat of his lower abdomen.

Colt's moan told me that movement did not go unnoticed either.

We tumbled downward to sin in this manner, one reaction from either of us pushing the other into further depravity. The captain and I would descend until there was nowhere left to go.

But hell.

We were unwed. We weren't even courting. We were nothing to each other but captor and captive. Should I return home despoiled, would Daniel even want me? And what became of a lady who could not marry? The options were limited.

I broke our kiss. "Please," I pled, turning my head to the side. "Please. No more. It's sinful."

I felt Colt's chest rise and fall against me as he tried to steady his heavy breathing.

"Alright," he agreed, voice husky. "I'll demand less sin from your mouth if you start working it toward salvation. Tell me the truth."

I froze. "I…"

"Don't you tire of this game, Charlotte?" he asked, weary.

There is no choice, I wanted to scream. *Because there is no game.* I looked about the waves as if they provided a way out.

"Shall we go farther away from shore?" Colt taunted, paddling us toward the mouth of the inlet. "Deeper? Where the sharks play?"

"No!" *Damn him.* I clung tighter around his neck.

"Tell me what happened that night," he said softly, almost pleading. "If I'm to protect you from the men, you have to give me something. Redhands wants to whip the truth from your back. Murdering Maurice might not rile them, half the crew felt as you did. But if he lets them know about the Eye and they put your fate to vote? Give me something to help protect you, Charlotte."

My stomach knotted at the mention of Redhands and the lash. "I can't."

Colt sighed heavily. "Alright, we have a little longer. Tell me something else, instead. Tell me the truth about what you want, Charlotte."

I blinked. What could I possibly want except freedom?

"I want you to release me. Let me return to my home, unharmed."

Unharmed any further, I corrected in my head. Although I wasn't quite sure where to draw the line between Colt's punishments and his pleasures.

His eyes narrowed. "The truth, Charlotte."

"I don't know what you mean."

"For as long as you've hated me, for as much as you hate me still… you desire me."

My cheeks flamed. "I—I…"

"*Say it.*" His order was accompanied by more squeezing of my rear. Every time he touched me there it brought forth memories of the harsher ways he touched my backside.

Turning my head to my shoulder, I whispered with defeat, "I desire you."

"No. Look at me. I want to see your eyes when you speak."

The mere command made me shudder. Colt's wet fingertips found my chin, guiding it upwards. His black eyes were both impenetrable and piercing at the same time—a shield and a sword.

Imagine such a man as a husband, I couldn't help but think. To his lady, he'd be exactly that. A shield and a sword.

The thought made my heart beat a little faster.

I averted my eyes and Colt gently squeezed my chin—a reminder to look up.

How could I not desire him? How could any woman resist? It wasn't fair. *The Lord shouldn't make men this horrible, this handsome.*

He'd take nothing from the words and yet he'd take everything. I'd rather have him molest me than make me say it.

Cocky, arrogant eyebrows raised impatiently over dark eyes. The sun set behind him, haloing him like a bloody god.

I licked my salty lips. "I desire you."

The smug smile I knew would appear did not disappoint. His face lit with triumph.

"Was that so difficult?"

"Would it matter if it was?"

"Of course. I rather enjoy causing you difficulty."

Huffing, I attempted to push myself off his body, but he didn't relent his grip. I relaxed only slightly, expecting more molestation, but Colt unnerved me even more by not groping my breast or squeezing my rear. He stroked my cheekbones gently, almost reverently, staring at me with awe. Somehow, it was more intimate than if he'd slid his fingers into my open sex.

But if he had… he wouldn't have met with any resistance.

HAVING RECENTLY WON A BATTLE and with the impending arrival at port, spirits were high on the ship that evening. News spread of my assistance with Colt in slaying my attacker, and the crew seemed friendlier toward me throughout the night. No one dared engage me in conversation, but I received many smiles or at least a tip of the head in acknowledgement of my service.

For the first time, I shared a table above deck—with Miguel, Conks, Johnson, and Colt. I didn't speak much but I couldn't deny it felt nice to be included. The stars shone brightly, seeming to bless the meal. With the promise of replenishing our stores on the morn, Miguel used a bevy of citrus fruits to enhance the rum, and we all drank happily, though not too heartily, at the captain's command. *Save it for tomorrow night, boys,* he advised.

When tables were cleared, someone broke out the fiddles and the men laughed and sang. I did not want to be enchanted, but such is the nature of enchantments that a victim is helpless to the spell.

Was it the rum?

Each song became a longing tune in my heart, subtle at first, then faster and faster, as if I swirled and danced under the magical incantation. I hadn't moved from my seat on the bench, but I felt swept away into a realm so different from the one I'd known that I might as well have been in another world.

A dream world, with pirate captains so handsome, they make my heart ache just to look upon them. A world with captains who do things such wickedly delicious between my legs, it makes my body shake and spasm until I fall apart. A world with a man like Colt, whose gaze makes me feel like he can see into my soul.

Maybe it all was just a dream and if so, my actions had no consequence. It didn't matter that I succumbed to the magical swirl.

Grasping my skirts, I stood—

—and I sang.

I began a wistful, melancholic sea shanty, singing for these pirates as I had sung many nights for the men in our tavern.

Immediate silence fell. I nearly faltered, scared I'd horrified them, until I saw the looks on their faces. From the surprise, I guessed that I had never given them a song in my past. Gathering my courage, I continued, moving away from the bench and to the center of the tables.

I poured my soul into that song, closing my eyes at parts that meant the most to me.

When I opened them as I finished, I was again met with total silence.

It was Johnson who clapped first. Conks quickly followed, hooting and cheering. I broke into a relieved smile as the rest of the men joined in. Looking them over, I met Colt's eyes.

He wasn't clapping. He wasn't even moving. He stared at me like he'd never seen me before. Whatever I'd done in the past, I was now sure I'd never sung for these men.

"Another!" someone shouted. "Give us another!"

Smiling tentatively, I ripped my gaze from Colt's. The fiddle struck up a familiar tune and the rum warmed my blood. I sang again, and again, to the pleasure of the men. Sometimes they joined in a chorus, sometimes they simply stared. It was like my nights in the tavern, but much more enchanting beneath the shining stars and above the rollicking sea. A light breeze blew, fanning my hair, and I felt like I was the wind too, like my voice carried out and through the men, joining them.

We were connected in those moments. I felt a part of the crew.

I've never felt a part of anything before. Not like this.

Sadly, the connection began to fade as the spell ended with my singing. And yet, something had irrevocably changed. Something began to forge that wasn't there before.

When I could sing no more, the men crowded me, congratulating my talent. Some clapped me on the back, as if I were one of them. From the corner of my eye, I noted that Colt hadn't moved. He sat on the bench like a statue, staring at me with wide eyes.

I felt someone edge close to my body and turned to see Robert the Red amongst my crowd of raucous admirers. My stomach instantly tightened.

"My, my," Redhands whispered in my ear, "look at what you can do, Charlotte. I can't wait to hear how prettily you'll sing under the lash."

I felt Colt's protective grip on my arm. *God, he was fast.*

"Lady Charlotte is tired from the gift of her entertainment this evening," he announced. "She will retire to my cabin now."

Colt's proclamation was met with groans and protests, but he quickly escorted me away from Robert and below deck. Colt didn't speak a word to me. His jaw remained clenched, his grip on my arm almost painful.

Slamming his cabin door behind us, Colt said, "You're just full of secrets and surprises, aren't you?" His lips were inches from mine as he demanded, "What other talents have you hidden from me all these years?"

Taken aback and a little fired up from the rum, I countered, "They are my talents to hide, captain. It is for me to decide what to share and with whom."

"And what have you shared, Charlotte? Your lips? Your cunt? Answer me!" He squeezed my arm and wild, frantic eyes searched my face. I could smell the rum on his breath too. "You've always been a liar, are you a lying whore as well? Do you sing men to sleep at night, fuck them, steal their gold? What have you been doing these past two years?" he shouted, squeezing my arm harder. "I deserve an answer!"

I almost didn't blame Colt for his anger and confusion, and that scared me more than anything.

"Stop acting as if you own me," I shouted back. "I am not one of your crew you can command!"

"You are correct, Lady Charlotte," he said, sneering. "You haven't the privilege of my crew, you are my captive."

"Then lock me away!" I cried, hating my helplessness. In an effort to seize back some control, I demanded it before he had the chance. "Put me back in the brig."

I'll escape tomorrow, somewhere in town. Forget my plans for justice. I can't stay on this ship any longer.

"You think I'd shy away from it?" he scoffed. "You think you haven't earned it?"

I lifted my chin and taunted, "Do it then. I do not wish to stay here tonight. Will you tie me to the bed to keep me? Tell me, if you're incapable of being without me this night, which of us is truly the captive?"

Colt jerked his head back, eyes full of rage. He opened his mouth to speak, but a knock on the door interrupted us.

Until then, I hadn't realized how loud we'd been shouting.

"Captain?" Conks's voice rang out from the other side. "You alright in there?"

"No, we are not," I proclaimed, lifting my head higher.

A pause, and then, Conks *opened the door.* I was sure Colt looked incredulous at his crewman's audacity, but I didn't spare the captain a look.

Stepping away boldly, I declared, "I would like to sleep in the brig this evening. I think I've earned a night of peace."

"That is not for you to decide," Colt growled, grabbing my arm and yanking me back to him.

My stomach sank. I had no way to fight the captain and I'd only hoped he wouldn't protest too much in front of Conks. Clearly, I was mistaken.

"Technically, it's for the men to decide," Conks said, rubbing his gray beard. "Do you really want to put it to vote and chance them overruling you?"

Was it true? My chest filled with hope. *Colt did say a ship is a democracy and a captain had less exclusive authority than I'd once believed.*

"A few songs and she's enchanted you?" Colt asked in disbelief. "Don't forget who she is. What she's capable of."

"She was capable of saving your life," Conks pointed out.

"Which only needed saving because I came to save hers!"

Conks shrugged. "That's not the story you sold to the crew. Johnson emphasized *her* heroism. I don't think the men will ever be voting to let her go, but they'd vote to give her a night's rest at her request. So I ask again—do you really want to give them the opportunity?"

I could practically feel Colt's anger coming off his skin as he released my arm.

I didn't look back as I brushed past Conks and said, "Good evening, captain."

"Lock her up tight," I heard Colt grit through clenched teeth.

You can't lock me up forever, I thought. *Tomorrow when we're in town, I'll escape.*

I *had* to leave. I couldn't let Redhands whip me upon departing Nassau and I couldn't allow myself to succumb to Colt's nightly… attentions. He'd already tarnished my body. How long until the devil corrupted my heart as well?

CHAPTER 23

CHARLOTTE

AFTER A FITFUL night's sleep in the brig, I was released in the late morning to a bustle of activity as the crew ferried to and fro, transporting men to the boisterous merriment of Nassau's lawless port, and carrying goods and supplies from town aboard *The Dread Night*.

It would be easy to get lost in that bustling town just beyond the beach, but where exactly? *And what would I do next?* I had no coin nor any items of value to trade. Finding a fellow woman would be wisest. Someone sympathetic to my plight. Someone refined.

I frowned. *Or as civil as one could get in a port of such debauchery and corruption.*

If I could negotiate assistance in hiding, and the eventual transport back to my settlement, then I could guarantee payment from Mrs. Penningham upon my delivery to whomever helped escort me.

Though staying at the tavern is no longer an option. Colt knows where to find me.

I chewed my lip and resolved to think about that later. Perhaps Mrs. Penningham could help me come up with a plan.

The sun had nearly set by the time it was my turn to stretch my legs, and Colt had cooled down enough to escort me to the docks. Contrary to what I expected, he looked a little excited to share Nassau with me as the captain, Johnson, Conks and I all climbed into the jolly boat and rowed through the calm, sparkling waves of the harbor. In the distance, pelicans swooped and dove from the sky, searching for their dinner amongst the turquoise water.

"We're headed to a special tavern tonight," Colt said, with a gleam in his eye and an annoyingly handsome smile tugging at his lips. "Unfamiliar to a lady such as yourself," he teased, "but I knew a girl once and it was her favorite establishment for their fried cod."

The captain watched me carefully for a reaction, but I only stared. Eventually, he shook his head and scoffed, gazing up to the skies with a *why me* question in his eyes, as if I were nothing more than a troublesome burden he'd been forced to contend with, as if he suffered my presence, instead of having required me to be at his side.

Well, I thought, proudly, *you'll soon be rid of me.*

It wasn't a far walk into town and to the dining establishment Colt chose. I ate whilst plotting my escape—I wasn't foolish enough to run on an empty stomach—and the captain was infuriatingly correct. The fish was delicious. As it was placed before me, my mouth watered at the smell, and I had to resist the urge to lick the salty, greasy crumbs from my fingers once I'd finished. Fortifying my courage, I washed my meal down with a generous pint of ale.

Standing quickly, I stumbled a bit upon my feet. Perhaps the ale hit me harder than I thought.

"Excuse me gentlemen," I said. "I have needs to which I must attend."

"That way," Johnson said, tilting his head to the rear of the tavern.

I smiled gratefully and nodded. To my surprise, Colt followed me with his eyes, but allowed me to leave without protest. I supposed he didn't have much choice, given what I inferred I was going to do. Also, enough patrons saw us dine together, so I doubted a single man would try anything untoward. And I supposed Colt didn't think me stupid enough to try to run.

Well, my dear captain, you have no idea how wrong you are.

Wait. That sounded wrong.

Brave, bold, clever, I corrected, as I rounded the corner and ducked out of Colt's sight.

In fact, I thought, gathering my skirts to pick up the pace, *I know the best place to hide for a while.* The place where Colt would least expect to find a lady.

Under the moonless night, I slipped through the crowded street as quickly as I dared and headed directly toward the flickering torches of the brothel we'd passed on our way to dine.

It was the last place in Nassau Colt would ever think to check. I'd simply hide until he gave up the search for the night, and then find myself a kind ear in the morning.

I ENTERED THE WICKED ESTABLISHMENT and immediately found what I believed to be the proprietor. Dressed stations above the others, the lady couldn't be missed. As I approached, she made no attempt to hide her perusal of my body with both the boldness of a man and the calculation of a businesswoman. Her scrutiny ended with one side of her lips pulling up into a small smile.

I dusted my skirts and tried not to fidget.

"Hello, my name is Constance," I introduced myself falsely.

"Lady Wick," she replied, evenly, and I couldn't tell if she'd bought my lie.

My heart sped up as I didn't like speaking in the open room where I could get caught at any moment. I resisted the urge to look over my shoulder, sure that would tip her off to the fact that I was hiding.

"I need a place to spend the night and was hoping you'd be so kind as to assist. I was separated from my party during a scuffle and lost my purse…"

Lady Wick snorted.

"Rooms upstairs are for clients only and you're distracting from my girls down 'ere," she said, unabashedly giving me another once-over. Lady Wick crooked an eyebrow. "Unless you're lookin' to earn back some of that coin you lost? Seems to me you shouldn't be turnin' away any chances you have to improve your situation."

I blinked, shocked. *My she worked fast to seize upon an opportunity and turn it to her favor.*

The door opened behind me and I jumped a little, exhaling when two men I didn't recognize stumbled into the room.

Running out of time and not wanting to be tossed onto the street, I lied, "Yes, yes, fine. I'm amenable to work." I thought that squaring my shoulders and tossing my hair as I spoke gave me the bold look of a fallen woman, but Lady Wick only laughed.

"Clearly, you're a shiny new pearl. Why hide it? You'll fetch a bigger price. My terms are more generous than any other establishment you'll find. And for a fresh maid such as yourself?" Lady Wick winked. "Fifty-fifty. Though I doubt we'll find a man to pay such a price as I'm going to ask. There's always tomorrow evening, and the next, for as long as you'd like to stay."

How easily she could lure new girls to the work, I marveled. *The prospect of a soft bed and a hot meal each night were powerful motivators.*

Sweat gathered at the back of my neck as the seconds ticked by—seconds in which I could get caught. Two facts worked in my favor if I accepted. One, she'd said it was unlikely that we'd find the appropriate customer in one night. Clearly, she took me for an unsoiled woman and wanted to charge the maximum price for a man to do the soiling. And two, if what I'd heard from the crew was true, the exchange between a lady and a gentlemen had to be mutually agreed upon—meaning I could reject any customer who repulsed me. Which would be all of them.

Lady Wick struck out her hand.

"Fair?" she asked.

"Fair," I whispered, shaking it and wondering what I'd gotten myself into. *The hour grows late,* I reassured myself. *I can reasonably hide for the remainder of the evening.*

"You're fresh as the morning dew, but those clothes won't work," Lady Wick said, signaling to someone over my shoulder. "Get upstairs and get yourself into a new dress. Anna will take you."

I followed a shy girl up a set of stairs, grateful to find a place to stay for the evening. I shed my clothes as if I could shed my memories of Colt along with them, though I wasn't keen on the scandalous dress I was offered.

Properly attired, I reluctantly returned to the bar downstairs and was pleased to see it had further emptied for the evening.

Sequestered in the darkest corner, I hid, biding my time.

CHAPTER 24

COLT

A PRETTY MAID IS *hard to hide*, I mused, scanning the town, trying to temper my panic at the thought of someone else finding her first.

Where would she go? She wasn't the same scrawny girl I'd once known; she wouldn't find it possible to pull the same tricks.

Like cannon fire, an idea flashed in my mind and I let a slow smile spread across my face. *But she'd be capable of pulling more womanly ones now.*

Turning on my heel, I walked briskly in the direction of The Pink Pearl, beckoning beneath flickering torchlights about two hundred feet up the dusty road. Easily distinguished from the rest of the buildings, bright pink desert roses flanked her door. It was an appropriate choice as the flowering plant was both beautiful and highly toxic. Not many who passed through the foliage knew, but I'd often wondered if the cutthroat proprietor simply collected the poisonous sap and served it up to any patrons who got too rough with her girls or tried to skip out on a bill.

I thanked whatever god listened to a man like me when I entered the salon and, quickly scanning, found none of my own men lingering. Either they'd already taken a whore to bed or they'd finished their pleasure, and, running low on coin had moved on to the lively night I'd heard coming from The Crooked Crow up the road. Ale was cheaper than women and in these parts, enough of the former and a man might find himself lucky with the latter, *en gratis*.

Panic stabbed my chest again as I worried that another man had already found her, taken her, hurt her -

Before my thoughts could escalate into me exploding and making a scene, I spied Charlotte in a corner, shoulders rolled as she hunched into herself, trying to be inconspicuous. Half-turned, she didn't see me enter.

My chest tightened.

The neck of her dress draped low in a provocative manner, revealing the tops of her ample breasts; breasts she now tried to cover in an attempt to blend into the background, to not be selected for an evening's pleasure.

Not smart, Charlotte, I thought, cocking my head. *How did you find yourself in this predicament?*

Oh, yes. Your impulsive nature.

Before Charlotte might spy me, I flagged the proprietor, Lady Wick—though she was no more a lady than Wick was her real surname. Who knew what it once was? In these wild territories, who cared?

"Capt'n Pearce," she gushed, eyes scanning my attire to assess any damage from recent battles and, with a keen eye, the possibility for having won a boon of treasure. At the same time, she smoothed her black hair, checking for any loose strands coming from the elaborate twists and pins before dusting her skirts.

Giving her a nod to the left, Lady Wick quickly understood my intention and sequestered us both in a more secluded alcove, tight enough to fit no more than a small table and two stools, and thoroughly out of Charlotte's view. As we sat, a tavern maid approached, placing a bottle of rum on the wooden table. Lady Wick waved it off so sharply, she nearly swatted the girl.

"The real stuff for the capt'n," she ordered, giving me a friendly wink.

The girl quickly disappeared to retrieve what I assumed to be a bottle of liquor that *hadn't* been watered down.

"Whatcha be needin'?" Lady Wick asked, once we'd been appropriately served and afforded privacy.

"I noticed you have a new girl this evening. The tall one in the corner with honeyed hair and a blue dress."

Lady Wick grinned so widely I caught the snaggletooth near the back of her mouth.

"Not just new to The Pink Pearl," she declared with satisfaction. "A freshly discovered pearl for all men, if ya catch my drift."

Oh, Charlotte. What have *you gotten yourself into this time?*

Playing dumb, I raised my eyebrows and asked, "A virgin, you say? But how can you be sure? Many girls will claim the same to increase their value. Few can prove it."

Lady Wick snorted. "You think I've been in the trade this long without knowing when a whore's lyin'? The pearl's never been rubbed on that one."

Oh, but it has, I thought. *Though I've never demanded entrance to the world just beyond.* Idly drumming my fingers on the tabletop, I vowed, *that changes tonight.*

"Are ye interested in the girl or no?" Lady Wick asked, and I realized I'd been adrift in my thoughts. "If she's out there much longer, someone else is gunna want her. I can cut a special price. Only for the capt'n."

Leaning back, I took a slow drink of rum. The price she named would be special for *her,* seeing as how she knew I could pay more than anyone else who might wander into the establishment that night. It was likely on the hope of a patron like me that no one had yet seized Charlotte.

I said nothing, choosing to take another drink instead.

How lucky Lady Wick must have thought herself, graced with both a new virgin for the evening and a man with enough coin to pay for her.

Working my jaw, I considered my options. I could tell the madam the truth, collect what was rightfully mine, and march Charlotte out of here without any drain on my bag o' bits. Lady Wick would never stand in the way of me and my men.

But I'd miss the chance Charlotte herself had inadvertently arranged. Taking her like a whore beneath the brothel's drafty roof. The temptation was too delicious, the ironic opportunity too irresistible.

"A hundred and twenty-five pieces of eight," Lady Wick bargained.

I chuckled, not because of the price being high, but because paying any price at all for what I could freely have had in my cabin was a laughable absurdity making me a fool. I laughed because I knew that once I'd had her, I was going to have to offer Lady Wick a queen's ransom to buy Charlotte outright and drag her back to the ship.

Oh, Charlotte. If you think I've been making you pay up 'till now, just wait. I'm going to make you earn back every bit of that ransom. With your hands, your mouth, that sweet little cunt and even your arse.

There was no scenario where Lady Wick wouldn't wring every last coin from my pockets. I'd paid for Charlotte once the night I took her, instead of a fee for not attacking her settlement, and I was going to pay for her again now.

Devil's bones, I'd been paying for her in some way or other ever since I'd had the misfortune of crossing her path.

"A hundred," Lady Wick offered, surprising me. She was a better negotiator than this. Whatever she heard in my laugh and read in my elongated pause, she'd misread.

"I'm interested," I hedged, watching her smooth the worried crease between her brows. "But if she's as virginal as you claim, I suspect she might have misgivings when it comes down to it. I don't fancy wasting my time. I don't want some hellcat scratching my eyes out."

I fought not to grin as I continued. *You really brought this on yourself, Charlotte.*

"I want fresh sheets laid. I want her brought to your best room. And I want her bound and gagged."

Lady Wick, bless her, balked. She might be as greedy as any other madam—nah, as a pirate—but she had a soft spot in her heart for her girls.

"I'll give you a hundred and fifty pieces of eight," I said. "And you have my word I won't hurt her. Think about it. Have any of *my* men ever given you trouble before? What would it do to my welcome in this place if you knew I'd damage your goods? I just don't want any lip from the girl. Once we're done, I'll happily accompany her back downstairs and you can see with your own eyes that she's unharmed. In fact, she can tell you with her own mouth how good a time I gave her."

Toying with her glass, Lady Wick hesitated.

"Two hundred pieces of eight," I offered. "And my word as captain that I won't hurt the girl. If I know myself and what I can do, I think she's going to enjoy herself."

Lady Wick narrowed her eyes. "She musta really caught your attention," she said, suspiciously. "Can't remember the last time you came in here wantin' a girl and now you're ready to empty your bag o' bits for this one."

I leaned back in my chair, letting my legs fall wide. "It's been several long months at sea and I've got needs just like everyone else. But unlike everyone else, I want to ensure I'm not walking out of here with anything more than I bargained for."

I'd meant diseases I speculated some girls may carry, but I had to chuckle because I already knew I was walking out with more than I'd bargained for. To get Charlotte out of this place, and quietly, Lady Wick was going to shake me down for all I was worth.

The tough-minded proprietor finally gave a curt nod and I tampered the grin I wanted to allow. After I paid the required sum , she waved two men to our table, whispering in their ears. Presuming she was giving them instructions on how to prepare Charlotte, I almost felt bad for my little escapee.

Almost.

Charlotte was about to be seized, restrained, and thrown into a bed to be raped by a stranger.

You brought this on yourself, I chided. *You could have been taken beneath the stars and above the rollicking sea, as is proper for our kind.*

I consoled myself by arguing, *perhaps being fucked for the first time while bound in a brothel is a fitting punishment for your crimes.*

CHAPTER 25

CHARLOTTE

FEAR WASHED OVER me like a rolling sea, making it difficult to find balance. Or air.

The rope tying my hands together didn't help. Scanning the surprisingly large bedroom, I found little I could use to cut it. She'd betrayed me. Lady Wick had ordered me tied and delivered to this bedroom, violating the code between a whore and a madam. I did not consent to this treatment nor to whatever man desired it.

Stupid, stupid, Charlotte.

I'd have given anything to be back on Colt's ship. To never have run. To not have my own pretending get me into a mess. A second mess.

If I have to lose my virtue, I thought, *I'd rather it be to* him, *than to whatever horrible cad walked through that door.*

Bitter tears rolled down my cheeks. *Not like this,* I prayed. *Please, God, not like this.*

It wasn't a question of whether or not it would hurt. I knew it would. The question was only how much. Colt's fingers had caused some discomfort at first, but he'd given me time to adjust and then it'd felt…

Good, I thought, with resentment. *Divine.*

I had no hope that whatever man came to ruin me would show any patience. Not if he'd already ordered me tied. Only a monster could be storming up the whorehouse stairs.

What could I possibly do to escape? I thought, frantically searching the dimly lit room again and again.

Perhaps… perhaps I could save myself the disgrace. Slowly, with my heart drumming against my ribcage, I crossed the floor. What if I pitched myself out the window? Was choosing death over defilement a sin worthy of eternal condemnation to the flames of hell?

I peered out the dust-covered glass. Even if I could find a way to open it, the two-story fall probably wouldn't kill me. I slumped, disappointed.

I should never have left *The Dread Night.*

Footsteps sounded in the hall outside the bedroom and my stomach dropped so sharply I doubled over in pain. Eyes glued to that ominous door, I waited.

The door handle turned, creaking.

The door opened, scraping the floor with a high pitch, like a squeal of warning.

I gasped to see Colt, then blinked several times to make sure it wasn't a mirage.

What is he doing here?

My heart stopped beating at the sight of my monster standing in the doorway. He was practically tall enough to hit the low frame and he emanated so much danger it seemed to fill the room as a palpable threat. He advanced and the world around faded as I heard only my panting and the *clop* of his boots as he stomped across the wooden floor. We moved in tandem as we always did, him stalking toward me causing my accompanying retreat with each step, sweating and shaking until my back hit the wall. I felt as if every fiber in my body hummed as Colt neared close enough to touch.

I'd angered him—that was easy enough to read in his face. But his eyes were wild with something else too. Hunger? Colt's presence was like a sea storm, summoning energy to its core and channeling it outward for others to tremble at the force. With hands bound and mouth gagged, I was just as helpless as a jolly boat at the mercy of a mighty squall.

Forced to gaze upwards to meet his eyes, I gulped.

What are you going to do to me? I asked silently, blinking in terror.

Colt didn't answer the unspoken question.

I thought he'd unleash a barrage of insults, admonishments, or at the very least jests at my expense. That he said nothing only frightened me more.

His eyes lowered, roving my chest. My jumbled thoughts flew so quickly around my head it was impossible to hold onto just one, though I kept repeating, *what are you doing here?*

With a quick, firm yank, Colt tore my dress downward, baring my breasts to his greedy gaze and to his bold hands, which quickly cupped them. My initial squeal at the exposure morphed into a moan I couldn't stop and I prayed sounded too muffled to be deciphered beneath the gag. But I couldn't hide my hardened peaks and the fluttering of my eyelids in ecstasy. I hated that Colt's hands felt so right as they stroked my breasts and teased my nipples. I hated that he felt free to do it. I hated that I *liked* that he felt that way.

Not your mouth, I silently begged. But I arched into Colt's strong hands, begging the opposite. I told myself rising passion was just an unintended consequence of relief that some random scoundrel hadn't come to defile me. But that couldn't be true because wasn't having Colt appear in this room *worse?*

Colt's grin was diabolical as he asked, "What have you gotten yourself into this time, Charlotte?"

To allow my answer, he ripped the gag from my mouth and I worked my jaw before gasping, "What are you doing here?"

"Didn't I just ask you the same?"

I licked my lips, looking around nervously. "I–I tried to escape. I thought I could hide..."

"In a brothel," he concluded.

Eyes downcast, I admitted, "Yes. Can you take me back to the ship, please?"

There was a pause and then Colt uttered one ominous word.

"After."

I looked up to see his black eyes burning.

"After?" I echoed.

"After you fulfill your purpose here," he said, taking my breast in his hand once more. "After I get what I paid for."

"You... you... paid for me?"

Colt brought his lips to my nipple, muttering, "Mm-hm."

I hadn't the strength not to moan, but I made myself step back. Colt's eyes narrowed, looking at me with almost boyish displeasure and impishness.

"No more games, Charlotte," Colt warned. "It's time to earn your fee."

With a pounding heart, I wondered—what did that mean, exactly?

"Like this," he rasped, hoarse, eyeing my torn dress. "I want you like this as you please me. Half-exposed, ready to be ravished."

"What do you mean, *please you?*" I asked.

"I paid for a whore and I expected to be serviced by one," he said, stroking my face with the backs of his knuckles.

"Kneel, Lady Charlotte. Like you're praying to your beloved God. But God can't hear prayers in this den of sin so you will pray to me. Use those plump lips and that little pink tongue to beseech me. And if you pray hard enough, I just might show you mercy and untie your hands."

My eyes widened.

"Ah, so you know."

"I worked in a tavern," I snapped. "I've heard drunken men talk. Of course I know."

"And isn't it time you repaid me with the same act I've performed upon you?" he taunted, reminding me of the pleasure his mouth brought me between my legs.

I gave Colt a sly smirk. "Why, yes, I think it is." Furrowing my brow as if pretending to think back upon it, I said, "If I remember correctly, the tortuous delay of gratification could certainly use repayment."

Colt waved a frustrated hand. "I meant the completion of the act, not the teasing," he growled.

Despite my fear, I laughed. I was still laughing when Colt pushed down his breeches and grabbed my jaw—not hard enough to hurt, but enough to command my attention. His other hand pressed my shoulders, forcing me to my knees.

"You're going to take my whole cock in your mouth. I don't care if it hurts. It will hurt less than if I stick it in any of your other holes, keep that in mind." As Colt spoke he stroked his large, thick member in his hand, mesmerizing me. I couldn't tear my eyes from the vulgar act. "And when I come, you're going to swallow every salty drop down your virgin throat."

Shocked and aroused, I stared up at Colt with an increasingly dry mouth. Lewd fascination at his profane words and perverse pumping riveted me.

"And after that, I want you to thank me for my seed. If you don't, we'll do it all over again until you learn gratitude. Are you clear on the instructions, my pretty little whore?"

"I—I'm clear." I licked my lips and swallowed a few times. A dry mouth wasn't going to help in what he'd ordered me to do. "If I do this, will you untie me and bring me back to the ship?"

"Aye," he agreed, boldly stroking his massive erection mere inches from my lips. "Lick me, first. Get it good and wet with your tongue."

The combination of arousal and fear was so potent within me, I nearly swooned. Tentatively, I reached out my tongue and gave his cock a few flecks.

Colt groaned. "From the base," he commanded. "Lick from the base to the tip."

Unsure, I placed the flat of my tongue on the base of his cock and gave a long lick upward.

Colt threw back his head and groaned again, eyes closed.

How much power I have over him, I thought. *Just from my tongue.*

I might have… liked it. Encouraged, I licked some more. There was a slightly manly, musky scent to Colt, but it wasn't unclean or unpleasant.

"Take me in your mouth," Colt commanded, working just the tip inside.

I sucked a little, marveling at the lewd act of having his cock inside my mouth.

"You don't have much leverage with your hands restrained," Colt panted, above me. His hands found the back of my head and the hair on my neck rose in nervous anticipation. "I'm going to have to fuck your mouth, I'm afraid. Now open wide and relax your throat."

Dear God, did other men talk like this?

I did as I was told and Colt rammed his cock to the hilt inside me. Instant tears sprang as I gagged. I thrashed, struggling to push him out, but my hands were tied.

"Easy, girl, easy," Colt said, withdrawing slightly. I fought to catch my breath.

"Again," he warned. "Breathe through your nose."

I had no choice but to accept his intruding erection as he shoved it past my limits once more. This time, he kept it there while I flailed and whined in panic.

Looking down, Colt stroked my face. "Can't lie when your mouth is stuffed with my cock, can you?"

He's punishing me, I realized. *Not just for escaping but for the past. Would he ever forgive whatever I'd done?*

Slowly, painfully slowly, Colt backed up. I looked up at him imploringly, tears welling in my eyes.

Please.

"One more time, my darling whore," he said with such loving cruelty, I didn't know what to make of it. I whimpered around his erection and the next moment, he rammed his cock to the fullest again, poking the back of my throat and making me panic. I pulled fruitlessly against the rope and tried moving my head, but he held it too tightly.

"A cock in your mouth is a sure-fire way to stop your lies, isn't it?" Tears leaked and several agonizing seconds passed before Colt withdrew his engorged member at a painfully slow pace. I gasped, trying to keep the snot from running down my nose but unable to stop the tears.

His violation hurt my throat. So why did my pussy ache?

I wasn't given much recovery time as Colt began moving halfway in and out of my mouth. "Do penance with your tongue, Charlotte," he said, "penance for all your lies."

He didn't thrust as deeply as before, but Colt was so large it was still difficult, at even a reduced depth.

What choice did I have?

No, I realized. *I never once said the word no. I'd licked my lips in anticipation when he'd presented me with his rigid member.* But even if I liked it, that didn't mean it was easy. I sucked as commanded, to the best of my ability. *The better you perform,* I told myself, *the faster he'll finish.*

Sure enough, Colt only lasted a few minutes, but when his body tightened, he once again strengthened his grip on the back of my head and shoved his cock further than I was comfortable of receiving. Lodged too deep, he released jets of warm, salty fluid down my throat.

My eyes widened at the taste.

"That's a good whore," Colt cooed, above me. "Swallow it all down."

Despite my wet, throbbing pussy, I thought angrily, *as if I have a choice.*

Colt withdrew from my lips as the last of his salty fluid ran down my throat and coated my tongue.

To my surprise, Colt pulled up his breeches, retrieved a carafe of fresh water, and poured a glass. I was still on my knees when he pressed it to my lips. I drank, greedily and gratefully. I was further shocked when he grabbed his dirk and cut my bonds.

"Thank you," I whispered vaguely, remembering his command before we began.

We can go back to the ship now, I thought with relief. *And perhaps the ache between my legs will fade by the time we return.*

"Onto the bed," Colt said.

Quickly, I found my feet. "Why?"

"No more games, Lady Charlotte," Colt rasped, stroking my face. "I'm taking you tonight."

My eyes widened, searching his face for mercy, but none could be found. *Yet if I wanted mercy... why didn't I ask?*

Instead, I parted my lips for his tongue when it descended. He kissed like he commanded, without question that orders would be obeyed. My heart pounded as he moved us toward the bed and laid me down without breaking our kiss.

Positioned flat on my back, I looked up at Colt, still disbelieving.

"You told me if I... did that to you, you wouldn't... wouldn't..."

"I lied," he grinned. "Pirate, remember?"

"How can I trust a man like you!" I hurled the accusation that was not truly a question.

"Because you can trust that I know what's best for you, even when it takes a lie to get there," he said, lifting the skirts of my dress. "Because I'm only playing your game Charlotte. It's always your game, isn't it, making us your players?"

Before I could make sense of that, Colt asked, "Tell me,

Lady Charlotte, is your cunt not dripping from the act of servicing me?"

Dammit. An obvious shiver ran down my body.

Staring up at his sinfully handsome face, I declared, "This is why your kind is so hated. You have no honor, captain."

Colt cocked his head. "We spare some for outsiders and offer plenty amongst our own. But alas, you claim you're not of the latter so I can offer you little."

I narrowed my eyes at his pretty way of speaking, determined not to be swayed by it. Colt had surely been a gentleman at one time, possessing a gentleman's upbringing and education. What had happened to turn him into this?

"I'll make you a fair deal," Colt said, further pushing my skirts out of the way. "Look me in the eyes right now and tell me your cunt isn't throbbing. Tell me you don't want me to satiate that burning need by tearing into it, making it mine forever. Tell me, and I'll allow you to re-dress and we'll leave this room together."

Mine forever. Those words made my heart ache. Heat rose on my cheeks and I averted my eyes as Colt stroked my bare legs. I couldn't convincingly lie. Not when one dip of his fingers would cover them in evidence to the contrary.

When I said nothing, he yanked my legs apart, causing me to squeal. In a flash, Colt inserted himself between my parted thighs, making it impossible to close them.

"It will hurt," I protested, panicking.

Foolishly, I expected Colt to argue—whether it be a chart-able attempt at soothing me or an outright lie to get his way. But he did the opposite.

"I want to hurt you," he said. "You have no idea how much I want to hurt you for what you've done, Charlotte."

Colt seized my thighs and spread my legs further, exposing my bare cunt to his will. "And I think you know you deserve it. I think you seek penance. I think you want me to hurt you too."

I shook my head rapidly back and forth, denying his decree. *So why do you say nothing, Charlotte? Why do you only watch, wide-eyed, as his fingers dig into your whorish thighs and his eyes sear your wet cunt?*

"I'm afraid," I tried.

"I can see that and it only makes me harder," Colt said, clasping my wrists to pin my arms up above my head.

"I hate you," I spat, but it came out like a breathy sigh.

"Yes, I think a part of you does. And that too only stiffens my cock."

"Is there anything I can say that doesn't excite you?" I cried, as Colt rubbed the tip of his manhood against my defenseless entrance in an effort to bringing it to fully erect.

Leaning down to whisper in my ear, he replied, "I could ask the same of you. Everything I utter seems to soak you," he said, rubbing his rough stubble against my cheek while his hard cock pressed against my slippery folds.

"*Lady,*" he began, teasing his cock up toward my clit.

"*Whore,*" he rasped, sliding up and down my wet center.

Suddenly pausing at the threshold of my entrance, Colt met my gaze. Guessing what he intended, I had just enough time to widen my eyes in anticipation.

"*Mine,*" he declared, pushing into me with a thrust hard enough to steal my breath.

Instinctively, I flinched against the mattress in an attempt to escape the pain, but there was nowhere to go, nor did Colt relent his firm caging of my body. He was the one hurting me, yet I had no choice but to cling to him, seeking comfort from the only other person I could.

"Shhh…" Colt's throaty whisper reached my ears, almost from a distance. He might have been whispering it awhile before I actually heard him. I noticed he laid very still, bracing himself so that his weight wouldn't crush me.

"Shhh…" he soothed, kissing my sweaty brow. "The worst is over." Despite his calming tone, I could hear the exaltation in his voice, as well as the strain. Colt was smug at having defiled me and physically pained from holding back.

"Charlotte." He sounded drunk on pleasure. "Charlotte, relax. I've pulled back, I'm only halfway inside you now. Can't you feel it? The worst is over."

"I-" I began, then stopped, focusing. Colt was right, that searing pain had abated.

How odd it was to be filled in a region never before having had such fullness.

"Relax," Colt soothed, kissing my sweaty brow. He brushed aside the hair sticking to my face. His breathing grew labored.

"Charlotte," Colt said between gritted teeth. "I'm going to push back inside you again."

My body squirmed with indecision. I wanted to experience that fullness again and my desire was obvious, but I was scared too. Just like the times Colt had punished me, the penetration inside me hurt a little, but it felt good too.

"I want you to relax and accept me," he insisted with his firm, captain's command. "It will hurt less once you learn to take it."

Nodding, I took Colt's advice and he began slowly inching back inside me.

"That's it," he instructed. "Relax and accept me. Take it."

I was grateful he moved so slowly, then angry at myself for feeling gratitude toward a monster who shouldn't have been inside me at all. He'd despoiled me. I was as bound to him through this act as I'd have been through matrimony.

And he made my whorish cunt want it.

Oh god, that admittance was the worst of it. No one could blame a woman who'd found herself the victim on some plundering pirate, but a woman who wanted it? Who relished the pleasure his cock brought her?

"Christ, Charlotte, you're so fucking tight. You feel so fucking good."

I lit up at his praise before growing angry at myself for the twisted idea of wanting to please him, the man pillaging me.

Was it supposed to be this confusing?

Maybe it was for us, because our relationship itself was confusing as hell.

Fully seated inside me, Colt groaned, "I want to feel you hold me."

"That will be difficult to do unless you release my wrists," I quipped.

"Not a chance," Colt chuckled. "I want to feel you squeeze this tight little cunt around my cock."

I nearly choked, face heating. Neither my nipples nor my clit had ever felt so stiff before. They throbbed, needing touch.

"I'm not backing up again until you do it. If you refuse me, I will stay buried deep inside this cunt of mine until we fall asleep."

"I'm not a whore, captain," I insisted.

"The whorehouse in which you're getting fucked says something to the contrary."

Wriggling, I tried to escape from beneath Colt, but he tightened his grip. I averted my eyes, terribly shamed… and that's when Colt did something I never expected. As sworn, he didn't slide his cock from me, but instead he rocked his hips, causing the immensely pleasurable pressure of his lower abdomen against my clit. Gasping, I looked up at the same time I instinctively clenched my core tight around his invading member, as if I wanted to hold it inside me.

"That's it," he coaxed, and I could hear the grin in his voice as he continued to move. "Say my name again."

Had I said it once already?

"C—Colt," I whispered, barely finishing before his mouth claimed mine. Kissing Colt made my hips buck up as if in request, as if wanting a deeper joining, as if wanting the same friction below as he gave above.

Why did he have to affect me this way?

Releasing my mouth, Colt said, "I'm going to fuck you now. Are you ready?"

"If I say no will you remove yourself from me?" I asked, a part of me praying he wouldn't.

A large part.

Maybe the whole part.

Could he tell?

Colt scrutinized my face and I wondered what game we were playing. Was it his? Or mine, as he'd said?

Both?

"No," he replied, gaze hard. "But I won't move until you tell me you're ready."

With a huff, I turned my head to the side, disengaging. "Do whatever you want," I said evenly, determined to show him I was only waiting to get it over with, only stuck in this position because he wouldn't allow me to leave.

Colt *laughed* as if that pleased him. He rocked his hips again and this time he didn't stop.

"Oh!" I exclaimed, before a moan escaped my lips.

"There she is. My sweet little whore who can't get enough." Colt began thrusting in and out, fucking me as promised. It made me struggle in the wrong direction, not away from him but toward. It made me arch and groan.

"I hate you," I swore, wrapping my legs around his strong back. Our mouths clashed, tongues seeking each other. "I hate you so much," I repeated between kisses.

"I think you'll hate me even more if I stop."

It almost sounded like a threat, making me instinctively beg, "Don't. Please."

"Say it again," he coaxed.

"Don't?" I asked confused. Then more confidently, I whispered, "Don't stop. Please."

Colt groaned. "As my lady commands."

I hadn't realized that sometime in our fucking, he'd let go of my wrists and our fingers had threaded. I didn't know until Colt reached his climax and squeezed my hands as he released his seed into me for a second time that evening.

It happened so quickly that I was left wanting. The astonishment of it being my first time seemed to interfere with my ability to finish as he had.

"Are you okay?" Colt asked, brow furrowed with concern. He took my chin between his fingers. "Are you hurting?"

"No, it's not that." I averted my eyes. "I didn't reach the same heights of pleasure as you, captain."

"Oh," he said, pulling his shirt above his head and tossing it onto the upholstered chair. "I'm aware. And we're not leaving this room until you do."

Gently lifting my torso from the bed, he slid my dress off my body and swore, "Many times over."

CHAPTER 26

CHARLOTTE

MY CHEEKS STILL flamed at the memories the next morning. Colt made good on his promise and didn't allow me to leave the room until I'd climaxed so many times that my legs shook when I tried to walk down the whorehouse stairs and he had to support my weight to make it to the bottom. By that time the roosters had long since crowed and the sun was high above the hills. Never in my life did I imagine I'd find pleasure in a pirate's arms.

But he's not just a pirate, my heart argued. *He's… everything.*

Bewilderingly, Colt made me confess to the proprietor, Lady Wick, what a jolly time I'd had the night before. To further shame me, I was sure of it, though I wasn't sure why he spoke with the madam privately in a little alcove, whilst bidding me to wait alone. I suspected Colt was going to tell the madam about the mix-up, to whisk me from the brothel without trouble, but he acted strangely.

Never having excelled at following orders, I crept along the wall until I could spy on the pair whilst remaining hidden.

I frowned as I saw Colt push his bag o' bits across the table to the proprietor. Was he buying me outright? A hard look flashed across Colt's face and then I watched him work a sapphire ring from his finger and toss it onto the tabletop.

A small fortune, I thought, watching Lady Wick snatch up the jewel. Colt didn't wear much jewelry and what little I'd seen had been precious.

Was this for me?

Colt managed a gracious smile and a dip of his head before spinning out of the alcove to collect me. He moved so fast, I hadn't time to re-position myself and a jolt ran through me at Colt's admonishing scowl.

"You'll pay for that later," he warned, dragging me out of the brothel.

The reminder his words brought to mind made my stomach lurch—not for the threat from Colt, but at what Redhands wanted to do to me once we departed.

Yanking my hand from Colt's, I shook my head vehemently and declared, "No. I cannot return to your ship. Not if you plan on sailing anytime soon. Did you forget your bargain with Robert?"

Colt ran a hand down his face, sighing.

"I can handle Robert, but I'm not in total disagreement with him. I'm playing your game Charlotte because I'm hoping you'll grow weary and confess."

Scowling, I returned, "I play no game, captain, but if I were, surely you'd be playing it because you like what transpired between us last night."

The captain cocked a brow. "Are you going to dare tell me you did not? Because every whimper, every moan and cry and scream told me something else last night."

Blushing, I averted my eyes.

Colt sighed again. Reaching out one finger, he lifted the gold locket around my neck, tracing the oval with his thumb.

"Listen to me, Charlotte. Nobody cares about my lost bag o' bits and half of the men are glad you killed Maurice. But they don't know you stole the Eye because they don't know it exists. The sooner you tell me where you hid it, the better I can protect you."

I swallowed. Shuffled my feet. *What could I possibly say?* Other than the truth, and I didn't see a happy outcome to that. Either Colt wouldn't believe me, and I'd enrage him for the lie, or he would believe me, and I'd enrage him for the deception up until then.

I had no plan, other than to wait and hope. Earn his trust, maybe.

Colt sighed a third time as he took my hand and led me back to *The Dread Night*.

OUR RETURN TO THE COLONIES was very different than our departure. Perhaps not outwardly, but within. I no longer fought the hot rivers of desire running through my veins whenever Colt set his dark gaze upon me. We made no attempt to hide from the crew our lingering glances, our overlong disappearances.

The nights became a wonder of exploration.

In Colt's increasing boldness, one evening he spread me upon the bed before supper, teasing my slit until I dripped. Captain Colt took that same wetness and spread it across my neck like perfume. He even ringed his own neck with my sticky lubrication, inhaling deeply. Without any shame he told me he wanted to smell my arousal as we dined, as a reminder of what was to come after. And he did—leaning over and inhaling at my neck throughout our meal, until I'd turned as red as an apple imagining the whole table could scent me.

True to his word, Colt spoke with Redhands and put him off his plan to whip me. For now. I knew I'd only bought time, but I prayed for a miracle to help guide me to my lost memories or at least, to the Crimson Eye itself. When Colt turned his back as he undressed at night, I'd kneel and pray beside our bed. But I wasn't sure if God's ears reached a pirate's cabin, so I prayed upon the forecastle deck as well. With wide seas and open skies, where better to have my pleas reach the heavens?

The only problem was, having succumbed to sin so thoroughly, I wasn't sure the almighty listened any longer.

Yet if my soul was tarnished, half-claimed by the devil, I'd never felt more alive.

Something I hadn't truly known before came over me as we sailed. Beyond contentment, beyond happiness. A feeling like bliss surged through me when Colt took me to bed. A feeling of finding home soothed my soul in a way I'd never imagined. In the evenings, we read to one another or Colt told me stories of his youth. As I suspected, Colt was raised to be a gentleman. By his mother, at least. His father preferred a bottle of whiskey over the company of his family and the more their money slipped away the more he raised his voice… and then, his fists. When his mother passed away, Colt ran away. Maurice had found him and taken him under his wing. Maurice was an even more brutal man, but he was never cruel to Colt, or Robert, his other adopted son.

It wasn't just my pirate captain; the ship and the sea worked its magic on me too. I'd awaken to the crisp salt air each morning and sing the men my favorite shanties as the moon rose and the endless glitter of stars shone above.

When we finally reached my settlement… my home… it looked curiously smaller than when I'd left it. Dirtier, even.

I dreaded facing Daniel at our rendezvous. For some reason, I was sure Mrs. Penningham would understand. A part of me wondered if she even knew before I knew, if she'd read something in Colt the night he whisked me away, if she'd recognized that a passion borne of the wilds existed between us—or could, if we let it.

But sweet Daniel… I was about to break his faith in me, and his heart.

WE ARRIVED LATE INTO A sleepy port, and I was glad. I wouldn't face the many questions of the townsfolk who'd long since retired for the evening.

The steadfast torchlights of our tavern still flickered, of course.

Mrs. Penningham rushed to greet me, wrapping me in the tightest hug anyone had ever given. She fussed over me like a child returning to her mother, which, I supposed in a way, I was. When Colt stepped behind me and wrapped his arms around my waist, a knowing smile touched her lips.

"Have a seat, have a seat," she said, with a knowing smile playing at her gently wrinkling lips. "I'll fetch some ale for you."

Noting the crew filing in behind us, she added, "For all of you."

I fidgeted nervously upon my stool as Colt regaled Mr. and Mrs. Penningham with anecdotes of our battle on the crossing to Nassau, as well as tidbits from other journeys. The conversation flowed with unusual ease, making me surer that Mrs. Penningham had suspected this outcome.

It didn't take long before I spied a head of light-brown hair peeking around the corner to the kitchens and my heart thumped.

"Mrs. Penningham," I said, interrupting the happy flow of conversation. "Thank you for the drink but I have had too much ale and must excuse myself."

Colt's gaze was immediately suspicious as I rose, and I couldn't blame him, given what I'd recently done. But he made no move to stop me.

There's nowhere to hide in this small settlement and you can't think I'd run away now, could you?

For a few seconds we stared in a tense stalemate until Johnson burst through the door.

"Captain," he called, hurrying over to us.

I froze. *Had they caught Daniel? Did someone know what I was up to?*

"You're needed back on the ship. There's been an issue with the rigging and a dispute has broken out."

"I'll be there in a moment," Colt gritted out. "When Charlotte is ready."

"No," I quickly protested. With a feigned smile, I said, "Please. Go on. I need to take care of myself and then I'd like to speak with Mrs. Penningham and collect my things… half your crew is here, I'm quite safe. *And I'm not going anywhere.*"

Don't you trust me? I asked with my eyes. *Where would I escape to anyway?*

"Johnson can escort me back once I'm ready," I added, helpfully.

It was difficult not to wither under Colt's hard, dark stare. But he said nothing as he turned to Johnson and gave a curt nod. My whole chest sank in relief with the breath I released. It would be easier to speak with Daniel now. Smiling, I gave Colt a quick kiss.

"Please trust me," I whispered in his ear as I hugged him. "I'm not trying to give you the slip. Where would I go?"

"Wait for her," Colt said to Johnson, tilting his head in my direction as he turned to leave.

Walking slowly and with purpose, I slipped through the door from the tavern's main seating area and into the hall leading to the privy, the kitchens, and the rear of the building. Stepping through the darkened hall, I saw no one.

"Daniel?" I whispered.

No answer.

Forced to travel further, I walked all the way to the back of the tavern and slipped out the door.

"Daniel?" I asked again, this time a little louder.

From my right he appeared, grabbing and hugging me.

"Daniel!" I cried, annoyed at the lack of propriety.

But why was I so shocked when I'd promised to consider his proposal? Why was I outraged when Colt had done far worse, far faster?

I had no time to consider as Daniel leaned in to kiss me and I was forced to push him away. What in the world made him so bold?

I remembered the possessive caress of Colt's fingers, low

on my back as we sat. I'd grown so accustomed I hadn't thought about it at the time. But surely, Daniel had spied the intimacy.

"Stop," I demanded, holding him at arm's length.

"Are you unharmed?" Daniel asked. "Did he hurt you? Touch you? What have you learned?"

A barrage of questions followed, but I was only half-listening. My stomach knotted as I prepared to confess the truth.

"Daniel," I began. "Know that I'm sorry for everything I'm about to tell you."

Quickly, I thought. *Best to get it over quickly.*

"But I cannot marry you and I—I don't know anything that might help us bring an end to Colt's piracy and… and… I'm not sure he's as bad as we all thought…"

Perhaps the truth behind my words was obvious as I averted my eyes. It didn't take Daniel more than a moment to accuse me. Perhaps the truth was obvious in whatever he saw between Colt and me as he spied on us from the kitchens.

"He's had you, hasn't he?" Daniel spat, fighting a sneer.

"That's none of your business!" I scolded. "And no gentleman would ask such a question."

"No lady would find herself in a position where it needed to be asked," he returned. "You're a ruined woman now."

His words stung. Maybe because they were true. Who would have me now, if not Colt, who was not my husband and had not made any such proposal? And all my hopes of being a lady… I'd dashed them upon the rocks myself.

But I still had my pride. "So be it," I said, falsely brave. "I am ruined. Too far beneath you to be a desirable bride."

I couldn't make sense of the emotions crossing Daniel's face. He seemed to have difficulty finding words.

"And what of our plan, hm?" he finally demanded. "Will thousands more lose their livelihoods, lose their lives, all because you want to spread your legs for some scoundrel of the seas?" Before I could reply, he pressed, "How many times did he have you, Charlotte?"

"It doesn't matter. All that matters is that I cannot betray Colt and his crew. You don't understand. You don't know them like I do."

"I should have known what you were the day I found you," Daniel said with disgust.

I shouldn't let it hurt, but Daniel was growing to be a respected young man in our community. He'd been clever enough to develop the wealth he'd come into. He'd been my savior that day. And he'd been my friend and companion ever since.

"You're no mermaid, no goddess of the sea. You're less than a pirate, even," he declared. "You're nothing but a pirate's whore."

Tears welled in my eyes and Daniel's face softened.

He shook his head and covered his eyes, ashamed. "I'm sorry, that was cruel. But you're... I can't..."

He gave me a lingering look and I could see the pain, anger, and disappointment on his face, along with a host of other emotions I couldn't identify.

"Daniel, I-" I began, but he cut me off.

"I can't even look at you," he said, re-covering his mouth as if it sickened him. Daniel spun on his heel and left before I could say more.

I swallowed back the lump in my throat as he scurried away. If Daniel felt this way about me, surely the rest of the townsfolk would as well. I'd participated in my own ruination and would have nowhere to turn if Colt turned me out. Mrs. Penningham would never shun me, but perhaps she'd be forced to, if everyone shunned the tavern, should I continue to be associated with it.

It doesn't matter, I told myself, standing alone in the darkness. *Because I don't want this life or any of them. I only want Colt.*

I heard a noise coming from the shadowed trees behind the tavern—the snap of a twig. My stomach knotted in fear as a familiar and unwelcome face appeared from woods.

I should have known Colt had me followed.

CHAPTER 27
COLT

THE STEADY DRUMMING of my fingertips against the tabletop belied my fear. Fear that Charlotte was in love with Daniel. Fear that she planned to betray us to him. Fear that she planned to run away with him, that she was lying…

Of course she's always lying, I thought. *But maybe about more than I'd ever guess.*

I sat behind my desk, feigning calm, when my door finally opened. Robert's casual gait into my cabin told me nothing. He was curating his appearance as much as I was. I'd wondered again if I should have sent Johnson to spy on Charlotte, but my pride had gotten the better of me.

Twirling his dagger, Robert sauntered to my bookshelves, as if interested in examining their spines.

So, we're both playing a game of who's going to show their hand first? I thought, aggravated.

He knew I desperately wanted information and I would be forced to speak.

Well, then. Purposeful misinterpretation of your silence it is.

I sighed dramatically and declared, "You were unsuccessful."

Robert's head snapped in my direction and I bit back the grin.

"'Course I wasn't." He squared his shoulders. "You were right. I caught her talking to that Daniel boy."

"And?" I gritted out, unable to keep from clutching the edge of the table.

"She's plotting somethin' alright. But I couldn't hear what. Sounded like they were having a disagreement about the terms of whatever game she's up to this time."

Ignoring the ache in my chest and the rage burning through my veins, I focused on getting matters under control, getting Charlotte under control. Quickly.

"Bring her back to the ship, I'll need-"

"Already brought her," Robert said, twirling his dagger once more. "Couldn't very well leave her running about the tavern spilling our secrets."

"Where is she now?" I demanded, unsure who I was angrier with at the moment—Charlotte, for whatever plotting she was doing, or Robert, for touching her.

"The brig," he answered with relish.

I'd leapt to my feet before I even had the conscious thought to stand.

"Ready to tie her to the mast now?" Robert asked, practically salivating.

When we'd departed Nassau, I had to bargain more lashes in order to stay Robert's hand, had to convince him that I'd convince Charlotte to talk. *Give me a few more weeks,* I'd negotiated, *or else you can give her five more lashes to the five you've already planned.*

I'd never let it come to that, of course, but just the image of Charlotte's back torn to shreds by the cruel bite of leather was enough to make me want to tear the flesh from Robert's bones.

When had we become so adversarial? Was it always? Maurice had groomed the two of us like his own sons, like we were brothers, but we'd never had similar natures.

"Set a course for Charles Town," I ordered, ignoring his comment. I wanted to put as much distance as possible between Charlotte and her schemes.

Between Charlotte and Daniel.

CHARLOTTE WAS WEEPING before she even saw me.

Save your tears, I thought. *You're going to need them.*

"Please, let me explain," Charlotte cried, shooting to her feet as I came into view. Her hair fell from her bun in clumps, her nose was swollen, her eyes red. She looked genuinely miserable, but then, I knew well how much of an act she could put on.

She's pretending even as she pleads, I thought, incredulously. *Acting the lady who's never before set foot upon a ship.*

I raked my hands through my hair. "Go on then. Let's hear you spin this story. I might enjoy seeing how you form your lies. That way, I'll be better prepared to stop them before they start." I folded my arms across my chest. "Tell me your lies, Charlotte. I know you were arguing with that boy. Tell me you weren't planning to betray us all."

Charlotte's face softened with desperate longing. "No lies, Colt," she breathed. "I *was* planning to betray you. *Before.*"

My stomach filled with dread.

"Before I stepped upon the ship," she quickly explained. "Can you blame me? You kidnapped me! I needed a plan. Any one of your men would have done the same. Would you respect a crewmember who couldn't conspire?"

I narrowed my eyes at her.

"Is it not both a man's valuation of his freedom as well as his innate loyalty that makes a good shipmate to begin with?"

Oh, but how she could wield her tongue to shape the story.

As if sensing my rejection of such manipulative arguments (even if they were true), Charlotte changed tactics.

"Yes, I meant to betray you. But that was before… before what we shared," she whispered.

I didn't bat an eye but I couldn't stop the twitching in my lips.

Did she see it?

Charging forth from another angle yet again, Charlotte insisted, "You said it yourself, you heard I was arguing with Daniel. That was me telling him I couldn't go through with it. Why else would we quarrel?"

"Why?" I scoffed. "There's a hundred reasons why. You disputed your payment. You didn't like a part of the plan. Who knows?"

"No," Charlotte insisted. "It's because I told him no. Because I couldn't betray you," she held a hand to her breast and whispered, "here."

God, she sounded like she'd meant it. I badly wanted her to mean it.

"I risk the whip to stay aboard your ship," Charlotte declared, grasping the bars of the cell. "I'm entirely at the mercy of your protection. Do you not see?"

"Then prove it," I ordered, voice low. "Stop this charade and tell me where the Crimson Eye is? Did you find a buyer? Then what have you done with the gold? Is it spent?"

Charlotte's shoulders slumped and her gaze fell upon the floor.

"I cannot tell you that now. But I promise, I will. Soon."

I'd clenched my jaw so hard I thought I might crack a tooth. In the silence, I heard a floorboard creak, just outside the door. It could have been someone listening or it could have been the natural noises of the ship, but I didn't want to chance it.

Forcing myself to relax, I grit out, "We'll finish this discussion in my cabin. And I should punish you until you can't walk for this planned betrayal, executed or not."

My words had the intended effect. Charlotte cowed. Or so I thought.

"Yes," she said, gazing up at me with her doe eyes. "I want you to."

CHAPTER 28

COLT

B ACK IN MY cabin I eyed my little liar as ideas swarmed my head. The rising excitement tempered my anger, yet I was still enraged at what she'd done.

"I'm going to give you the most severe punishment of your life," I told her.

Charlotte gulped before reaching for the hem of her shirt and lifting it over her head.

"Yes," she whispered. "Absolve me."

She unlaced the ties on her skirt and shoved it to the floor. "Punish me."

Standing only in her chemise, she gazed at me with unobstructed longing in her eyes.

"Belt me, whip me. Do whatever you must. Whatever you desire."

I was losing focus on her words as she lifted the soft slip over her head and off her body, standing completely naked before me, *asking* me to punish her.

"Only… make love to me after."

The room spun as if I'd drank more than my fill.

Crossing the distance between us in two strides, I grabbed her elegant neck and shoved her backwards. She didn't fight me or yell or even complain.

She *moaned*. It was full of yearning. Submission.

"You don't know what you're asking."

"I don't," she agreed. "But it's not for me to know. It's for you to decide and deliver."

Fuck, my cock was hard from her words and from the meaning behind them I saw in her adoring eyes.

"I want you on the bed," I ordered. "You're to remain there until I return."

Though Charlotte scurried to obey, her submission wasn't complete (I doubted it would ever be) as she asked, "Where are you going?"

I grinned. "To the galley."

THE SIGHT OF CHARLOTTE waiting obediently, naked on my bed, sent a rush of pleasure and power to my head.

"Turn this way," I instructed, positioning her so that her arse touched the side of the bed. "Spread your legs and bend at the knees."

Charlotte complied without protest, revealing all of her soft, pink cunt to me.

"Arms up. Place your hands against the wall and do not move them. If you do, we'll have to repeat the punishment."

Her eyes widened and her lip quivered with trepidation, but she slowly raised her arms and placed her hands flat against the wood. I could see her confusion in the crease of her brow.

"What you've done is no minor offense and for it you will receive no minor punishment."

"I understand," she whispered.

"No, you don't. Not yet. But I'm about to explain it to you," I said, unbuckling my belt. "You acted like a naughty little cunt tonight and that is where we must punish you."

Charlotte's mouth fell in surprise.

"That's right," I said, cupping her pussy with my hand. "I'm going to belt you right between your legs. Ten strokes. Maybe fifteen." I watched her face flush with arousal and fear as I rubbed my fingers through her slick slit. "But first we need to get you ready. Bring your clit to attention." I rubbed in circles there, just the way I knew drove her mad with desire. "Do you know why, Lady Charlotte?"

Her eyes were half-lidded. She shook her head back and forth, dazed.

I gave her clit a soft pinch. "Because it's going to hurt more now that you're fully aroused."

No sound could ever be as sweet as the whimper she gave.

"Remember, hands stay on the wall or we'll repeat that stroke," I announced, backing up. "Now ask me to punish you."

"P–please punish me," she obediently requested.

"Where?" I grinned.

"On… between my legs?"

"You know what I want to hear. Or would you like me to add more strokes?"

"No! Please punish me on my… cunt," she said, face flaming.

"You're blushing harder than I'd thought possible, Lady Charlotte. Let's see if we can redden your cunt to match.

Brace yourself, girl, but do not attempt to close your legs or the stroke won't count."

Charlotte squeezed her eyes shut and pressed her fingertips hard against the wall.

I brought the belt down with medium force, testing. She yelped and brought her knees together.

"Legs spread! Knees up!" I ordered. "I warned you. Do that again and we'll repeat the stroke."

Charlotte groaned as she obeyed, offering me the target I desired. I brought the belt down again with the same force. Charlotte cried out, throwing her head back, but she didn't break position.

I gave her a third smack of the belt, slightly harder this time, and she whined harder, but her hips bucked with desire.

On the fourth smack I moved lower, letting the tip of the belt fully connect with her arsehole and she squealed.

"Don't, please! Don't hit me there!"

"Keep those legs spread and I'll hit you wherever I like."

Wherever you *like. You like this too, don't you?*

"Unless you'd like me not to absolve you?" I tested. "Just say the word, Charlotte, and we'll stop."

Eyes downcast, Charlotte shook her head and I realized I'd been holding my breath.

I raised my belt again.

On the fifth stroke tears began to gleam in her eyes, but her cunt glistened. I knew if I examined my leather, I'd find it wet with her juices.

Smack.

I laid a sixth stroke high, hoping to connect fully with her sensitive nub. When Charlotte screamed, I laid another and was rewarded with another scream as her legs folded.

"You have three seconds to spread your legs again or we'll repeat that stroke," I told her.

"Please, no more," she begged as she complied.

"Good girl," I said when she presented her pussy again.

"Please, Colt, no more, please."

"You have three more coming, but that was your last warning. If your legs collapse again, we'll repeat the stroke."

Gritting her teeth, I watched Charlotte resolve to take her punishment and I gave her the eighth and ninth strokes with medium force.

The tenth, however, was my hardest yet. I knew it was cruel, knew I was a bastard. But thinking about how she'd snuck off, how she'd endangered herself—endangered all of us, strengthened my resolve.

Charlotte broke position completely, crying and whining as she curled onto her side and held herself between her legs.

"Did I say you could rub?" I asked, incredulous.

"Noo…" she sobbed. "But I couldn't help it. I'm sorry! It just hurt so much."

"Back into position."

Her eyes widened. "No, Colt, please."

"Into position."

Charlotte obeyed slowly, as if her limbs were stuck in pitch. But she obeyed.

"I'm not going to belt you," I announced, grinning. *Oh, but I was cruel.* Retrieving my horse crop, I returned to Charlotte.

"I'm going to whip you."

Charlotte's mouth dropped in terror. I stroked the small, flat leather panel at the end of the crop.

"One stroke, right on your sweet, little clit. Would you like that, Charlotte? Ask me for it."

I watched her mouth work but no words came out. Charlotte licked her lips and had to try several times before I heard her mousy whisper.

"Please… please… whip me on my clit."

I gave Charlotte an indulgent look. "Only because you begged so sweetly. Now help me punish you by spreading those legs real wide this time. That's my girl, my good girl."

I tapped her clit a few times. She was so wet I could smell her without bending down. I'd never punished a girl in such a manner before, and didn't know how much Charlotte could take, so I erred on the side of caution and only struck her with medium force. Her cry was loud enough that I knew any man nearby would have heard it. But it tapered off into a deep, throaty moan, the sound of which went straight to my cock.

I couldn't wait any longer.

Freeing my erection, I bent down and slid gently into her pussy. I was unsure whether Charlotte saw as it as a reward—quenching some of her throbbing desire—or as a punishment, the rough scratch of my hair chafing her sore and swollen cunt.

"Tell me you like it," I coaxed, driving in and out of her slowly. "Tell me you like it when I punish you."

"It–it hurts," she moaned.

"But you like the pain, don't you?"

When she didn't answer, I rammed her hard.

"Don't you?"

"Yes! I do," she cried, tapering off in another moan.

"The first part of your punishment is over," I said, reluctantly withdrawing from her cunt.

"F—first?" she echoed, eyes wide as a doe's.

Ignoring her, I retrieved what was necessary from the small set of drawers built into the ship's walls and serving to hold my wardrobe. I made quick work of tying Charlotte's wrists together and securing them to the hook behind the bed. I let her see the handkerchief and long sash.

"What are you doing?" she asked in a timid, suspicious voice.

Not replying, I watched her face color with surprise and confusion as I began pumping my cock. It took a minute, but I spilled my seed into the handkerchief, filling and soaking it.

Poor Charlotte had no idea what was coming.

"Don't worry," I said, grinning. "I'll be hard again in a few minutes. In the meantime…"

I grabbed Charlotte by the hair, shoved the soiled handkerchief into her mouth, and tied the sash around her head, securing the wad of cum within. Charlotte scrunched up her face in displeasure.

"I should be offended," I mocked. "But we'll have plenty of time to train you to like my taste. And I don't think you'll be thinking about it soon enough…"

Her eyes widened when I withdrew my dagger, but she relaxed when she saw I only meant to pare the ginger.

"This is going in your arse," I explained as I peeled. "You've never had anything in there before. It's going to feel uncomfortable. But that alone isn't punishment enough."

Charlotte's eyes bulged as I used her juices to lubricate her anus, sliding my own finger in to prepare it for the ginger. She squealed and tried to move away, but I grabbed her hips to keep her in place. With purposeful slowness, I slid the ginger inside and stood above her.

I looked down at Charlotte, trussed up upon my bed. Her mouth was filled with my seed and her heavy breasts swelled, begging for attention. Her face reddened with embarrassment and desire as ginger root stuck lewdly out of her arse.

I'd never seen her more beautiful.

When her eyes rounded, I knew it had started to work.

"It burns, doesn't it?" I grinned.

I took her moaning and head-thrashing as a reply.

"I'm going to really fuck you now. It might hurt your sore cunt and I imagine the pain in your rectum is even worse. But I have a reward for you too, Charlotte," I said, grinning. I wasn't sure if she'd see it as a reward in the moment. In fact, it would be further punishment, for now. But later… later, she'd come to look back on it and thank me.

I hoped.

"I'm not going to stop fucking you until you come." Her eyes snapped to mine. "You're going to have to find a way to relax, to enjoy the pain and to enjoy what I'm doing to you. Because the longer you take to come, the more it's going to hurt. And if you take too long, I'll simply replace this ginger with a fresh one."

I needed to be careful not to burn myself in the process. This was a punishment for her, not me, and Charlotte was so wet that her juices were spreading over her thighs and dripping down to the bed.

She actually trembled when I entered her, deepening my groan.

"Are you filled everywhere, Charlotte? It hurts a little in each hole, doesn't it?" I demanded, ramming her mercilessly.

Her eyes rolled back in her head as I thrust. "No other man would fuck you like this. No other man would bring out the whore I knew was inside you all this time."

Thrust.

"My whore."

Slam.

"Mine."

Charlotte's head lolled like a ragdoll's, but her cunt tightened, telling me she was near her pinnacle.

I chuckled in her ear, delighted. "I thought it might take some time but look at you. What a perfect little pain slut you are."

No words could describe the sound Charlotte made beneath her gag.

"That's my perfect little whore," I said, talking her through the last seconds before her orgasm sent her into oblivion. "Coming on my cock, with my punishment in your arse and my seed in your mouth. Look at how trainable you are. Look at how you're mine."

Charlotte's screams were muffled by the handkerchief, but she shook as if seized with the most powerful climax of her life. I had no hope of holding back at that sight; she pulled me over the edge with her the moment after she began her descent.

CHAPTER 29

CHARLOTTE

I FLOATED IN A sea of rapture. Colt wrapped his arms around me as we lay naked together in his bed. Everything ached deliciously. Even my heart.

"Tell me true," Colt whispered in my ear. His scruff scraped my cheek. "Don't play the lady. For one moment, drop the act."

My stomach fluttered at the vulnerability in Colt's gravelly voice. It was strange coming from such a powerful man. *Eyes so black, reputation so cruel.* He didn't have to do anything to intimidate anyone, he could merely appear and a person knew they were in the presence of someone to be reckoned with.

"I am begging you, Charlotte. Not as your captain, not as your punisher."

I held my breath as I awaited his next words.

"But as a man who's been longing for truth from you for years. As the man who's been trying to get past your walls for ages," Colt pled. "Do you forgive me for what I've done to you?"

My heart thumped in my breast. *Forgive him?* I didn't know how to explain that not only did I forgive him his past treatment—however many punishments I'd suffered under his hands—I welcomed them now. I *loved* them. Even when I hated them. Whatever Colt saw in me all those years ago… he knew before I did.

"I more than forgive you," I whispered. "I *understand.* I understand why you did what you did."

Colt's entire body relaxed, as if he'd been carrying the tension for a lifetime. Which might have been the case.

"Do you forgive me?" I asked, eyes wide. "For not understanding before?"

Colt's arms tightened around me. "There's nothing to forgive. Everything is as it should be. As it was meant to be."

My heart thumped wildly at his words and I looked up into those black, bottomless eyes. Colt was wild and I must be wild as well, for what I was about to say.

"I love you," I whispered, swallowing the lump in my throat. "I don't know when I fell in love with you. But I know that I do." I chewed my lip before continuing. "Do you think you could… love me, as well?"

Colt's thumb swept my cheekbone. "Charlotte, I've been in love with you for years."

My breath came out in a rush, along with tears of joy. "Since when?" I laughed.

Colt shook his head, laughing. "I don't know. Maybe since I first saw you strung to the whipping mast and knew I could."

Mention of a whipping mast made me shiver. I bore no marks. I hadn't been whipped. At least, not enough to scar. So what had happened? I badly wanted to ask Colt about it, but every question I formed in my mind gave me away.

I knew that I was running out of time and that Colt would eventually insist I confess about my supposed thievery… and murder.

But the last thing I wanted to do when we'd just found each other was to push him away by admitting I'd been conducting a ruse since I'd stepped aboard this ship.

I just needed a little more time, I reasoned.

A few days, maybe a week.

Maybe some miracle would happen before then.

CHAPTER 30

COLT

IN THE MORNING we looked out across the bay to the walls of Charles Town. Even in daylight I could spy smoke pluming into the sky from the many hearths cooking breakfast, or from smithies getting an early start to work, forging steel in the flames.

Steel meant to fight pirates like us, I thought, grinning.

We'd struck the colors and sailed under the flag of a safe and forgettable merchant ship out the Port of London. I dressed Charlotte in the finest attire we had and her skirted presence above deck helped squash the suspicions of soldiers who'd sailed out to take our information, asking a bit too many questions.

"Though we live so nearby, I've never been to Charles Town," Charlotte remarked, gazing at the sprawling city. "Have you?"

Charlie had been to Charles Town a few times, but I supposed the invented Lady Charlotte had not. I guessed we were back to playing her game this morning and, truth be told, I found it beyond frustrating.

After everything we'd shared the night before, how could she still insist upon the ruse we all knew to be false? What was the point?

Ire rose within me.

"Though you may not have known my purpose at the time," I declared, "I spent days here searching for the truth about your mother."

I threw out the statement abruptly, maybe a little coldly, hoping to jolt her out of her act.

Charlotte blinked up at me, expression blank.

You confessed love, yet you still lie. What kind of love is that?

A wicked seed planted inside me and the tendrils of something evil unfurled, making me want to push Charlotte, to jar her into confession or at least to break this shield she'd reassembled around herself.

"I thought something horrendous might have happened to her," I said, flippantly. "That she'd died horrifically, painfully. But I suppose the truth of her disgrace, for someone godly like you, is even worse."

It was a low blow, meant to wound, and still Charlotte's mask didn't crack. Her brow furrowed and the corners of her mouth turned down, but she remained composed. She neither wept nor attacked me.

Since we'd already discussed her father the night before, I thought mention of her mother might have some effect. *It should have.*

I didn't realize I'd clutched Charlotte's arms until my hands tightened on her biceps. Charlotte barely met my eyes. Her gaze would flick to mine, then dart downward or to the sea. I froze. My gut tightened with dread and déjà vu. It was like before. Just when I thought we'd made progress, when

I thought something real happened between us… the world was going to show me that men like me were not permitted happiness.

I should have never let down my guard. Charlotte was going to do something to make fools of us all for a third time. Three bloody times she would play us.

Finally, Charlotte met my gaze with something like pleading.

Why did she look up at me with such adoration in her eyes? What was the *point* of her lady act anyway? What could she possibly hope to gain? I clenched my jaw. Unless something else entirely was going on.

But what?

Who was this creature before me, who could hear mention of her mother and not bat an eye?

Impossible, wild ideas ran though my head—too nonsensical to even fully conceive, yet they nagged at me.

I was ashamed to even voice them aloud to anyone.

Insanity.

And yet…

When I told Charlotte to remain aboard while I attended to some business in town, I said nothing of my true intentions to anyone.

Nonsense.

When Conks asked me what I sought, I shrugged him off.

What foolishness.

Striding through various taverns with a clear purpose and coin in hand, I found what I was looking for in the third establishment. I bought the man a drink and we sat down to chat. I paid him more than he'd hope to see in a week and promised the second half once the task was complete.

I returned to *The Dread Night* with a young man bearing a passing resemblance to Charlotte and led him to my cabin.

Perhaps I'd lost my mind. But whatever happened, I vowed not to leave my quarters until I had the full truth from Charlotte.

CHAPTER 31

CHARLOTTE

"HOW DO YOU do?" I greeted the man accompanying Colt as pleasantly as possible, offering a welcoming smile. "Pleased to meet you…"

"Charlotte," Colt said, voice as hard as his stare. "Are you really going to play the lady when you haven't seen your brother in years? He's just sailed in from Boston. Won't you give George a true greeting?"

I folded my lips between my teeth to avoid gasping and tried to calm my racing heart.

Brother? What should I do?

"Charlotte?" George asked tentatively. "Is something wrong? Stop this, please." He held out his arms and crooked the fingers of one hand with a *come* motion. His eyes were round and pleading, brow furrowed with confusion.

"I—"

What to do?

"Please, sister." He looked so pitifully sad as he spoke. "Tell me what's wrong and I can help. I've missed you."

The pang in my heart made me gush, "Yes, *of course*. It's just been so long. My dear, dear, George." I threw myself forward, preparing to embrace the stranger as my own relative, when Colt withdrew his sabre and extended the blade perilously close to my throat, forcing me to halt.

I couldn't help my gasp, but quickly recovered and flashed a fake smile. "What—what are you doing?"

"Who are you?" Colt demanded, face wild with hostility. "What devilry is this?" He advanced, forcing me to back up to avoid the sharp blade.

"What in the hell is going on? A twin? Some kind of witchcraft?" he cried. His rage-filled eyes searched my body. "Have you possessed her? Is this even Charlotte's body? Speak! Now, witch, or I'll cut you in two."

Pressed against the wall, I panted, "I don't understand. What do you *mean?*"

"Charlotte has no brother," Colt growled.

I could actually feel the color drain from my face. *Oh God. I'd been fooled.*

"Who are you really, what trick is this?" Colt demanded.

I licked my quivering lips as tears formed. My mind, always an asset I could count upon, utterly failed me. Painfully long seconds passed.

Gazing into Colt's impossibly black eyes, I whispered, "I'm not a witch. At least, not that I remember." I swiped the back of my hand across my cheeks to remove the tears.

"I'm Charlotte." I touched my locket. "I think. The truth is... I don't remember."

Colt stared, hard, accusing. He did not lower his sword from beneath my chin.

Shaking my head, I wiped more tears. "I was found on a beach one day. I—I possessed no memory of what came before. The Penninghams gave me shelter and work at the inn. I've never known who I was or what happened before that day. I possessed nothing of my life here, save this locket. Until you stormed our tavern two months ago, I didn't know of—" I gestured broadly "—any of this."

Colt blinked, mouth parted in surprise. "Amnesia?" he whispered, body slumping. He lowered his sword, staring with more wide-eyed horror than if I'd declared myself a witch.

I nodded. "I was afraid. Afraid of what you'd tell me, what you might make me believe if you knew the truth. I feared you'd take advantage of me. So I pretended that I hadn't forgotten. Only, I needed something to cover up my lack of knowledge and familiarity with," I shrugged again, "all this. So I played the lady. The lady I hoped I had been before I lost my memory. The lady I always wanted to be."

Colt's sword clattered to the floor. He was only half-listening. His eyes glazed over, dazed. Conks appeared in the doorway, perhaps lured by Colt's shouting, and pulled the man pretending to be my brother out of the room. Colt and I couldn't be bothered to care.

"You don't remember…" Colt whispered, as if lost in his own memory.

"I don't remember who I was before the day I was found on the beach," I confessed.

I watched Colt's face crumple in pain. Two agonized hands tore through his hair. His eyes rose back to mine, wild, wounded.

"You don't remember," he repeated, wincing.

I stepped forward and he stumbled back, as if I were a threat. I reached out my arms, "Colt, I-"

He stepped back again, hands raised, refusing me. One hand smacked his forehead, half covering his closed eyes. His fingers tensed and his brow was creased with pain, as if he tried to subdue an unbearable headache.

I froze. It seemed like an eternity passed in those seconds. Beneath his large hands I could see Colt's face crinkled in distress. *Despair.*

Finally, Colt's hand moved, swiping down his face and neck. His eyes snapped open. New eyes. Eyes that saw something else as they focused on me. They were no longer the blackness of pitch, ready to suck me in and trap me forever, but the blackness of an abyss providing nothing to stop my fall, offering nothing for me cling to. No warmth or light, just endless nothing.

"Since your jig is up, I suppose mine can end as well."

What? I drew in a shaky breath and swallowed. I didn't know what those words meant, and I didn't like his ominous tone.

"I thank you for confessing, Miss Charlotte, and I thank you for the jolly time you gave me while forcing you to do so." Colt winked. "I won't soon forget it. At least, not until I've had my next turn to crack jenny's cup."

"Stop it," I said, fear rising in me with as overpowering as the tide. "What do you mean?"

"I mean as you're through pretending, so am I."

I wanted to slap my hands over my ears and stop hearing his words. I wanted to close my eyes and stop seeing the truth, plain upon his cruel face. So *cold;* his face was so cold it could scarcely be called human.

"Pretending? Stop it," I ordered. "We haven't been. You haven't been…"

"Treating you with affection to wrest the truth from you?" he said. "There's no further need."

The room spun. *What was he saying?*

Colt sneered. My heart screamed.

"You haven't been doing that," I repeated.

"Oh, but I have. Did you think I couldn't best you? Are you forlorn to have been beaten at your own game? Did you think it was real?" he mocked. "Aw, you did? I'm sorry about that. We'll return you to your port and keep it quiet, you have my word as a pirate," he winked again.

What in the world was happening?

"Stop it!" I sobbed so hard, so childishly hard. "Don't treat me like this. Like I'm some whore you've used and discarded. That's not what we had. It was real, I felt it. You felt it." Blubbering, I continued, "I know it's true. It *is* real! It hasn't changed."

Shrugging, Colt said, "You might not have been a whore when you stepped onto this ship but you sure as hell are one now. Do you honestly think I'd marry you? A girl who'd sully herself as you have? Even a pirate has better standards than that."

Oh God, it hurt so badly I couldn't stand the pain. I threw myself at Colt, beating him and wailing, "That's a lie! It was real."

What we shared was unlike anything I'd ever felt.

Colt clasped my wrists in one of his hands, restraining me. *What was he doing? Why?*

"Real? How would you know? Have you been whoring so much with the scoundrels passing through your inn these past two years, that a few tumbles in a captain's bed made you believe it was love?"

I wailed, throwing my head back. Colt seized the top of my shirt and ripped it in two, right down the middle. My hands flew to hold the shirt back together. Colt fisted my hair instead, yanking it and causing the pins to fall.

"I could take you now and you'd love it, wouldn't you, you filthy whore? After I'm done I could invite my men in here to take their turns."

I barely heard his horrible words above my sobbing. "Please…"

"Say the word and I'll drop you off at the nearest brothel. You haven't been used too much; you can still fetch a good price. Even better if you let 'em treat you as rough as I have. Let 'em know you like it. Many men will want to rough up a pretty little thing like you."

Impossibly, I wept harder.

"Let me know if you'd rather I deposit you at the nearest brothel, instead of back with your Daniel." With obvious disgust, Colt shoved me off his body and I crumpled onto the hard floor, weeping pathetically.

"Makes no difference to me," he declared, as calmly as if he discussed selecting one pair of breeches over another. I'd broken to pieces, never to be reassembled, and the entire matter hadn't even made a dent in his day. "I have the truth from you now, Charlotte. You're only weeping because you've lost. And if there's more to it than that… well then. You have my pity at least. Pity for what an easy mark you've become."

"It was real," I babbled, over and over. "It was real to me."

Colt shrugged, turned, and opened the door.

I didn't think I could fall any lower, but I was wrong.

Lunging for Colt a second time, I screamed while attacking him, "I'm not a whore! Liar! It was real!"

The more my fists flew in pathetic attempts to injure him, the harder he smacked them away and eventually, he clamped my wrists. Using my own flailing against me, Colt spun me around, locked my arm behind my back, and gave me a shove so fierce I was sent sprawling. Pain erupted on my palms and knees, but I didn't care. I lost the will to battle Colt and crumpled into a pitiful ball.

"Put her in the brig," I heard Colt tell someone. I hadn't even realized we had company. "If she wakes in the morning ready to behave like a lady, she can leave. If she attacks me again, she'll stay there until we reach land."

Crying into my hands, I felt Conks touch my elbow and help me rise on wobbly legs. I barely had the strength to stand or walk, but I didn't have the strength to refuse the guidance either. I certainly had no power to fight Colt again. I did not struggle as I was led to the brig. In that moment, I could have been led off the plank and I wouldn't have protested. My heart may have already taken such a plunge, right to the bottom of the ocean. That was what it felt like—as if my heart was drowning, screaming in pain, but the rest of my body was above the surface and wouldn't let me die, forcing me to live in continual, unbearable agony.

It was real, it was real.

It was real… to me.

I didn't even make it to the brig's hammock. When the metal door closed behind me with a *clank,* I crumbled to the floor, covering my face and wailing.

I did not move all night.

CHAPTER 32

CHARLOTTE

WHAT WOULD BECOME *of me now? Could I convince Daniel to want me?*

I did not need to ask the question, *did I want him?* The answer was no. I didn't want anyone but Colt. Not this Colt, the one who cruelly tore my heart from chest. I laughed, mirthlessly. I wanted the Colt who cruelly tore my innocence from my body. Who tore screams of pleasure and pain from my lips.

Perhaps Daniel was right and I was no better than a whore. Maybe it was my nature. I knew nothing of my previous desires. Maybe the strumpet lurked within and I'd only needed Colt's hands to coax her forth.

Because I was a wretched thing. And my wretchedness wasn't from my wanton nights with Colt.

It was from his rejection.

Now, nothing was left for me on *The Dread Night*. Yet I couldn't face Mrs. Penningham with what I'd become, leaving me nowhere to go. Maybe Daniel would still want me if I hadn't disgusted him enough on our last meeting. I could beg and plead; tell him I'd been deceived.

No. My heart sank. Daniel was a good man, despite what he'd said to me. Those words came from the pain of betrayal. I *had* betrayed him, our plans.

What became of a woman who couldn't marry and couldn't find work in her settlement?

I knew the sound of those boots upon the floorboards before I even saw his face, and my heart beat in time to each thump.

"Are you going to behave?" Colt asked, rounding the corner and coming into view.

Head bent, I nodded.

"Good. Then you can come out. But raise one hand to me and you'll spend the rest of the journey in here, is that clear?"

I nodded again.

Colt unlocked my cell and stepped back. He turned abruptly on his heel and walked out of the small chambers.

Shuffling my feet, I exited the unlocked cell slowly. Part of me wanted to stay because I was afraid that, now free, I couldn't restrain myself from jumping overboard and letting the sea take me. I wandered the ship like a ghost, trying to hide from everyone. I didn't want my face to betray my shame, my pain. It might have been five minutes or five hours later when I stood upon the quarterdeck, nearing the rail as I stared despairingly at the sea.

My stomach had just grazed the wooden rail when I felt a painful grip on my bicep and whipped my head up to see Colt, eyes narrowed. He shook his head ever so slightly. His eyes glowed with… concern? That couldn't be. But the message in that dark gaze was clear. *Don't you dare do anything stupid.*

Did you think I would jump? Why do you care? I wanted to cry, and my face must have asked the question.

"If I return without you, Mr. Clayton will be disinclined to pay the tribute I've decided we're going to demand, and we'll start a battle that could have easily been avoided."

Tears welled and a half-mad laugh tore from my throat. *You're returning an empty husk,* I thought. *My heart and spirit have been ripped from this shell. But what care men about such things, as long as I appear whole on the outside?*

Colt's eyes narrowed further and he yanked me from the railing. Mistaking my despair for defiance and believing it gave strength to my empty-husk body, he pulled too hard and I stumbled. Forced to catch me or let me fall, instinct took over and Colt's strong arms found my waist. Pain ripped through my heart as I desperately longed to remain in his embrace.

Looking up at his cold expression with pathetic, pleading eyes, a lump formed in my throat.

"If you return me, you condemn me. If Daniel tells the town about my betrayal, I'll be shunned."

"Mrs. Penningham will never let that happen," Colt said.

"She might not have a choice, should everyone shun the tavern."

Colt shook his head. "I'll be returning you with enough coin for her pocket to make any concerns disappear."

"You're bribing her to shelter me," I said, flatly.

"Call it what you like." Colt shrugged and strode off, boots stomping across the wooden deck.

Why do you care? I screamed the question in my head as I watched his retreating back.

I made it safely to the isolation of the galley and let my tears fall again.

———◆———

HOURS LATER WE REACHED MY settlement and I'd never seen such a hateful sight. The stocky, ugly little buildings. The dusty paths. And aside from a select few, such as the Penninghams, the small-minded people. It had all changed in the past two days to become a threat.

I didn't belong there. I belonged with Colt. My head fit perfectly into the small dip of his chest, just below his shoulders. His cock fit perfectly into the secret places beneath my skirts. My heart fit perfectly into the safe cocoon of his.

Or it had, until this.

The sky, heavy with storm clouds, mirrored my heart. I wished the winds had died down and left us floating in the doldrums, rather than carry me back. But all too soon we'd arrived. I'd run out of ideas. And time. Colt was going to deposit me ashore like cargo, sail away, and never return.

From behind me, I heard arguing, low at first, but increasing in volume.

"...can't let her go without the information," Robert shouted.

"She doesn't have it!" Colt shouted.

More voices joined in—arguing, asking questions, or offering grunts of agreement or denial.

Resolved, I joined them, only to be roughly grabbed by Colt and shoved in the direction of the jolly boat.

"Time to go, Charlotte," he ordered, coldly.

"No," I insisted, chin raised. "I won't leave. Not until you tell me why."

"She ain't leavin' 'till she talks," Robert yelled. His declaration stirred two of the men near him. The hair on my neck stood upright at the same time shame rose at Colt's harsh dismissal of me. But panicked desperation overrode my pride.

"Stop this, please," I begged, grabbing the neck of Colt's waistcoat and speaking in a low, urgent voice. "I'm not taking one step; I won't leave this ship until you talk to me. Not as *this*. This monster without conscience. I want my Colt back, my captain. The one who held me in his arms all night. Please, talk to me."

"Conks, take her back," Colt ordered. "Drag her if you have to."

Conks didn't move, other than to stroke his gray whiskers.

"Dammit!" Colt roared. "This is my ship! You'll obey my orders!"

Conks stared defiantly at his captain.

"We're not releasing her anywhere," Robert cried. "Lash her, lash her! She killed Maurice! She knows where the Crimson Eye is!"

Three or four men gathered to back Robert, and for the first time since Colt betrayed me, I felt an emotion other than despair.

Fear.

"Thief!" Robert shouted. "Murderer."

From seemingly nowhere, a whip appeared, and I thought I might faint.

"We'll lash her 'till she talks," Robert decreed.

A fight erupted so suddenly it was hard to tell what was happening amidst the fast-moving chaos. I was shoved, separated from Colt's arms, while two of the men who'd been backing Robert moved to block Colt from reaching me. They weren't forcibly attacking the captain, but they were arguing passionately. Almost at the same time, Robert lunged, attempting to grab me, but I leapt out of his reach. There was nowhere else to go on a deck full of men, so I scrambled aboard the ship's rail. Robert reached for me again and I shuffled left, holding onto the rigging with one hand.

The boom of a pistol rang out as Colt fired a shot, hitting Robert square in the chest.

Everyone fell quiet in shocked silence. Using his last few breaths, Robert made a final attempt to grab me, but his attack knocked me off balance.

With a scream, I fell overboard.

Into the murky sea.

Into the shadowed past.

Part II

Concealed

CHAPTER 33

CHARLOTTE,
THE PAST, AGED 16

ONE DAY, I'LL *be a lady.*

I tugged at my unruly mop of hair as I made the vow for the thousandth time. *With fine silver combs.* I smacked at the dirt upon my breeches. *And gowns of pink.*

Or gowns of any color, at least.

I owned but one dress, and while it hung to dry I made do with the hand-me-down shirt and breeches of a boy I never knew, two sizes too big. I tightened the belt at my waist. Had I some curves or muscle or any meat on my body at all, the tattered clothing would at least fit better. But to build meat on my bones, I needed to eat more often than I did.

Leaning down in the town square to retrieve my basket of eggs, I flinched as something flew by my head, narrowly missing.

"Charlotte's a boy, Charlotte's a boy!" came the chant from my right. I turned to see the three girls I least wanted to see. Despite our ages—ranging from fifteen to sixteen—they acted like children, often forcing me to respond in kind. I hated them all as much as they hated me. *More.* Because I had reason and they'd despised me all my life when I'd given them none.

"Have you been sleeping with the cows again?" Rebecca mocked, knowing full well we couldn't afford our own cows… though I had been known to nap in George's barn some afternoons.

Behavior I planned to cease. As soon as I was a lady, of course.

Father and I lived on the outskirts of town, on a small plot of land we helped farm. It was my job to bring the produce to market each day, but days like this were bad, bringing these three girls taunting, laughing, and twirling in their finery. Rebecca was the worst.

"You're just a cow yourself, aren't you?" she smirked, ostentatiously playing with the blue silk ribbons on her dress. "Isn't she, girls? She looks like a cow and smells like a cow. Must be a cow."

My hands itched to box her ears. Or better yet, to use my fists. It wasn't a ladylike thought, but I couldn't be bothered with that now.

"She's too skinny to be a heifer and where are her teats?" one of the girls behind Rebecca taunted. "Cows have teats for milking. She looks more like a bull."

The barb smarted and they knew it. Malnourished and underdeveloped, I didn't look like the other girls, and wearing boys' breeches didn't help the matter.

"I'm not a cow and certainly not a bull," I cried, finding my voice.

Rebecca's grin was pure malice. "Go on then," she urged, advancing. "Take off your shirt and show us your teats."

Heart pounding, I realized the imminent threat these three girls posed. As they eyed me maliciously, I got the sense that if I didn't strip my clothing, they would pin my arms and do it for me. Glancing down in panic, I saw Rebecca had tossed a rotten onion at my head. I almost reached down to throw it back, but I had a better idea and retrieved an egg from my basket.

Quickly, I drew the largest and took aim.

Splat.

It landed right in the middle of her chest, splitting open and sending yellow yolk running down her blue bodice in gooey trails.

Rebecca bared her perfect teeth. "You'll pay for this!" she swore "I'll tell my father what you've done and I'll see you whipped!"

"Go ahead," I challenged. My father, a gentle man, would never raise a hand to me… though I did worry about *hers,* and what trouble he might cause. Rebecca screamed and started toward me, but I grabbed another egg.

"Stay back, unless you be wanting more," I yelled.

The threat wasn't effective.

All three girls charged, reaching me before I could escape. In the tussle, Rebecca knocked my eggs from my grip, smashing them all as the basket clattered to the ground and out of my reach, and sending my heart breaking along with them. We needed that money.

I had only enough time to retrieve the basket of ruined eggs or run, so I ran, hot tears streaming down my cheeks as I heard the girls laugh behind me.

By the time I made it to the safety of George's barn, I was sobbing. It wasn't like what happened was anything new, but once I started crying, I couldn't stop. *I am just so tired of it all. So hungry all the time.* The girls were right—my underfed body didn't resemble that of a woman's. Some days I was so frail I thought I barely looked human. In the summer, when we ate better, I still had no breasts to speak of, my hips were as narrow as a boy's and my curses hadn't come about yet. But in the winter, when food was less plentiful, my cheeks hallowed, my shoulder blades stuck out, and my legs looked like sticks.

Father said I was blessed to have my mother's wild waves of hair and her soft, full lips. But I didn't even have a picture to know if that was true.

That afternoon, I cried myself into a deep sleep.

BLINKING MY EYES OPEN IN George's barn revealed I'd been asleep for maybe two or three hours. The barn stank, but the space was better than the cramped hovel I shared with Father. As I moved, the underside of my arm brushed against something sticky in my hair and I furrowed my brow, bringing my hands to my head.

The shrill scream I released would have rattled the devil.

Stickiness. All over my head.

My stomach sank as horror washed over me.

Tar.

Whilst I slept, someone had covered my beautiful hair in tar. Hot tears sprang in my eyes. *Covered it to the root.*

Sobbing hysterically, I ran though the fields toward our home. By the time I threw open the door, I was inconsolable.

"Oh, my sweet girl," my father sighed upon seeing me. "What trouble have you gotten yourself into now?"

"It wasn't my fault!" I cried, running into his arms like a child.

"Careful, now," he cautioned, retrieving his blade. "We don't want to get that sticking anywhere."

Over the next hour, my father hacked my hair. Tarred, matted chunks fell onto the floor. I sobbed all the while, feeling like I was six and not recently turned sixteen. It was gone. My mother's pretty hair, gone.

"Shh, you're still my beautiful girl," my father said. "It will grow back in no time. You'll see."

"It will take years," I wept. "I shall never marry. I have no dowry and now I have lost my best feature. I have nothing to offer a husband."

"Hush," my father chided. "You have everything to offer, my daughter, and I'm more concerned with what he be offering you." Finishing up the area around the back of my neck, my father said, "I wanted it to be a surprise, but I've been saving up. We can go to the shop next week and pick out a bolt of cloth for a dress, a *new* dress. All your own, one that's never been worn before."

Who cares about a new gown, now? I thought, *when I look like this?* But I didn't want to disappoint Father, who worked so hard to cheer me. Instead, I said nothing when we set the table for dinner and I ate nothing as we sat.

Finishing up our meal, the last rays of the dying sun still shone through our greasy windows when we heard a noise coming from outside our small house. It sounded like several loud men approached. My father immediately tensed, but I wasn't alarmed. After all, anyone who'd meant harm would approach stealthily, I decided.

My father raced to the window and stumbled back, stricken.

"Quiet!" he whisper-shouted, making me jump. "Hide! There, behind the dresser!"

What was happening?

The color had drained from his face as Father looked me over. "If anyone finds you, you're Charlie, you hear me? Charlie, my only son."

Who was outside?

Father shook my shoulders. "What's your name? Say it!"

"Ch—Charlie," I repeated.

Shocked, I watched father retrieve a pistol from beneath the same mattress upon which the two of us had slept when I was a child. Now nearly grown, my father usually dozed in the armchair at night, giving me space. *Had I slept above a weapon nightly, never knowing?*

"Do what I say, no matter what!"

My father released me and I scurried behind the chest-of-drawers with my heart pounding so loudly it seemed to fill our home. Curling into a tight ball, I did as I was told. Seconds later, I heard the door creak open and the ominous, heavy fall of boots upon our wooden floor as three or four men entered our tiny dwelling. I knew I would never forget that sound as long as I lived. It was the sound of dire fate.

"Don't do anything stupid and we won't harm you," announced a man's gravelly voice.

In our small hovel, I could smell the men, wafting into the room with so much ale and rum in their bellies it leaked from their breath, their pores, and scented the already-stale air. Crouching, I peeked beneath the chest-of-drawers and could see three pairs of dirt-caked black boots, as well as the prints of fresh mud they trailed behind them.

I realized there was another reason men might not bother to hide their approach—*confidence.* They had nothing to fear from us and sauntered into our home with all the bravado afforded by their sense of security and superiority.

I hated them. I feared them.

"May I introduce Captain Colt," one of the men said. "We've only come to get some information about your town. Give it to us and we'll be on our way."

"On your way to plunder it," my father countered with anger. "On your way to *kill.*"

I heard Father move, feet sliding against the floor of our hovel, causing the pirates to quickly move in turn.

"Don't fight, old man," one of the men warned. "We promise you no harm if you do as we say. In fact, the more you help us the more lives will be spared. I give you my word."

"The word of a pirate," Father spat. "Did my wife have the same vow when your kind killed her?"

What? I froze, chills running down my spine and locking me in place. *Mother died in childbirth. Didn't she?*

"I'm Captain Colt," a deep voice said. "Not whoever that was. And when I make a vow, I keep it."

My head spun. It was hard to keep up with what was happening mere feet from my hiding place *and* process what my father had said about my mother's death *and* suppress my rising terror.

"We should kill him," someone said. "It'd be doing him a favor, judging from this hovel."

I can't let them kill Father. I'd rather they kill me.

I heard a noise and moved without thinking.

"No!" I shouted, jumping from my hiding place and coming to my father's defense. My arms were raised wide as I prepared to throw myself in front of him as a sacrifice.

I saw the blood drain from my father's face before I fully faced the men.

"Charlie, no!" he shouted, pushing me out of the way. "Charlie, don't do it, *Charlie,* my boy, no."

"What's this?" Captain Colt asked, stepping forward. He'd gripped his pistol but hadn't raised it, like the others. Still, that left two pistols aimed at us from the men behind the captain. One was especially muscular and had a head of sandy hair and a pierced ear. The other was brown-haired and not as tall as Colt or as strong as the other man, but far meaner-looking than both.

Father pushed me back toward our rear window and threw himself between us.

"Kill 'em and be done with it," that gruff voice said. It belonged to the snarling man with brown hair and blue eyes, standing behind Colt.

"Robert, nobody's ki-", Colt began with a sigh, but my father cut him off.

"Run!" he cried, holding up his hands. "Run and save yourself. Tell them they're coming. Do as you're told, boy!"

For a moment, I froze with indecision. I didn't want to leave father. But I didn't want to disobey him either and I'd made a vow. Thinking I could bring help, I leapt for the window.

I was yanked back by Colt's rough grip on my shirt. He was impossibly fast. Deciding to make a leap for me, however, caused him to be preoccupied while my father raised his pistol.

Wrapped in his arms, Colt could have used my body to block the shot. But out of instinct, I supposed, he ducked and shoved me sprawling onto my hands and knees. And the same time, he raised his own pistol —

— and fired directly into my father's chest.

In the span of three seconds, my world changed forever.

"Father!" I screamed, throwing myself at my father's lifeless corpse. "Father, Father, Father!" I wept.

"Shut the boy up," Robert grumbled. "He's giving me a headache."

"You killed him!" My red face was covered in tears and snot. I could barely choke out the accusation.

"He tried to attack us," Colt said, voice full of pity, if not remorse. "We told him not to fight."

"He was protecting me," I sobbed, clutching my father's lifeless body.

"We promised him no harm if he didn't raise a hand."

"And–and he was to believe you?" I choked. "Pirates!"

I didn't know how long I cried before the realization of the danger I was in washed over me. Slowly, I looked up.

Captain Colt stood, indecisive as he considered me. His gaze burned.

"We've as good as killed the boy if he's got no one to look after him," he said, speaking to the men and not me. "Take him. We could use a new swab on deck."

What? He couldn't mean that.

One of the men shrugged, then stepped forward as if to grab me.

"I won't go with you!" I shouted. "Please, let me bury my father. He needs a proper burial!"

Father, father, father. My only family in the world.

"There's no time," Captain Colt said. "Your townsfolk will take care of him."

Baring my teeth in rage, I declared, "I'd rather die than go with you."

"We don't have time for this," Robert argued, but the third man approached anyway, ready to rip my world from me.

"Father!" I yelled, clutching at his body, helpless as I was pulled away. "Please, no!"

"You'd rather stay here?" the captain asked. "There will be nothing left of your town if things go sour and there's nothing left in this house from the looks of it."

"Please, no, wait! Let me have his handkerchief."

The crewman holding me allowed me to stretch forward and grab the handkerchief from my father's pocket before quickly whisking me back while I screamed.

"Gag him or he'll alert the whole town to our arrival."

Someone produced a gag as well as rope. Colt's two men held me down while my wrists and ankles were bound. Still sobbing, I was tossed over the strong man's shoulder.

"Bring him back to the ship and leave him with Miguel. Hurry back to finish the job here."

Bouncing roughly over the pirate's shoulder, I cried too hard to notice much of the journey. The blood rushing to my head made me woozy. I heard the call of gulls and smelled the sea when we neared the harbor and I began my struggles anew. Once deposited on that ship, I'd have no hope of escape. No hope of seeing my father ever again.

But the man carrying me was too strong. After a quick ride in the jolly boat, I was hoisted onto *The Dark Blade* like cargo.

Pirates. I despised their kind. Pirates had killed my mother *and* my father.

I curled into a ball in the brig.

They'd probably kill me too.

CHAPTER 34

CHARLOTTE,
THE PAST

F OR WEEKS, I barely ate or drank. Counting my ribs pleased me. Maybe I'd shrink so much, I'd disappear. If I grew too weak to work, I thought Captain Colt would abandon me to die at the nearest desolate island. I was not so lucky.

Colt looked at me strangely, like I was a puzzle to solve.

"Eat, boy," he ordered one evening, shoving a plate of biscuits under my lowered head. "You can eat on your own or I can force it down your throat."

"I'll throw it back up," I spat, snarling.

"Do it and I'll make you lick it up," he said, calmly. "I'm sure the crew would like to watch that, seeing as how you're not pulling even your own meager weight around here."

Confusion pierced through my anger. Though I didn't doubt Colt's words, his concern puzzled me. Why did he care if I ate? Why did he insist on bringing me on their voyages though

I did almost nothing to contribute throughout? Why defend me against the crew when they—rightfully—pointed it out?

I studied the man who killed my father.

He was very tall, but not burly. His hair was neatly groomed, his fingernails clean, and his face clean-shaven. His clothing was slightly rumpled and smelled of salt and sweat, but none of it was tattered or torn. Dark eyes gazed at me from a finely chiseled face. It wasn't a soft, gentleman's face, but rather a face with a savage, ancient sort of nobility. His eyes were hooded, haughty, and so dark and cold they were like the bottom of a black pond or the ocean itself. His movements were too measured to speak of an upbringing other than one of refinement at *some* point.

A pirate shouldn't look like that.

We stared at one another in a battle of wills I was sure to lose. With the crew looking on, Colt couldn't afford any disobedience to a command. Not that I'd have fared much better in private.

Capitulating, I brought the bread to my mouth and chewed. It tasted like nothing.

Like my future. Like all that was left for me now.

Nothing.

THAT NIGHT I stood alone on the stern deck, hidden from the watchman's view as best as possible. The moon glistened off the soft night waves, beckoning. I wanted to dissolve into that bubbling sea foam or those glistening beams of moonlight. My hands clutched the railing. I placed one foot on a wooden beam, then another, stepping up, closer to my destiny.

Death.

Holding onto the ropes for balance, I climbed barefoot onto the rail. I let my head fall back, taking one last deep breath of air.

Father, I'm coming, I thought.

My muscles tensed, ready to leap —

— a hand roughly grabbed my arm and yanked me off the railing, making my stomach flip.

Shaken, the blood drained from my face as I met Colt's fierce black eyes staring down at me.

"If you ever try that again, I'll beat your arse so hard you won't be able to walk," he swore. "Do you hear me?" Colt shook me with his last words. I could only nod frantically.

"Say it!"

"I–I hear you," I stammered.

"You want death? Have we treated you so poorly on this ship that you seek to end your life?"

The fire in my breast rekindled and I shouted, "No, captain, it's what you did before you kidnapped me onto this ship! Or did his life mean so little to you that you've forgotten?"

Colt's eyes narrowed. "He was an inadequate father. He could barely provide for his only son. We did you a favor."

"That was for God to decide, not you!"

He scoffed. Colt seemed to disdain religion of any kind. "Maybe God sent us to you."

I didn't know how to argue that, so I cried, "I hate you so much! One day I'll have my vengeance, do you hear me? I will avenge my father."

Colt loosened his grip on my arm. "I look forward to it," he mocked. "But how, boy, do you intend to avenge your father if you're dead?" Colt tipped his head in the direction of the ocean. He raised his eyebrows once. Then he spun on his heel and left me shouting curses at his back.

I hated that he was right. I couldn't avenge father from the grave.

I'll be patient, I vowed to Colt's back. *I'll remain quiet and watch for an opportunity. Then one day… I'll make you sorry.*

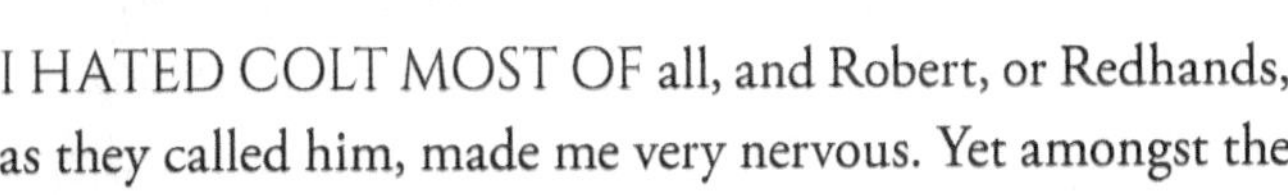

I HATED COLT MOST OF all, and Robert, or Redhands, as they called him, made me very nervous. Yet amongst the crew, another man stood out as more fearsome than all the rest. And he didn't even lift a finger to do it.

Maurice was older than Colt by a good twenty years, and he seemed to function as a sort of father or authority figure to both Colt and Robert, and perhaps the entire crew. Lean, quiet, and watchful, Maurice often stood back, observing Colt and Robert, whom I noted often looked to him for a sort of permission to proceed in an endeavor.

I learned there was some history between the three men, Maurice having brought Colt and Robert into piracy years before and acting as a sort of mentor. At some point, Maurice had supported Colt's rise to captain and it wasn't hard to see why. Colt was quick-witted, clever, and possessed a restraint Robert lacked. But Robert's taste for violence was the one area in which he beat Colt and matched Maurice. It was as if Maurice would like to have forged the perfect boy to mentor, could he merge the two men. Whenever the crew raided, Colt's careful planning enabled the win, making Maurice crook a small smile. But Robert's bloodlust—often leading to slaughtering a choice few crewmates or townsfolk who'd peacefully surrendered—brought a gleam to Maurice's eye.

Captain Colt always looked displeased about the breach of honor but said nothing. The killings earned him more of a reputation for cruelty than he would have gained if he'd murdered a crew en masse. The arbitrary selection of those put to the sword had a distinct malice for its casual unpredictability.

Once, I'd heard Colt argue with Maurice about it.

"It's smarter this way and you should be smart enough to see it," Maurice said. "Never draw blood and the merchants won't fear you enough to surrender. Draw it too often and they'll put up a fight every time, rather than lose their lives."

I could hear the self-satisfaction in Maurice's voice as he concluded, "But never knowing, giving them a dose of hope and fear together, and they'll bend to your will. Give a man that perfect mixture and you've got a man you can control."

My heart pounded as, hidden in the shadows, I listened to them talk.

I had hope—the hope to kill Colt and all his men to avenge my father. But other than the fear of failure, I had no fear.

Liar, said a voice in my head. *You don't want to die. Not any longer.*

Scurrying below deck, I pondered that voice. Months had passed on the ship and I'd learned to work as a part of the crew, albeit, not as well. I was smart and quick, but never as strong as they desired or expected, and only I knew the reason why.

I was nearly down the stairs when I heard the captain.

"Stop," he said. I turned to see him standing at the top of the stairs. "You think I didn't know you were eavesdropping?"

My stomach twisted. Would he punish me? I must have paled because Colt laughed.

"If I whipped every man for listening in on conversations not his own, I'd have a shipful of bloody backs," he said, as if reading my thoughts.

Colt stalked down the stairs and I froze, unsure what to say or do.

"You've been eating," he remarked, looking me up and down.

I blinked. So?

"You're settling in. Still want to kill me?" he asked.

"More than ever," I swore.

"He drew first," Colt said, for the hundredth time.

"He was protecting me!" I shouted, so angry I forgot to deepen my voice as I usually did. Luckily, Colt didn't notice.

"That's my job now," he said, almost sneering at the declaration, as if he resented it. "I'll do a better one than he did."

"On a pirate ship?" I asked, disbelieving. "If you care so much for my well-being, dump me off at the nearest port and I'll be on my way."

Colt laughed. "You'd get yourself killed in a day. And if you didn't, you'd just be waiting for the chance to kill me. Maybe you'd even succeed someday. Better to keep you here, keep you close."

The pronunciation brought angry tears to my eyes. The idea that I might never escape Colt made my heart sink. Rather than allow him to see it, I turned on my heel to scurry away.

"There's something else I've been doing in port," Colt called after me. I stopped, curious at his tone. Almost… kind.

"I've been asking around the other crews," he said. "We'll find out who killed your mother, Charlie. It's my… gift to you."

At the mention of my mother, tears pooled in my eyes.

"You mean it's your attempt at recompense for my father's life," I whispered. "And a pitiful one at that."

"Call it what you like. I vow to find out who killed her."

I shook my head and continued down the hall, even though I burned to know the truth about my mother.

I hated that Colt might be able to access this knowledge. Was it more hope? Was he instilling hope in me, in order to control me, as Maurice had said?

It didn't matter. I had no way to escape the captain either way.

CHAPTER 35

CHARLOTTE,

THE PAST

WHEN I AWOKE in the morning, blood blossomed between my spread legs, staining the tan breeches before my widened eyes. With the way my legs shifted in the night, blood spread down my thighs, impossible to ignore.

"No, God, please no," I whimpered. Waves of horror and panic washed over me.

What should I do? Why had my curses come upon me now?

They'd been so delayed, I'd wondered if they'd ever come at all.

This blood wouldn't wash out and the crew would surely see. We were so far from shore… the danger I'd be in…

Crying softly, I found a clean rag and stuffed it between my legs to staunch the flow. I pulled my shirt free from my belt, letting it hang low enough to cover the apex of my thighs, but it wasn't long enough to hide the stains.

What to do?

I spied the knife on the galley table. My stomach flipped as I resolved, *if I can't make it better, I'll make it worse.*

Before I had time to back out, I grabbed the knife and steeled my courage. Wincing, I sliced from my palm, up my forearm, careful to avoid my veins.

The blood-curdling scream I let out woke Miguel and everyone else on the ship. It was no act as I crumbled into a ball and further spread the blood all over myself, clutching my arm in a fruitless attempt to stifle the searing pain.

He couldn't have arrived first—not when Miguel was also sleeping in the galley. But somehow, Colt was the first face I focused on as I came in and out of a haze of pain.

"What have you done to yourself?" he asked, eyes blown wide in fear.

"N–not intentional," I protested. "Was… cutting an apple…"

"Jesus, Charlie," Colt said, scooping me up in his arms. "To the infirmary," he commanded Miguel.

The infirmary was only one small staircase down from the galley, an oft-used little room in which I'd seen many shipmates patched up over the months. Once we arrived, Colt laid me on a makeshift table and Miguel turned my arm, examining. Then his gaze roved over the rest of my body. The hair on my neck rose.

"I need everyone out," Miguel said calmly, quietly. "You too captain."

I hadn't noticed the crowd gathered at the door and spilling into the small room. At Miguel's request, everyone departed, including a reluctant captain.

Miguel uncorked the rum—something I'd seen him do many times before and an act which no longer surprised me. I turned my head and winced again, knowing he was going to pour the spirit onto my wound.

It stung worse than I anticipated and I screamed.

"I don't think you need sewing up," Miguel said, "but we'll bandage this arm and you won't be able to use it for week, possibly a fortnight."

I nodded, glad his proclamation might grant me a reprieve from work I needed to tend to the new problem leaking between my legs.

Scanning my body, Miguel said, "Considering you didn't hit a vital artery, that's a lot of blood coming from one cut."

I smiled weakly. "I've always been a bleeder." My voice rose at the end, like a question.

Do you believe me? I seemed to ask.

Miguel's warm eyes danced, as if to reply, *no. But your secret's safe with me.*

My shoulders slumped, part from relief, part defeat. If anyone on this Godforsaken ship was going to know the truth, Miguel would be my first choice. But it would have been better if no one knew at all. It felt like dominoes were falling, too fast for me to stop.

I'd put on weight from the steady meals and my breasts were beginning to grow. The onset of my monthly bleeding arrived. Miguel knew the truth.

How many more dominoes would fall before I was exposed?

IT BECAME A ROUTINE EACH month where I'd use the cargo hold to take care of what I needed to. I wore longer, looser clothing to hide the evidence of my cycles and my increasingly fuller breasts. They weren't large yet. But they *existed* where none ever existed before and where they shouldn't reside on a scrawny *boy*. I swiped gauze from the infirmary to bind my breasts flatter and to help soak up the extra blood. It was the only thing I could think to do.

Even with Miguel possibly on my side, it was brought to the captain's attention that someone was pillaging the supply. Yet I had no better option. My prolonged and frequent absences during my cycles were noticed, but it was a necessary risk. I couldn't allow the curve of my breasts to show beneath my shirts and I couldn't get caught with blood between my legs.

Sometimes, for all the fear they brought, I lingered in the dark safety of the cargo hold and admired my breasts, examining them. They were the size of small apples now, the tips of my nipples growing and deepening into a dusky pink. I wished I had someone to talk to about the changes in my body. Not that I'd have fared better in the past, with only my father to look out for me, but it was a lonely existence on a ship full of men with no hope of female company.

Perhaps I'd stayed too long in the hull one evening, when I heard shouts from the crew echoing through the cavernous room.

"There he is!" Robert shouted, pointing at me. "Charlie's been stealing!"

Terror roiled in my gut as I shot to my feet. Luckily, I'd just re-dressed, but I had no ready excuse as to what I'd been doing.

Quickly, the crew formed a semi-circle around me, blocking my exit. Redhands turned to address them. "I told you Charlie's a thief!"

"And what am I purportedly stealing?" I cried.

"Rations," Redhands declared with gleeful malice. "Someone's been pilfering from the food supplies and taking gauze from the infirmary."

My heart stuttered. Rations were missing? On a ship with a limited food supply, that was a far greater offense than thieving some extra strips of cloth.

"I—haven't." I stammered.

Where was Colt?

I looked around but the captain was nowhere to be found.

"Then why have you been sneaking off in here?" Robert asked. "What are you hiding?"

Having no acceptable answer, I could only shout, "I haven't been stealing, it wasn't me!"

Frantic, I searched the crew for a friendly face, but found none. At this hour Miguel was asleep, Colt must have been up to something in his cabin, and even Conks and Johnson were mysteriously absent.

"You've been stealing the food," Redhands accused.

"I haven't," I swore. "You have no evidence."

"You ate it! We know you've been sneaking off. What else could you have been doing down here?"

His words seemed to rally the men, which worsened when I had no acceptable answer.

"Punish him," someone in the back of the semi-circle insisted.

Desperate, I looked to Maurice as the highest in command, but he wore an expression of satisfaction.

"The lash!" I heard James yell. "Give him the lash until he talks."

"No!" I cried, but the crew had been whipped into a frenzy. I'd raised too much suspicion with my inability to explain my actions.

"Tie him up! Whip him! It's the lash for him," the crew chanted, eager to spill blood.

"Let me go!" I shouted as the first hand grabbed me. But too many hands followed, hauling me above deck. I couldn't fight the men when they turned and shoved me against the mast. In the blink of an eye, my hands were tied together and then tied to the mast. The men were in such haste to see me whipped, they'd forgotten to remove my shirt and I felt the cool air as Robert carelessly knifed it open in the back.

My binding.

I pressed myself tighter against the mast in both fear of the lash and terror of being discovered.

"I told you, he's the thief!" Robert proclaimed with gleeful malice, spying the gauze. "See for yourself."

My stomach flipped wildly as Robert quickly slipped the knife beneath the cloth and cut upwards, stripping me of that last protection.

Oh God, oh God. Could they see in the darkness?

It was a moonless night and the torches glowed far from where we stood.

No one paid too much attention to my body as Robert held up the gauzy bands as proof. "The boy's a thief, just like I said."

I was sweating and shaking with fear, hearing the men either grumble in confusion or cheer Robert on. Feeling the air move behind me when Robert stepped back, I cringed.

As I braced for unbearable pain, the ship rocked, riding an errant wave. It forced me to stumble backwards, away from the mast as much as the rope allowed.

"Stop."

Captain Colt's command sent chills up my spine. I hadn't even known he'd arrived above deck. I heard the shock in his voice. The crew was behind me, but the captain had arrived from the side.

What had he seen?

CHAPTER 36

COLT,
THE PAST

I GLIMPSED THE SIDE curvature of a small, milky breast, and blinked, attempting to clear my vision.

Why did Charlie have breasts? Why was he being whipped? And why hadn't Robert come to me first?

Charlie spun and thrust himself back against the wood, but not before I caught sight of a pert, pink nipple. *A supple female breast and nipple.*

What the fuck was going on?

I must have gone mad, I thought, storming across the deck and shoving Robert aside.

Had I thought about it rationally, I might have made an attempt to protect any modesty necessary, but I was possessed with disbelief as I spun Charlie forward and tore the remainder of his shirt from his boyish torso.

As I stared at two small, pert breasts, I shook my head, sure I was dreaming.

What the fuck is going on?

With his hands tied high, Charlie whimpered, hiding his face against his shoulder.

Her. Her? Could it really be? Tilting Charlie's head up by the chin, I gazed at his face, studying the delicate, feminine nose and soft jawline that never failed to catch my attention and confound me. Those long lashes framing wide, hazel eyes and pink, full lips. I turned his—her—head left and right, studying Charlie's fright. He—she?—had been rib-thin when we'd taken him, but tall, like a boy. Or was it that Charlie was average height for a boy and unusually tall for a girl?

Jesus. A girl. Her curves stunted from malnourishment or stress, blossoming when fully fed upon our ship.

I released a short laugh at myself. There'd be time later to indulge privately in a longer one and to maybe smash something. I couldn't decide between humor and rage. She'd fooled me. Fooled us all.

Oh, you lying little wench.

"Punish him for stealing!" someone in the back yelled. "Get on w' it!"

I realized only those nearest could see the truth and I set my mind, making the cruel decision to continue her exposure.

"Him?" I asked, stepping aside so that the remainder of the crew could see for themselves what I'd glimpsed from the side. Charlie's arms reflexively tried to cover her chest, but they were tied. She again buried her head against her shoulder. I could hear her crying softly above the stunned silence.

You brought this on yourself, I thought. *Would you prefer I kept your secret and let them whip you?*

"A girl?" they echoed, scratching their heads.

"It's her fault for that mess back in Nassau. Bad luck to have a woman aboard!"

"Toss her into the sea!"

"Whip her anyway!"

"Punish her for lying!"

"He ain't no girl. Let's see the rest of 'im," Robert demanded, stepping forward as if to pull down his breeches.

I wondered if it was instinct when Charlie cringed toward my chest for protection, as if deciding I was the lesser of two evils.

It was my instinct to protect her. But it was my decision that I become her punisher, as well.

The lesser of two evils.

"I can see with my own eyes, my *captain's* eyes, that this is a girl. And I'll further confirm it after she's sufficiently punished back in my cabin. In a manner befitting her status as a woman," I said, feeling Charlie shudder against me.

"Punish her for stealing!"

"I wasn't stealing," Charlie whimpered. "I just needed to change my soiled… rags." She turned her head down, clearly embarrassed and scared.

Good. How dare she lie to us for almost two years? Make a bloody fool of my captaincy?

A girl. Charlie is a girl.

"Punish her, captain!" the crew cried, echoing the desire rising in my chest. We wanted the same thing, I just wanted it in a manner I had difficulty sorting out as I mentally shifted from thinking of Charlie as a boy, to seeing her as the girl she was.

There was another emotion I didn't want to admit.

Relief.

How many times had I stared long at Charlie with a fondness other than friendly? Other than one of mentorship and protectiveness, just like any other member of my crew? How many times had I questioned things about myself for my attraction to a boy?

Could this even be real? Or was she some mystery of the sea? A siren or enchantress?

Still forced on display, Charlie sobbed, and I spared some pity. Using my dirk, I cut her ropes, quickly shrugged out of my coat, and covered her.

"Colt." Maurice's voice was a caution, a warning.

"I've got it under control," I dismissed. I looked over my shoulder to see him standing above everyone, surveying the chaos. *Allowing it.* The bloodthirsty side of Maurice had likely given Robert the permission he needed. Maybe this was another of Maurice's games, pitting Robert and I against each other or using Robert to test me. Perhaps the men would be stirred to replace me if this didn't play out in my favor. Robert was always nipping at my heels to take my place as captain.

Devil's bones. Now was not the time to lose control of the crew. Not when I now had an errant girl loose on a ship full of men. Maurice would never hurt her in that particular manner—he had a type of woman and Charlie wasn't it. But he wouldn't protect her either. Besides, Maurice loved a good whipping.

I braced for an argument, but eyes locked, Maurice gave a dip of his head in something between permission and agreement. I was a little surprised that he didn't encourage the bloodlust of the crew, but I knew he had his reasons. Maurice did nothing without good reason.

No time to speculate on it now.

"Who are you?" I growled, turning back to Charlie.

"I'm Charlie!" she foolishly insisted. As if her breasts hadn't been in plain view seconds before.

My hand rose high in the air, a threat to strike, and Charlie cringed in anticipation. "Lie to me again and see what happens. For the last time, who are you?"

"I—I'm Charlotte Clarke. Daughter of Edmund Clarke, the man you slew in his own home!" she cried the words with a wrath I could practically feel coming off her in waves, as if she'd waited years to declare them with her true tongue.

"How old are you, really?"

"Eighteen," she whispered.

A girl of eighteen, passing as a boy of sixteen. She'd been scrawny enough to look fourteen when we found her. Eighteen. Jesus. Just coming into womanhood and finding it harder to hide her distinction aboard a ship full of men.

A woman with a mere few years of difference between our ages. Old enough to marry, to bear children.

With me, came the unexpected and desirous thought.

No. We were but a few years apart in age but leagues apart in life experience—save whatever she'd learned aboard a pirate's ship for the past year and a half. Charlie possessed no ability to read and had little experience with the world outside her small town or *The Dark Blade.*

What would she look like if her hair grew out? What did she look like underneath those breeches?

What to do with her now?

How could I have mistaken her for the past year and a half? Those full, pink lips and those high cheekbones. The way she moved.

It moved things inside me I'd hated to admit. I'd resented those thoughts, late at night in the darkness of my cabin. It hadn't stopped them.

Now I understood.

Charlie made fools of us all, but no one more than me. If I didn't punish her, if I didn't reassert my authority, it would weaken my command. If that happened and someone like Robert organized a mutiny, she'd truly be in trouble. Even now, I could easily guess which of my men would be glad if I commanded she was to be raped and thrown overboard this night.

Charlie gave me no choice but to punish her. Loudly. Thoroughly. Shamefully.

And truthfully, my fury was glad for it.

CHAPTER 37

COLT,
THE PAST

"WHAT ARE YOU going to do to me?" she demanded, after I marched her to my cabin. Following my rescue, it seemed some of her spirit returned. I think Charlie was more frightened of the men above than the one in front of her.

I'd change that soon enough.

"I'm going to punish you as a woman is to be punished."

At her widened eyes I realized she thought I meant something else entirely. It was with both cruelty and kindness that I clarified, "Relax. You can keep your breeches on for your spanking."

Ah, there was the terror I desired. Though I wasn't sure if her horror was more from fear of the impending pain or humiliation.

"Don't you dare lay a hand on me," Charlie ordered, backing up.

"Oh, I'm going to lay my hand on you. Forcefully. Repeatedly. Until you scream and cry loud enough for every man out there to know you've been suitably punished for your actions. Enough to satisfy *me* that you've been sufficiently punished."

"I will never cry for your satisfaction," Charlotte declared, her laughter an attempt at boldness.

I grabbed her arm and she squealed.

"I do love a challenge," I said, easily throwing her across my ample thighs.

She yelled but I ignored her, staring at the rounded bottom before me. *A girl's rear.* She bore somewhat undernourished hips, but her backside was ample enough to punish. With relish, I raised my hand high and smacked it down. The pleasure hit me like a shot of whisky to my brain. Charlotte yelped at my force, kicking fruitlessly to free herself.

Smack. I struck again. And again. Occasionally my fingers curled as I struck, grabbing the meat of her arse. The pleasure of punishing Charlotte was so intense, I grew focused on nothing but her rear and her grunts. It was hard to judge if she'd had enough as her breeches blocked my view. When Charlotte's shouts of protest morphed into cries of pain, I stopped, curious.

Some instinct made me abruptly draw Charlotte up into a sitting position on my lap. Perhaps shocked, she didn't move. Wide, wet eyes stared at me, but there was more defiance than contrition in them, telling me I'd stopped too soon. I also doubted anyone had heard her.

"Why did you hide the truth the day we found you?" I asked. I desperately wanted to know everything that went on in her head. All she hid, all she had ever thought. I wanted to examine it, shape it, mold it, play with it.

"And what would you have done if I'd confessed I was a girl? Raped me?"

"My men do not rape," I stated. "You know this. Their needs are seen to at every port, even if it cost them the better portion of their wages. I see that they have it."

"So I'd have been left on my own? Too old to be adopted yet an orphan at the mercy of a town that hated me? You'd have left me to starve and die!"

I raised my brows. "So you'd rather your fate on this ship?"

"I'd rather you spared my father, you murderer!"

"He drew first."

I'd repeated it so many times. It was true that I defended myself, but there was more at play than she understood. If I hadn't killed him, I'd have lost the respect of my men. Maybe not at that moment, but eventually. And if, one day, they set upon a town without me to rein them in, who knew what slaughter they'd unleash? This was the life I was given, as she was given hers. And was it so much worse? Didn't she see how ill-equipped her father was to take care of her? It was almost willful negligence.

"He was protecting me," she countered, as I knew she would.

"He failed," I said, a bit cruelly.

Charlotte's lip quivered before she lunged, beating me with her small fists. "I hate you! I hope you burn in hell for your sins!"

Unbelievable. I'd just spanked her and she attacked me again.

Well then. If that punishment wasn't hard enough to subdue her, I'd happily increase her discipline.

"Stop it this instant," I ordered, "or I'll spank you again."

Fair warning. Your choice.

Charlotte's eyes blazed and she fought not to snarl. Then, like the challenging little minx she was proving to be, she drew back her hand and smacked me across the face.

I grinned slowly. *You brought this on yourself. And really, the men need to hear.*

Charlotte flailed and shrieked as I picked her up and threw her over my lap once more. Since it wasn't enough the first time, I yanked down her breeches, instantly meeting the sight of Charlotte's bare arse.

She's a girl, my mind repeated, stupidly. I knew when I was alone later that night, I'd still be echoing the barely believable truth in my head while drinking deeply.

Charlotte's hand splayed behind her, attempting to protect her rear, so I pinned it to the small of her back.

Pull apart her thighs, came the thought, *and see what truly lay between her legs.*

I shook it away.

"I won't scream for your pleasure," she vowed. "Smack me all you desire but I will not give you the satisfaction."

What a delicious little spitfire. She was also putting herself in a bad position, although, judging from the past year I'd say Charlie was probably good at that. Should she fake it and scream out her shame and pain more readily, I'd have little excuse to continue punishing her.

She was all but forcing my hand.

I had two choices. I could either bring her above deck and punish her in front of the men, or she needed to scream loud enough so they could hear that she'd been satisfactorily disciplined.

With one hand, I unbuckled my belt.

She brought this on herself, said a voice in my head.

As if she ever had a better option, argued another.

I folded the belt in half.

If Robert uses this fiasco to sway more men to his side, to rally them and overthrow my command… they'll do far worse to her than dole out a spanking.

I raised my hand.

The more I hurt you, the safer you'll be.

With that vow, I cracked the belt across her bare arse.

Charlie screeched and did her best to scramble from my lap. *Now we're getting somewhere.*

I held her tighter and brought down the belt again on the fullness of her cheeks. I couldn't wield full force from this close angle, but I didn't want to either. Judging from her wails, it was enough.

I whipped her backside enough to leave marks for days. Angry red strips bloomed across her pert rear. Charlie shrieked the loudest when I struck her thighs. The sight of her helpless bottom and the sound of her cries sent bursts of almost blinding pleasure in my brain. As she kicked, I caught fuller glimpses of her cunt, each one like a draught of rum heating my blood, until I was drunk on the sight of her sweet sex.

I didn't stop until she stopped struggling. When she submitted and lay sobbing over my knees, I put the belt down. I hadn't before a more intense sexual experience, yet I hadn't even touched one milky breast, nor had she even laid a finger upon my stiff cock.

For several long moments, neither of us moved. Charlotte was too humbled and I was too entranced. Her wails must have brought all work to a standstill. But I didn't want to leave any room for doubt.

I licked my lips, realizing my mouth had gone dry staring at Charlie's well-striped arse. Gently, I guided her to her feet. Charlie refused to meet my eyes, staring at the floor.

"Will you ever lie to me again?" I asked.

"No, captain," she whispered.

"Will you ever strike me again?"

"No, captain," she repeated.

"I will protect you. I won't allow any of the men to touch you. But I expect full obedience. Do you understand?"

She licked a tear by her lips. "Yes, captain."

As she re-dressed, I shook my head, plagued by the lingering image of Charlie the boy and possessed by the desire to claim Charlotte the girl.

This whole damn thing is too confusing.

Focusing on the matter at hand, I marched Charlie onto the quarterdeck.

"Let's get this over with," I ordered. "Hands on the mast."

Charlie obeyed without question. Sniffling, she grasped the mast as if the wood could provide some comfort. At least it gave a place for her to hide her head in her arms as I yanked down her breeches and drew up her shirt, displaying her thoroughly punished backside for all the crew to see.

You brought this on yourself. If I don't show them, they'll do worse.

"She's been punished and she'll continue to be dealt with by me and me alone," I announced to the crew. I let Charlie's shirt fall, quickly covering her backside against some of the more lecherous stares. "I will decide her fate," I declared, folding my arms and angling to stand in front of Charlie.

"If any man on this ship acts with anything less than the standards of propriety I've set forth concerning women, he will be shown no mercy and will have forfeit any claim on his life." I held each man's eyes as I scanned the crew and broke down the meaning. "You understand me. Touch her and you'll be lashed to death and tossed overboard."

"Robert," I said, hoping to keep my enemy close and drunk on the power I knew he relished. I hoped, if not to have him on my side, to at least neutralize him by offering a shiny toy I knew he enjoyed—the suffering of others and the ability to cause it. Like Maurice.

"You're in charge of any justice that needs meting out," I told him. "If you hear any griping or dissent from the crew, you have my permission to dole out however many warning lashes you think it merits."

Distracted for the time being, Robert grinned and nodded.

Turning to leave, I first stopped by Conks and whispered, "Bring salve from the infirmary to my room."

I grabbed Charlie's hand but on our return to my cabin, her legs wobbled so much that I had to half carry her. She was both too terrified and too tired to fight me. When we reached the threshold of my cabin, she tensed and tried to pull away.

"Shh…" I hushed. "I'm not going to punish you anymore." *Tonight,* qualified a voice in my head. *I can't make promises about the future.* "I'm only intending to keep you safe in here for the night, until I figure out what to do with you."

Charlotte's head fell in submission and I escorted her into my cabin. A knock came a moment later and I collected the jar of soothing ointment from Conks.

Charlotte didn't protest as I laid her flat on my bed. I pulled down her breeches once more and scooped a generous amount of the salve into my hand.

Even with the lightest of touches, Charlie gasped and whimpered as I spread the soothing ointment over her punished legs and arse. I was careful not to touch too deeply between her legs, though I had to dip my fingers slightly into her cheeks to rub the ointment where the tip of my belt had occasionally snapped. Whipped into compliance, she didn't protest. Between her soft whimpers, she sighed.

I'd meant to carry her into the brig, to sort out what to do with her on the morrow, but when I heard her even breathing, I realized she'd fallen asleep in my bed, bottom still on display. I started to lower her shirt to cover her, then thought better of it. It was nothing I hadn't seen already and it looked like any contact with cloth would be painful. I also couldn't make myself move her. Instead, I pulled one of the chairs next to the bed and watched Charlie as she slept. Her head was turned to the side and I let myself imagine what she'd look like with longer hair. Would it wave or curl, those long strands of honey whipping with the sea's winds?

Not that I could keep her aboard now. Could I?

My gaze fell upon her lips. How could I have been so foolish? How could we all? Those lashes, too. *Pretty boy,* we'd all called her when the sunlight reflected in her big eyes. *Useless boy,* when her muscles weren't strong enough to do what we thought she should have been capable of. I cringed, remembering how roughly the men shoved and kicked her when she wasn't quick enough with the day's work. No wonder she'd caked herself in dirt and grime whenever possible. No wonder she hid under her tricorn hat and the loosest clothing available.

Charlie didn't awaken, not even when I grabbed the salve and spread another layer on her skin.

And again, an hour or two later. Slowly, reverently, my hands moved.

What should I do with you, Charlie? Drop you at the nearest port?

Yes, of course. Women were bad luck upon a ship. *You deceived us. Nothing but trouble can come of you.*

I'd deposit her at Port Royal once we arrived. Though that still left the matter of her mother's murderer, whom I'd vowed to bring to justice. But I could do that on my own.

Again I spread a layer of ointment over the soft globes of her arse, dipping my fingers into the balm and working it delicately across her tender flesh.

I repeated the process until I'd used the entire jar and the sky outside lightened to the gray of pre-morn.

CHAPTER 38

COLT,
THE PAST

I COULDN'T VERY WELL turn her off the ship looking like a bedraggled swab, I reasoned. As soon as I cleaned her up, I'd let her go. Once she was made presentable again. The next day we'd dock in Port Royal anyway, and I knew just where to have her tidied.

I didn't want to parade Charlie through the wharfs, however, so *The Dark Blade* made berth in a favored inlet a quarter of a mile south of the main port. I bid the men to wait until our return. The imminent night of drinking and whoring kept the crew's grumbling about the additional walk from our distanced cove to a minimum. And the threat of my wrath dimmed the chatter about Charlie's newly revealed truth.

Charlie sulked, refusing to speak to me as I led her around the outskirts of town and beyond.

It wasn't called the Wickedest City on Earth for nothing. Every fourth building was a bar or a brothel. Men entered with the wealth of princes, only to be reduced to paupers, having emptied their bag o' bits on women and wine. Even at midday, revelry could be heard, carrying through the streets.

We made our way to Estelle's, an old friend who kept a house free of gossip—for a price. It was always a fair one for me, but still a price.

"I need access to your bath," I said, when the no-nonsense blonde opened the door. "I also need a new gown, stockings, shoes… and perhaps, a hairpin of some sort."

Estelle's eyes flicked to Charlie, resting there for a while. I could only imagine what she thought, taking in the boy-girl's filthy appearance, her ill-fitting clothing, and Charlie's unique expression of fear mixed with defiance.

After a moment, Estelle said, "No hairpin is going to work on that head as she's got no hair to make it stick." Opening the door to let us in, she said, "Tub's upstairs. I'll have someone fetch water. And I'll get her a clip."

"Thank you," I replied, tipping my head. "I'll see to payment on our way out."

Estelle shook her head. "This one's on me."

Sequestered in an upstairs room, I studied Charlie as a servant filled the tub with lukewarm water.

A woman, a woman, my mind repeated, flashing back to images of her bare rear.

No wonder she'd always been diligent in cutting her hair as we sailed. It was the very opposite of how negligent she'd been in keeping her body clean.

Once filled, her eyes flicked nervously to the tub, easily guessing what was to come. After we'd been left alone, I folded my arms and stated the obvious.

"You need a bath."

"Then leave me to bathe," Charlie ordered, jutting her chin.

Not a chance.

Those were the first words she'd spoken to me all day. She didn't hurl a single insult or mention one word about her punishment or her ongoing deception and its discovery. I didn't like admitting that it made me nervous to consider the calculation going on in her head. If she'd hidden the truth from us for this long, what else was she capable of?

"Alone so you can escape?" I asked. "Or do a shite job of cleaning and continue to hide behind your cover as a boy? You're getting a bath and I'll be the one doing the bathing."

I hadn't been sure I'd meant the words until I said them. I couldn't leave her alone, but I'd been torn on the of idea involving myself directly in her scrubbing.

A fire lit behind her eyes. "You can't clean me," she insisted, snarling.

I shrugged. "You can't seem to clean yourself."

You lied to me, I reasoned. *Made a fool of me. Threatened my command, my captaincy. Anyone else would do far worse.*

Charlie didn't budge.

"I would have been within my rights to lash you," I said. "To toss you overboard."

"Do it!" Charlie cried. "I'd rather die at sea then suffer your touch."

"Enough," I growled. "Strip your clothes or I'll strip them for you."

I was certain the little hellcat would make it as difficult for me as possible, screaming and thrashing. I readied myself for a fight I'd take pleasure in.

Perhaps she saw, and perhaps that was why Charlotte surprised me by changing course. She stripped her clothing as quickly as possible and jumped in the bath before I could get an eyeful, other than her striped rear.

I tried not to smirk. I didn't try to stop my erection. Any pirate worth his salt knew not to fight a battle he was sure to lose.

Charlie hissed as the water hit the sore flesh of her backside. Maybe that's why I took pity and amended, "Only your hair. You're free to wash the rest of you. I won't touch what's below your neck."

Scowling, Charlotte looked as if she'd claw my eyes out, given the chance. Instead, she gave me her back and drew her knees to her chest, hiding herself as best she could.

Using the pitcher, I poured water on her shorn hair. But when I began to wash with the soap, Charlie stiffened away, forcing me to place my hand on her neck to draw her back.

I washed Charlie's spikey hair, again wondering what it would look like grown out, and I let my hands clean behind her ears and down her neck.

"I revile your touch," she declared, sneering at me over her shoulder. The palpable hatred from Charlie seemed to emanate from every pore in her body. She conveyed the fury with every flash of her eyes. Every flare of her nostrils. Each angry twitch of her lips.

God, she was beautiful.

How could any of us mistake her for a boy? What a mockery she made of my leadership. *Jesus, was Robert stirring up the men to vote me out as captain, even now?*

The idea made me so angry I stepped away from the tub to stop myself from squeezing the very neck I washed. I'd worked so hard to secure command of *The Dark Blade* over Robert, and she might have stolen it all from me. A smarter captain might have given Charlotte over to the men to assuage their tempers at her ruse. Let them humiliate her for how she'd humiliated them.

Is that what you're doing for yourself? asked a voice in my head.

As Charlie finished washing I was unsure whether I wanted to continue her degradation by making her rise from the tub to dress in front of me, or whether I needed to step away to keep myself from belting her rear all over again.

I was saved from having to make a decision by a knock from Estelle, who appeared holding the requested gown and promptly ordered me to "leave the women to their business."

I grunted at her command, but obediently shuffled outside the door to wait.

And wait, I did. God only knew what took them so long. I had begun to worry that Charlie used her skillful tongue to convince Estelle to help her escape when the door finally opened.

A vision appeared before me, an angel. For several moments, I stood slack jawed.

Charlie wore a gown of white with tiny flowers of the palest blue. Ruffled trim hugged the outline of the dress, which hung a little loose on her slight frame. I'd briefly wondered if Estelle would produce a wig, but she'd arranged Charlie's stubby hair with a pearled clip and silvery hair net so artfully that it almost looked as if the girl had simply swept her hair into an elegant style one might find back in London. Estelle had fastened a blue-stoned earbob to each ear and applied a rouge to Charlie's lips and cheeks. I was sure other womanly tricks had been applied, but that was all I could discern.

Maybe I should keep her for a few more weeks, I reasoned. *Or perhaps months, as she needed more filling out for dresses such as this.*

Charlie wore a curious expression I couldn't read. The way her face hid her emotions vexed me, raised my guard. Did she like such a dress or resent being stuffed into it?

Conniving minx. Stunning beauty. Liar.

Lover.

She could be. All those confusing feelings Charlie always stirred in me—that need to protect—could be justified.

If she didn't hate me enough to wish my death.

Instead of paying Estelle on our way out, I instead requested yet another favor. Gossip often found its way to her home because there it found its end. Estelle knew a lot because of her very pride in keeping secrets. But I wanted Estelle to bend that honor. I wanted her to help me learn more about the pirate who killed Charlotte's mother. I'd always wanted to solve that mystery, but now…

Now if you help her, give her something she wants, she might soften for you. Look upon you with new eyes. Eyes filled with something other than hate.

Estelle nodded once, accepting my request. The motherly way she fixed Charlie's hairnet on her way out the door told me she agreed to help not for me, but for the girl with the shorn hair.

It was only a short walk back into town, but we made slow progress as Charlie grew accustomed to her new shoes.

We'd reached the midpoint when the world rocked, violently and completely without warning. The ground beneath our feet shook like the fires of hell were rising up to claim all that lay above it.

I'd never experienced an earthquake before but knew it at once.

I also knew this one was severe and we weren't quite at

the epicenter. But we were close, and cracks could spread in seconds.

Screams echoed from every corner of Port Royal. Not two hundred feet before us I watched one building, then another, and another, collapse to the ground. More screams of terror rang out in a chorus of horror I'd never forget.

Charlotte clung to me and I searched in desperation for somewhere to run, to keep us safe. But we were surrounded only by trees—trees which could fall upon us and kill us at any moment.

The shaking abruptly stopped, only to begin again.

Not here, I begged a god who surely didn't listen to men like me. *Don't let the quake spread this far inland.*

With no better option, Charlie and I were forced to stay in place, and I shielded her body beneath mine. From our location, I saw the tops of buildings disappear into the ocean, which, I presumed, had already gobbled up the wharves. The blood-curdling cries came from everywhere before us as countless men and women were swept away to sea, lost to the cracks in the earth, or even crushed between the ever-changing fissures.

When the ground stopped moving, the screams continued.

But Charlotte and I were safe.

"Thank God it's over," she breathed, slumping like a rag doll against me. My shoulders relaxed as I exhaled as well.

It's over.

I hadn't realized the silence enveloping us until it broke. Below, lizards scurried past our feet, heading east. Above, birds followed suit. The hair on my neck stood on end as I worked it out.

It's not over. The earthquake had been at sea. A tidal wave was coming.

How long? Minutes?

"Charlotte, we have to run. Now. I think a wave is coming."

"What?" she asked, looking up at me with round, disbelieving eyes.

Shit. Which way?

If I chose incorrectly, we might die.

I grabbed Charlotte's hand, adrenaline surging through my veins, and began pulling her toward town. "Come on. I need you to lift your skirts and run. *Now.*"

Charlotte pulled back. "No! The earthquake came from that direction and if all the animals are scurrying that way," she nodded her head east, away from town, "we should too."

I pulled her with more urgency and she stumbled after me. "Normally, yes, but there's no high ground there," I cried. "If the wave comes too far, we'll get swept away. It's a risk but we can make it back to town and onto a roof in a few minutes. Now pick up your skirts and run!"

Charlotte did the best she could with one hand while I dragged her with the other.

My men, I thought. *Would they be safe?*

"Faster!" I yelled. Charlotte cried out as somewhere along the way she lost her new shoes. Her feet took a beating, but better to be bruised than buried.

How long after an earthquake did it take for a tidal wave to come? If the animals were already running, it couldn't be more than a few minutes.

"Tell no one," I ordered when we reached the outer limits of town. "If you create a panic, I don't know what will happen. And if there's no room on the roof for us, we'll be swept away in a crowded fight for space!"

Charlotte looked horrified but clamped her lips together.

To say that Port Royal suffered devastation was an understatement. Glass and other debris littered what remained; everywhere I looked people wept.

It's about to get so much worse, I thought. *But even if I shouted, who'd believe me?*

I kicked open the door to the nearest tall building—one of the countless inns—swinging Charlie into the room with me. In the midst of chaos, no one was shocked by our entrance until I shouted, "Everyone needs to get to the roof, now! A tidal wave is coming and if we don't reach high ground in the next few minutes, we'll all be swept away."

Three or four minutes must have already passed. We'd been lucky to remain safe this long.

At the pause of surprise, I shouted, "I said now! What's the quickest way to the roof?"

A smart young woman called out, "This way. Follow me."

Anyone with any sense ran behind the girl as she guided a group of five of us into another room and up three flights of stairs. When we reached the top, the woman threw open a window and cried, "From here, we climb."

I watched as she scooted onto the ledge and disappeared upwards. Then I poked my head out the window to see it was a short climb onto the roof, but one in which Charlie would need help, especially in bare feet.

"I'll go first and pull you up," I told her. Panic-stricken, she only nodded.

Once I'd made it to the roof, I laid flat and reached down.

"Take my hands," I commanded.

Charlie hesitated. In mere seconds that seemed to last for minutes, she didn't move. Was she considering running away? Choosing to die?

"Hurry up!" a man behind her yelled, jarring Charlie to action and my heart to start beating again. She clasped my hands and I dragged her onto the roof as carefully as I could. Turning, I blinked with disbelief to see half of Port Royal had already sunk into the ocean. It was just *gone*.

We hadn't even processed our shock when we heard the screams.

The wave was coming.

The sea had pulled back and a horrifyingly large wave flew at rapid speed toward Port Royal. Beside me, Charlie gasped and turned as pale as death. The others on the roof with us made signs of the cross over their bodies. One man fell to his knees to pray.

My men, I thought again. *Were they safe? Would I lose them? How many?*

But there was nothing I could do to help them now.

"It's going to hit us," I calculated, searching desperately for something to hold onto. The best option—the brick chimney, was constructed too poorly to be reliable.

"Get down!" I commanded Charlie, flattening us to the roof and holding onto a beam by the edge.

Charlie was shaking as she clung to me, buried half-beneath me. Everyone screamed and wept, but she didn't say a word.

I'm not letting you go.

"Hold on tight!" I yelled, gripping the beam until my knuckles turned white. "When the wave comes, it will push us and continue to push us. Even after the initial hit, water will surge and try to rip us apart. You must hold onto me, Charlie, don't let go!"

I felt her tighten her grip around me and looked down to

see the blood still drained from her face. I hoped she didn't swoon; I needed her to hold on.

The screams from below us rose higher.

"It's coming!" I called. "Hold tight."

I heard the wave rush closer, heard the first contact with land—

—and then it slammed into our building.

Our saving graces were that we were both far back and high enough that the wave only blasted through to the top floors, breaking glass and sweeping away anyone beneath us. The building held through the initial surge, but more water swelled and instantly enveloped us; fierce currents tossing the other rooftop refugees about like rubbish thrown overboard.

Hold tight, I wanted to scream to Charlie as waves crashed over our heads. *Hold tight to me.* But I couldn't scream and could barely hold on. We sputtered water and clung to each other as the waves continued to rush. Something hard smacked my leg and I prayed it hadn't hit hers too.

For several minutes we gasped like that, fighting for air and to stay atop the roof as relentless wave after wave did its best to rip us apart and toss us off the building.

Finally, the water level sank, dipping beneath the roof and back to the second or third story of the building.

I stood, helping Charlie find her balance on shaking legs.

The water continued to recede, but the devastation all around us was unimaginable.

The earthquake had caused the majority, sinking half of Port Royal into the ocean, but it was as if that wasn't enough for the hungry seas. The wave came as a final sweep, clearing out whatever it could within its angry path.

Only two others remained on the roof with us. The rest had been swept away, though I couldn't say if they were alive or dead. When the water dispersed enough, we made our way back to the ground floor in stunned silence.

I half-carried Charlie, who'd lost her shoes to the sea. And her hairnet and each of the ear bobs. Her dress was torn and filthy. All the hard work from Estelle had been spoiled within minutes. It was as if the world had refused Charlie's gown, her appearance as a lady, and shoved her back with the likes of us.

Even in the wake of devastation, some looked to profit. Whether it be the finest city in the world or the most infamous, like this one, that could always be counted upon.

I spied a man with a horse, selling it at an exorbitant price, and I paid him.

"Wait," Charlie protested. "We have to help."

I shook my head. "My obligation is first to my crew and you're in no position to help anyone in your condition."

"These people are innocent," Charlie said, holding my eyes. "You're nothing but *pirates.*"

"There are many innocent here, aye, children and more—but if you think this town doesn't live up to its name you're more naïve than I imagined," I said. "Anyone you'd help has more chance of being a scoundrel than a saint."

Charlie scowled, some of her old spirit coming back as the shock abated.

"And you can barely stand," I pointed out, "let alone walk. Now we're returning to my men and I don't want to hear another word of protest. Or you can imagine what I'll do to you later."

I mounted the horse and Charlotte begrudgingly climbed up behind me, wincing as she put more weight on one lacerated foot. She hiked her tattered skirts up to her knees as she sat. No one noticed the impropriety with all the destruction around us.

With my heart in my throat, I rode as fast as I dared. My men and I had faced so many battles together, but this was different. It was as if God struck his hand down to spite our sinful city, and I knew that was exactly what the preachers would preach.

Conks, Johnson, Miguel, Maurice… even Robert, I thought. You may be my rival but you are like a brother. Maurice raised us as such.

When we crested the hill, I exhaled at the sight of my undamaged ship, floating in the protected inlet, away from the epicenter of the surge. I may have even thanked Charlie's vengeful god.

She's safe. The Dark Blade is safe. Hopefully, the men aboard fared as well.

Conks was the first to greet me when we reached my ship, clapping my back as he gave me a tight hug. "We're all accounted for," he said, before I could even ask the question. Maurice, usually sparse in giving affection, also wrapped me in a rare, fatherly-style hug.

"What's it like down there?" Conks asked. "How bad is it?" But before I could answer, Robert pushed his way to the front.

"I told you women are bad luck," he said, sneering. "If it weren't for her, we wouldn't even be here today."

"We needed to come to port anyway," Johnson argued. "If it weren't for her, we would have docked at the wharf and we'd be as good as dead with the rest of them."

The men murmured, divided.

It took some time and more than a little fast-talking on my part, but I managed to convince the crew that Charlie's presence was our salvation, the one thing that had kept us all alive. Putting it to vote, the men agreed that she could remain aboard, and a fair half did so with gratitude over resentment.

Charlie remained indignant, viewing herself as my captive—an attitude that didn't improve over the course of the next few weeks, which seamlessly turned into months.

It might not have helped that whenever she stepped out of line, I threatened to put her back over my knee.

And occasionally… I did.

It was never as harsh as the first time. For starters, I didn't use my belt and I didn't bare her bottom.

If I thought she'd be grateful for the mercy, she quickly disabused me of that notion. It riled her all the more that I did not treat her as I did the men.

"You think you're an exemption from the rules?" I'd ask her. "That you're allowed insubordination and to not expect punishment for it like any other man in this crew?"

"Then punish me like a man," she'd insist. "I want the mast!"

"No."

Dock my wages, she'd protest. *Assign me an extra shift. Throw me in the brig. I'd rather the lash than your hand.*

As if I'd mar her skin. But I took her over my knee. Knowing it made her hate me more didn't stop me. *She has the power to stop it herself if she would just be less obstinate*, I reasoned. *It's almost like she seeks it, then hates me for it.*

In the passing months, Charlie's hair grew below her ears. Only once had she threatened to cut it and I'd threatened to belt her. She'd put down her dagger at my words, declared her hate for the thousandth time, and stormed off sulking.

The men who'd agreed to her presence aboard the ship grew to tolerate Charlie, and some to even like her. She was quick, clever, and never grumbled about her work. She even won over those men whose minds hadn't yet been made.

But the few that held to Robert's side grew to resent her all the more.

I decided I'd improve Charlie's usefulness by teaching her to read. And then, when I'd better prepared her for a life outside our ship, somewhere back in the Carolinas perhaps… then I'd let her go.

I couldn't release her to the world ignorant of even the basic ability to read a sign, I reasoned.

Yes, I'd let her go as soon as soon as we developed her reading skills.

Just a few more weeks. Or months.

CHAPTER 39

CHARLOTTE,
THE PAST

AT NIGHT, I slept in the galley with Miguel. Colt said it was the safest place for me, though I didn't know why he cared. If he wanted me safe, he could simply let me go. Miguel slept in the galley to protect the food, and I slept with Miguel so that he could protect me.

"Only other option is the brig," Colt had informed me.

I might as well have slept there, I was a prisoner either way. Whenever I did anything to displease Colt, he used it as an excuse to threaten to punish me in a way he did not punish the men aboard. It was always done under the guise of needing to prove that I wasn't being shown any preferential treatment, to keep it fair. But any of the crew could vouch for the fact that I always pulled my weight and without complaint. The only area where I stepped even a toe out of line was with the captain himself.

I couldn't help it. How could I obey the man who murdered my father? At night, while the others slept, I thought up ways to kill him. I imagined his screams. They were like food or air, sustaining me throughout the long months.

When my insubordination supposedly threatened his command, Colt swept me over his legs and attended my rear until he'd *smacked the defiance out of me.*

I supposed I could have avoided those punishments if I bent more readily to his orders, but I couldn't stomach it. I couldn't stop my outbursts, even when I knew I was giving Colt the excuse he wanted, giving him just cause.

Especially during his required reading sessions.

Confined to his cabin, Colt would plop me down upon the chair and sit beside me or stand above me, pushing me to learn to read from one of the books in his small library. I resented that I found the skill an asset I'd appreciate once I escaped. Over the months, as the letters began to form words and the words turned into sentences, I resented that it would forever be Colt who'd given me this ability. He especially tempted me with etiquette books and lessons on manners I hoped to someday apply elsewhere, away from life at sea.

Conks, Johnson, and Miguel became my friends and my protectors, each looking after me like a father or a brother. Playing games and drinking with them beneath the moonlight was one of my favorite things to do. (Besides plotting my escape, of course.)

I had my first breakthrough after a raid like any other, when Captain Colt's luck turned into my own. I'd learned from my mistakes and this time, I was stealthier when eavesdropping on his nightly talk with Maurice.

"A prize like this will change the fates for all of us," the captain whispered in a low voice, tinged with excitement. "Our way of life changing; I can feel it. Maybe not tomorrow, maybe not for a number of years. But that tsunami signaled the beginning of the end for our kind."

I chanced a peek around the doorframe to see Colt held within his hands the largest ruby I'd seen in my life. I clamped my lips against my gasp.

Such a prize had been aboard the ship we attacked? No wonder her men had put up so much of a fight. We'd lost several of our crew in the process.

"It's no mean feat to find a discreet buyer for the Crimson Eye," Maurice cautioned, shaking his head. "If we break it up, we lose the value. It's going to take some time to sell it."

"Aye," Colt agreed. "But once we do, we can split the shares and all of us start a new life. A comfortable one. We'll keep it to us, for now. Conks, Johnson, you and me. No more."

My heart fluttered. I wanted that for Conks and Johnson and Miguel—a new life.

"Robert is already aware," Maurice said. "And some of the men who were there when you found the trunk may suspect."

Even from the doorway, I heard Colt's frustrated sigh. Keeping a secret aboard the close quarters of a ship was never easy. With several men already suspecting, it might be nigh impossible.

"And Charlie," Maurice said, off-handedly. A cold shock ran down my spine at the mention of my name. "She's been listening in the doorway this entire time."

My stomach sank as I heard the scrape of Colt's chair being roughly pushed back. A second later, he loomed, grabbing me by the scruff of my neck and shoving me within the small room in which the men spoke.

"Have you not an honest bone in your body?" the captain growled.

"Have you not a merciful one?" I returned. "Let me go and you'll never need to worry about my honesty again. Or lack thereof."

"I will lash you within an inch of your life if you speak a word of this to the crew," Colt threatened, ignoring my plea.

"Now, Colt," Maurice cautioned as if to soothe the captain. But he didn't wear an expression of calm. He looked as malicious as ever. More so. He drummed his fingers on the table with lazy exaggeration.

"Why don't you tell the girl what you learned today?"

Colt released me, turning his ire onto Maurice instead. "Dammit, now's not the time."

Another chill ran down my spine. I looked back and forth between the two men. Colt rarely took that tone with Maurice, who acted like a father to the captain.

"Tell me what?" I asked.

Colt raked a rough hand through his already-tousled hair. After an elongated pause, he said, "I've been making inquiries. About your mother." The captain ran his tongue along his lips, stalling in an atypical manner. "I found out what really happened to her. I'm sorry, Charlie. But your mother wasn't killed by pirates. She killed herself. Shortly after you were born and leaving you alone with your father."

I felt as if I'd absorbed a physical blow to my stomach. Something like a smile spread across my face, but even without looking I knew it was grotesque.

"Liar."

Colt shook his head. "I'm sorry Charlie. You can ask Estelle the next time we dock. She doesn't normally sell her secrets, but she took a liking to you and made some inquires on your behalf."

I scrambled to look for excuses, refusals, or holes in Colt's declaration. But it was the cruel look on Maurice's face that made me believe it. It was as if he took pleasure in the knowledge.

My lip quivered and hot tears filled my eyes. Colt looked pitying, but I knew it was fake.

I fled before anyone could see me cry.

IN MY DARKER moments I might have admitted that my father wasn't well-equipped to take care of me. But I'd always believed in my mother. How could she have left me alone?

Sometimes, in those dark nights at sea, I hated her. *She was weak, like my father.*

But I won't be.

A plan began to form in my mind, involving the Crimson Eye.

A FEW WEEKS after I'd learned about my mother, Colt summoned me to his cabin. It was too late for a reading lesson.

"I have a gift for you," he announced, a tinge of nerves touching his voice. The candlelight on his walls played upon his face, softening it.

A gift?

Slowly (Timidly, I wondered?) Colt produced a small box from his waistcoat.

I stepped back as if the thing could injure me.

"I want nothing you have to offer," I replied. "Except my freedom or your death. Preferably, both."

Colt's nostrils flared. He held the box aloft. My refusal to take it spurred his anger and he opened it himself.

Curiosity got the better of me and I peeked down to see the box contained a pretty gold locket.

Raising the necklace, Colt declared, "I bought this for you in port. It's engraved with your name on the back. See? Charlotte," he said, turning it to show me. Colt approached, fumbling with the necklace clasp. "I want you to wear it."

I snorted and stepped back again, this time hitting the wall. "And I want you to shove it up your arse but I have about the same odds of that happening as you do of putting that thing on me."

"Why are you so obstinate, Charlie? It's a *gift*. I wanted to do something to make you feel better about… what happened," he said vaguely, and I knew he meant my mother.

I could tell I'd wounded Colt's pride and that pleased me greatly. He had no right to speak of my father *or* my mother, let alone to purchase baubles in an attempt to soothe my pain.

"It's a horrid, ugly thing, as horrid and ugly as you." I smiled with venom, though neither statement was true. The necklace was stunning and Colt… I had to admit the cruel captain possessed an equally cruel beauty.

"You will put this necklace on right now," Colt insisted, now thoroughly insulted. "If you fight me, I will strip your clothing first and then put it on. Are we clear?"

I huffed, knowing he meant it. When Colt came closer, I hung my head in defeat. Deft, surprisingly gentle fingers brushed my neck as he fastened the necklace. The gold oval hung nearly to my breasts.

When I next looked upon the captain, he bore a strange expression. Maybe he simply gazed upon the necklace with appreciation. But it felt as if he gazed upon me, with… affection? *Attraction?*

The emotion in his eyes frightened me enough that I ducked past the captain and fumbled at his table, grabbing the best weapon I could find—a knife.

Was I overreacting? Or had he been wanting to… touch me?

Why was he making me wear a locket anyway?

"Don't come near me," I commanded, raising the sharp knife. "I'll cut you!"

Perplexed and annoyed, Colt advanced.

He was in for a surprise if he thought I wouldn't do it.

Colt raised one hand to grab me and I slashed it right across the palm.

Immediate panic set in. *Stupid Charlotte. Would he wrest the knife from my hand and cut me in retaliation?*

Blinking, Colt looked down at his hand. Wild eyes returned to my face and he charged. I had nowhere to go but scurried until my back was against the wall. Colt grabbed my wrist and squeezed, forcing me to drop the knife. He was so close our breath mingled as we both panted. I didn't feel much better with the blade on the floor. Colt could kill me with his bare hands. *One of which I'd just bloodied.*

The captain seized my necklace and I flinched at the unexpected move. With his good hand, he thumbed the locket open. Transfixed in terror, I watched as Colt brought his other hand to the necklace and fisted it. Blood dripped from his cut into the open locket. Smearing it to the edges for good measure, he clasped the oval shut and let it fall back against my flesh, where some extra blood stained my skin.

"Let this serve as a reminder. You will wear this locket around your neck for the rest of your life. You will never take it off. If I see you without it, I will strip all your clothing and this necklace will be the *only* thing you're allowed to wear."

Colt's thumb traced the golden locket, as if sealing in his words.

"You'll wear the blood you drew. And if you ever try to draw my blood again, I will draw yours, and I'll repay it tenfold."

Colt backed away, but it was as if a piece of him remained. The gold oval fell heavy upon my chest, like a collar that would not be ignored.

THE NEXT WEEK, MY ESCAPE plan began to grow.

I had no way to obtain poisons aboard the ship, but I did have access to the food stores.

First, I needed to figure out where Colt hid the Crimson Eye. I was sure it was in his cabin, and he never left anyone alone in his quarters.

Except he had allowed me to sleep there. Once.

Butterflies flew wildly about my stomach as the idea took hold.

I needed Colt to punish me as he'd done the first time. It was only when he'd belted me that he kept me in his cabin through the night. If he did it again, I'd be able to feign sleep and search for the Crimson Eye while Colt slumbered.

God, I hated the belt. It was awful. But it was my only way out.

Summoning my courage one evening, I found Captain Colt dining with the crew and resolved to provoke him that night… before cold fear claimed my heart, solidly freezing both that organ and my legs, which now seemed barely able to move forward at the sight of Colt's broad back alone.

I needed rum, perhaps, and lots of it.

I noticed my hands shook as I lifted the pitcher and poured myself a cup. Time moved at unnatural speeds as I downed it. I had no stomach for the meal before me; the scent of the chicken made me ill.

"Eat," Colt ordered, making me jump. I looked over to find his dark eyes scrutinizing me. Had he noticed that while I drank, I'd neglected to temper the alcohol with any food?

My heart pounded as I sneered my reply.

"No."

"I said eat," Colt repeated, firmer this time.

"And I said no. Have you so much seaweed between your ears that you cannot hear? Perhaps that is why you cannot lead well, either. Too much flotsam and jetsam clogging your brain."

Everyone around us fell silent at my insolence. Colt's eyes darkened. But he held his temper.

"This is the last time I'm going to repeat myself, Charlie," Colt warned. "You *will* eat. Now I'd choose your next words very carefully. I don't know what's gotten into you tonight."

The rum made me do what I did next.

"Well, it isn't cock, yet I'm on a ship full of men. Perhaps next time we dock I can visit the taverns whilst the rest of the crew visit the brothels. That way we can all return to the ship more satisfied than when we left it."

I'd needed to raise the stakes and somehow, I'd known that threat would rile Colt more than jabs at his ability to command. Rage flamed behind those dark eyes and my resolve nearly melted to nothingness. But before Colt could act, I stood, captivating the men at the table who all stared in rapt silence, watching the battle between the captain and me unfold.

"Perhaps I should go fuck myself, instead. Perhaps *you* should go fuck *yourself.*"

I grabbed the pitcher of rum.

"Or perhaps you should fuck right off this ship and die, like a murderer such as yourself deserves."

I tossed the rum in his face.

The time between Colt slamming his hand on the table and grabbing me was seemingly non-existent. One second I was safe, the next, I was being dragged below deck by the man who frightened me most in the world. When we reached his cabin, Colt slammed the door behind us and loomed in front of it, a tower of menace blocking any escape.

"I can see your punishments aren't making an impression on you," he declared. "So we'll remove the obstacles to learning. After all, you've made it very clear what a woman you are, haven't you? No small, childish spanking will be effective."

My heart skipped a beat. *I'd asked for this,* I reminded myself.

Yet my body's natural response was to fight.

You're just making it look real, I reasoned.

Colt lunged and I didn't have time to escape before we both tumbled to the floor. He made quick work of untying my breeches despite my pummeling fists. When he tucked his fingers into the waist to yank them down, the only thing I could do was flip over to protect my modesty. But my act of protection required the use of my arms and made it easier for him to tug, as well as gave access to the preferred target. The next moment, my breeches were bunched around my knees, locking them, and Colt had a clear view of my rear. He yanked me up and tossed me over his ample lap while I shrieked. The stupid breeches nearly immobilized my legs and Colt's strong hands immobilized my back.

Everything had happened so fast that I was surprised by the sudden stillness above me. I stilled in response. *What was Colt doing? Staring?*

I nearly jumped out of my skin when he laid a warm hand upon the lower half of my right globe.

It felt… confusing. My body ran hot and cold at once, making me sweat. His hand moved, stroking higher, and my heart raced upwards with it. Then Colt's strong hand shifted, running downwards, but my pulse didn't slide down along with it. Everything around the room faded into insignificance—everything but Colt's intrusive hand on my unwilling rear.

If I was unwilling, why didn't I want him to move it?

I did. I did. I was just… scared into silence.

"Get your bloody hands off me," I snarled, to confirm what I knew to be true, but my voice sounded heavy with need.

Or did it?

Colt's hand immediately disappeared and a part of me twinged with regret that he didn't fight it. Because I wanted to fight him… not for any other reason.

"I'm going to spank you," Colt said, voice raising at the end.

I froze. Why was he almost asking, like a question? He'd never done so before. I was shocked into stillness as I lay over his strong thighs.

It's a trick, I thought. *Some game he's playing.*

Well then, I could play right back.

"Go ahead," I challenged, softly. My voice cracked midway. Where had all the air in the room gone? "Do your worst."

Had I played my cards right? Because Colt did spank me, but he didn't do his worst, as I'd goaded. The spanking was long and hard, but he didn't use his belt. He didn't scold or admonish. No sound filled the cabin other than his smacks and my cries.

Or those other sounds I made. The ones that sounded like gasp-y little moans.

He's onto me, I worried. *Why else didn't he punish me harder?*

When it was over, Colt drew me up to sit in his lap again, like the first time. Except it was nothing like the first time. In fact, something was very different than the other times he'd spanked me. The air between us seemed to pulse. My stomach felt funny. Warm. The area between my legs grew hot. And my lips were curiously full. The more Colt's eyes flicked down to them the more they tingled.

I had the unbelievable thought that Colt was going to… kiss me?

It was with sincerity that I spit in his face and slapped it as hard as I could.

Unbelievably, Colt didn't toss me back over his legs. He simply *took it,* staring at me.

Was nothing I did this night going to earn me the belt?

Desperate, I began screaming. I jumped off Colt's lap and, yanking up my breeches, threw what must have looked like the tantrum of the century.

"I hate you!" I shouted, knocking glasses, maps, and important documents from Colt's desk.

He stood, calmly.

I kicked over chairs. I raged loudly enough for the men to hear, to force Colt's hand. And still he didn't threaten the belt.

I spied his small library and reached for a book. His favorite. That got his attention.

"Charlie, put that down," Colt ordered, brow furrowed in confusion. "Do you *want* me to belt you?"

In response, I smiled. Opened the book. And tore out the pages, ruining it forever.

Colt was on me in an instant. Within what felt like two seconds I was back over his knee with arse bared to his view and the sound of his belt being unbuckled.

"You want a good spanking, I'll oblige," he declared. But his voice wasn't full of anger, as I'd expected. He sounded… satisfied. "I don't know what's gotten into you." The first lick of the belt made me scream, made me reconsider my entire plan. "But whatever it is, I'll beat it out."

Colt, a man of his word, tried his best. Had my tantrum been genuine, I'd have been a very repentant girl by the end of Colt's lesson. My face was soaked with tears. I wouldn't sit down for a week.

Limp and sobbing by the time Colt stopped the awful strapping, I had no fight left in my body nor room in my heart for anything but two feelings. One was the desperation to stay awake long enough to find the Crimson Eye while

Colt slept. The other was a curious and nagging guilt that I'd destroyed Colt's favorite book.

The captain summoned Conks to retrieve the same salve he'd given me the first time he belted me, and I was allowed to stay in Colt's bed once more. This time, the captain climbed in beside me. But he did not touch me—not in that manner. He seemed as drained as I was and promptly fell asleep after one coating of the ointment on my punished rear.

When I heard Colt's even breathing, I rose from the bed, wincing.

It took the entire night to find the Crimson Eye, hidden beneath one of the floorboards in Colt's cabin.

Part one of my plan was complete. I was closer to freedom than I'd ever been.

So why, when I looked at my sleeping captor, did it feel like I'd just taken a giant leap back?

CHAPTER 40

CHARLOTTE,
THE PAST

SOMETHING WAS MISSING inside me, as if I'd left a piece of myself in Colt's room that night. He stole it from me when he touched my bare rear with his bare hand, as if he'd sucked it right out of my flesh and absorbed it into his.

But whatever happened between us in that moment when he'd sat me on his lap, only solidified my resolve to escape, quickly. To do so, I needed a time when *The Dark Blade* was close to land and hopefully, with the promise of inclement weather. Each day I watched the skies, looking for signs of impending rain, and I had my chance when we departed Saint Augustine.

Did I feel guilty when I let the chicken spoil and discreetly added it to the turtle soup, ensuring everyone would fall ill?

Maybe, but not so much for the men who'd wanted to see me whipped, more for Conks and Johnson and Miguel.

No guilt for Colt, either. He deserved it.

It was easy to refrain from eating the soup that evening, everyone knew I hated it.

I never heard a sweeter sound than that of the first crewman's groan. It was quickly followed by several more and I had to hide my smile. Soon, everyone retreated to their hammocks, desperate to find some comfort as the ache in their stomachs grew. By nightfall, I finally had a flash of good luck after years of misfortune. Rain pelted the ship hard enough to keep everyone below deck, yet the seas didn't toss so much that I wouldn't be able to escape in the jolly boat.

Dutifully, I flitted about the ship as I tended to the very men I'd sickened. I brought clean rags and fresh water, as well as emptied many soiled buckets. The smell of sick was so pungent I nearly vomited myself.

I wondered if the illness would come out the other end, and hoped I escaped beforehand.

The moon was high when most of the crew had fallen into a fitful slumber. Those who remained awake paid me no mind as they were too busy vomiting the contents of their stomachs every quarter hour. Not a single man climbed the rigs or stood watch upon the deck. I'd never heard the ship so quiet before.

It's time.

I crept down the stairs and into Colt's cabin. He was fast asleep in his bed, a sheen of sweat covering his body. The captain was bare from the waist up, and perhaps below as well, though I couldn't tell with the linens pulled across his midsection. Quietly, I retrieved the Crimson Eye from its hiding place beneath the floorboards and approached Colt's bed.

Slumbering, he didn't seem as much of a beast. His brow furrowed in pain and his face was deathly pale. Remembering he'd eaten my share of the turtle soup so it would not go to waste, I realized he was sicker than the others and I almost felt bad. Almost.

Quickly, I used my dirk to cut a small hole in the seam of Colt's mattress. Careful not to disturb him, I shoved the Crimson Eye inside and got to work on the longest part of my plan—sewing the mattress without allowing the stiches to give me away without closer examination. A normal man wouldn't notice something like that, but Colt was fastidious and I needed to keep him occupied in searching for the Eye. It would buy me time as I drifted… hopefully to shore.

I gulped. It was a huge risk. But I'd packed food and fresh water to keep myself alive for several days, if necessary.

I completed my sewing and had turned to leave when I spied Colt's dirk on the dining table. The shining blade beckoned, and, entranced, I slowly walked forward and grabbed it.

I could kill him before I escape.

Then I wouldn't have to worry about anyone chasing me; the men would be too busy fighting amongst themselves as to what to do next.

I crept back to Colt's sleeping form.

I could avenge my father. Myself.

I held the blade aloft.

All those times Colt put me over his knees. How he'd dared to look at my backside.

How it made me feel… confusing things.

God, how I hated him. I could do it. My grip tightened on the handle.

Kill him.

Colt suddenly moaned and my stomach dropped. The

world spun as his eyes fluttered open and locked on me. The terror I felt in that moment nearly made me swoon.

Oh god, my plan's over. Before it even began.

"Charlotte," Colt rasped, eyes unfocused.

He'd never called me by my name before. Did he not see the blade?

"Do you know how I love you?" Colt murmured.

My mouth fell and my heart gave a curious, achy beat against my ribcage.

For several moments I stood frozen in fear and immobilized by confusion.

Love me?

Insanity. It must have been the sickness talking.

"Can you ever forgive me for killing your father?" Colt mumbled, gaze unfocused in his fever-state.

No, I wanted to shout, *I hate you so much.*

But as angry tears sprung to my eyes, Colt closed his, returning to a fitful slumber.

For another few heartbeats, I remained still. Colt had never admitted any guilt in the murder of my father before and he'd certainly never asked forgiveness. The tiniest voice in my head said things I didn't want to hear. Things like, *what happened wasn't entirely Colt's fault.* But the voice was small enough that I was able to squash it.

Yet a worse voice took its place. Not quite forming words, but feelings. Horrid feelings to consider, like a ridiculous disappointment that Colt didn't fully awaken, see what I was doing, and punish me for it.

Move, Charlotte, I commanded myself, shaking my head. *You're wasting time.*

Rushing to Colt's chest of drawers and tossing aside his clothing, I grabbed his bag o' bits. There was enough gold in that purse to start a new life, one without beastly pirate captains trying to spank me.

With large, hard hands over strong, ample thighs.

I strapped the gold to my belt.

Thinner than his thick, supple leather.

Quietly, I crept to the cabin door.

With luck, while I sailed away, Colt and his crew would be too busy searching for the Crimson Eye to follow me. Whenever he next careened, he'd certainly scour and scrub the ship from top to bottom, including his mattress, as always. If he hadn't located the gem by that point, he most certainly would once the crew began their unusually thorough cleaning.

As much as I wanted to see Colt at the bottom of the ocean, I would never rob Conks or Johnson or Miguel of their future—a future that could be purchased with that stunning gem. And Colt knew it.

The captain and his bag o' bits, however… well, that was payment owed for everything he'd done to me.

My heart pounded in my ears as I made my way above deck with the gold, a sack of food, and a canteen of water. The moon broke through the rain clouds and I was thankful because, without the ship's torchlights, the world would have been utter darkness. Sick below deck, either no one had bothered to light them or they'd been put out by the rain.

I crossed the wet and slippery deck and headed straight for the jolly boat. I began pulling the ropes, alternating between fore and aft. It would be tricky without assistance, but I needed to lower the boat into the sea and jump. Then, safely aboard, I could cut the ropes and sail away to freedom.

I'd managed about halfway when the ropes stuck.

"Dammit," I cursed, wiping rain from my sweaty brow. I peered overboard to see the boat dangling about halfway to the sea. But no matter how hard I pulled, I couldn't muster the strength to free the ropes. I needed more muscle.

My pulse raced and an insistent pounding began in my head. Desperate, I sawed at the ropes with my dirk; first one, then the other. I figured I could cut the ropes enough so that when I jumped into the boat, maybe my weight would snap the final fibers and we'd plunge into the sea. If that failed, I could at least jump aboard and try to cut the ropes from below. But watching the jolly boat smack against the hull of the ship and imagining everything that could go wrong once I was inside make my gut twist in fear. If I couldn't get unstuck, I'd neither be free to sail away nor able to climb back aboard *The Dark Blade*.

"Going somewhere?" asked a voice behind me and I jumped, nearly dropping my dirk. With my heart in my throat, I turned to see Maurice.

"You know, I don't like turtle soup either," he drawled. Maurice looked more severe than usual with rain soaking his gaunt face. Sparse, graying hair stuck to his shiny forehead. "I guess it runs in the family."

The ship rocked with a wave and I braced myself on the rail.

"What are you talking about?" I mumbled. I wasn't really interested in listening, I just needed time to figure out how to thwart him and to continue readying the boat.

"You don't look a thing like her," Maurice said, shaking his head. "You don't look anything like me either."

A chill ran up my spine.

"But you do look like *my* mother," Maurice declared. "Now that you're starting to fill out."

My stomach knotted as Maurice drew closer. If he began shouting for the men, I'd lose my chance of escape. If he tried to grab and restrain me, I'd never be able to fight him off.

Unless… I tightened my grip on my dagger.

"I first saw your mother when she was visiting family in Jamestown," Maurice said, stalking closer. "She was much too stunning a beauty for your father. And what man leaves his lovely wife unchaperoned? I tried to tell her these things. I tried to show her, though she clawed at me and cried throughout."

Maurice cocked his head. "I thought she was a spirited woman from the fight she put up. But alas…"

What was Maurice saying? The pounding in my head grew unbearable, making it even more difficult to make sense of his words.

"By the time your mother reunited with her ridiculous husband, returning from whatever fool's endeavor he'd been upon, she was already ripening with my child." Maurice licked his lips. *"You."*

Nonsense, gibberish, insanity.

"You're crazy!" I spat. The ship rocked again and I hoped the jolly boat didn't drop into the sea without me.

Why was he saying these things?

"I don't know what you're talking about," I protested, stalling. "This is all some story to cover up the truth, isn't it? You killed my mother, didn't you?"

"The captain already told you," Maurice said calmly. "She killed herself."

"Liar!" My hands tightened on both the ropes and my

dirk, unsure about the best way to escape the looming threat of Maurice advancing.

"Well then, you could say you killed her, if you look at it another way," Maurice said evenly.

I wanted him to stop talking so badly, I fantasized about stabbing him in his malicious mouth. Each of his words felt like the prick of a blade into my heart. It hurt so much I pressed the heel of my hand into my chest. I was sure I bled, sure it would soak through my shirt at any moment.

"I was coming for her," Maurice insisted. He seemed the embodiment of blood-curdling evil as he spoke. "But she couldn't stand to be parted from you and she couldn't accept life with a pirate like myself," he mocked, sneering. "So when she received news I'd landed, she put a pistol to her head and pulled the trigger."

"Stop lying!" I cried.

"You were left alone with her now-widowed husband," Maurice said. "But he's no father of yours."

Tears soaked my face, indistinguishable from the rain.

"Deep down, I'd had the thought…" Maurice mused. "When you were first brought aboard. But that child had been female. And what were the odds that it lived? That it found its way onto my very ship? It wasn't until Robert tied you to the mast and we all saw the truth that I knew. Fate brought you to this ship. To me. To Colton."

I tensed my fingers around the dagger's handle once more.

"Colt wants you as I wanted your mother," Maurice said, smiling as if his words were happy ones. "I shouldn't be surprised he takes after me. I raised him like a son, after all. But you, my dear Charlotte, you are my actual daughter."

"Stop saying that!" I screamed. Before I knew what I was doing, my hand was flying sloppily toward Maurice and I'd stabbed him high, near his right shoulder.

He wasn't prepared for my rage, but he quickly recovered, lunging for me. I leapt backwards, dirk still in my hand, and scrambled onto the wet and slippery ship's rail. With one hand I clung to the rope above my head. I didn't have the chance to jump before I was forced to turn as Maurice attacked, face twisted in fury.

Had he determined to push me into the sea, it would have meant my eventual drowning. But either because he thought he was my father or because he wanted me for Colt, Maurice instead struggled to pull me back onto the ship. It gave me the opportunity to stab him once more, lower in his abdomen in what would hopefully be a fatal wound.

But it cost me my balance.

When Maurice tried to deflect the stab, he knocked me backwards.

By sheer luck, I fell into the jolly boat and not the dark sea. The fall was enough to snap the final frays of rope and plunge the boat itself into the waves.

But my luck had run out as when I fell backwards, my head smacked against the wooden railing with such force it not only knocked me unconscious, it knocked all sense of self from my head along with it.

That night the moon set upon the truth of Charlotte Clarke: orphaned daughter, pirate, thief, *murderess*. By the time the sun rose, I was Charlotte in name only—a name engraved upon the back of my locket, my only possession. I'd lost my rations and my bag o' bits to the sea.

Somehow, I'd even managed to lose my clothing.

I awoke ashore, bare and mysterious, like the goddess Aphrodite herself coming out of the waves.

I liked that story so much better, I'd wanted to believe it.

PART III

CLAIMED

CHAPTER 41

CHARLOTTE,
PRESENT DAY

S PUTTERING OUT SEA water, I blinked my eyes open to find myself sprawled upon the deck of *The Dread Night*. To the west, a terrible storm looked ready to burst from the clouds, rolling in with an early evening. Captain Colt lifted my torso and I flopped like a ragdoll into an embrace so tight it threatened to crush my lungs. A gathering assortment of crewmembers stared with rapt attention.

All of my memories came flooding back at once, making me gasp for air as if I were still drowning.

I was young Charlotte… the lie of Charlie… and Charlotte once more, as a woman grown. Before Colt had taken me again.

I pushed Colt's arm away.

"Don't touch me, don't you ever dare touch me."

When he didn't move, I pushed harder and screamed, "Murderer!" Fat tears leaked from my eyes. "You murdered my father!"

Colt released me, jumping back as if he'd been slapped. Torment clouded his eyes and despair covered his face. As if he had any right to feel those emotions. Everyone on deck fell utterly silent, watching the show. I didn't care.

"My father, my father," I covered my mouth with hands. "And you stole me! Made me work for you." Closing my eyes against the image, I sobbed, "And beat me…"

Oh god, it hurt. The truth hurt so much more than my not understanding why Colt pushed me away. This man, this scoundrel I'd allowed to touch me most intimately, had taken everything from me. He'd ripped me from my father's arms and the only home I ever knew.

Throughout my breakdown, Colt watched with a clenched jaw and tortured, glistening eyes. What right did he have to look as if he was sorry?

My hand flew to my locket—the locket I'd worn every day since I'd been found. Every day since Colt put it there. All this time, I'd thought it was dirt staining the edges within, but it was blood, a pirate captain's blood.

"You made me wear this," I accused, "like a golden chain around my neck." I tensed my hand to tear it off, but I couldn't do it. It had been a part of me so long, I wasn't ready.

"I hate you!" I cried. Memories charged me like vicious, wild animals. It was too much at once and I tried to fight them off as they attacked me, but their power was relentless. "I've always hated you."

I tugged my hair, unable to handle the onslaught. Pictures raced through my mind, endless days and nights aboard *The Dark Blade.* Strange, lingering looks from Colt I couldn't decipher at the time, and the escalating tension between us.

My boiling hatred was always present beneath the surface. Pushing me, motivating me…

…to escape.

I gasped as my mind caught up to the night I'd last seen Colt, the night I'd poisoned the crew.

"I… did steal the Crimson Eye," I whispered, covering my mouth with my hand. "But only for a moment, to hide. I thought you'd be distracted looking for it instead of chasing me. I never thought you'd think I took it. How could you?"

"You're a master of deceit," Colt whispered. "How could I not?"

"Because you knew I cared about the crew! I would never do anything to jeopardize their future."

"And I thought you averse to killing too, yet you slew Maurice."

"He deserved it!" I fought the tears, not wanting to explain the truth about Maurice when another realization hit me. "Wait, I don't understand. You never found the Eye?"

"No," Colt said in a low voice, scarcely breathing. "Where is it?"

"I sewed it into your mattress," I confessed, picturing the glittering ruby in my mind. "You careen without fail every three months and you always strip and wash the bedding, air your mattress… You perform such a thorough cleaning I thought you'd find it immediately."

At my confession, murmurs rose from the men.

Colt closed his eyes as he brought a hand to his head. "After you fled we sailed less-familiar waters looking for you. When we next careened it was in an unknown cove and we were attacked. It put a quick end to our scrubbing and after that, the men were too spooked for my overly thorough maintenance. We did the bare minimum the next two times we pulled her ashore and I cleaned the bedding but not the mattress," he said, groaning. "And then we traded her to Captain Arbuckle for *The Dread Night.* I thought we got the better end of the deal." Colt fisted his hands and yelled, "*Fuck!* I'd been sleeping above it the whole time."

I sucked in a breath. "So, the Eye might still be there? Aboard *The Dark Blade?*"

Colt cursed and demanded, "Are you lying to me?"

"No!"

"Swear it!" Colt ordered, grabbing me. "Swear to me the Eye is on my ship. My old ship."

"I swear it. Sewn directly into your old mattress. As long as no one else has found it first." I tried to dislodge Colt's grip but couldn't, so I attacked with words instead. "You can go fuck off and find it yourself! I don't care if you do, I don't care if you die on your journey. I *hope* you do."

Flinching, Colt released me just as roughly as he'd grabbed me. He took a long breath and stood, spinning away from me. He raked his hands through his hair and then placed them on his hips as he stared out to sea, deep in thought.

"They'll probably be in Nassau now," Johnson said. "Arbuckle always docks there this time of year. If we hurry, we might catch them."

Colt swore through gritted teeth. His shoulders rose and fell with a deep, frustrated breath.

"Set a course for Nassau." He spun around to face me. "She comes with us."

I lifted my chin as I stood and declared, "I will not. I'm leaving this ship just as you decreed and I never want to see you again." With a rigid back and fisted hands, I stood boldly before the murdering captain, challenging him. "If you keep me here, I will slit your throat in your sleep. And if you prevent me from doing so, I will slit my own throat before I ever spend one night in your presence."

I mean it.

I tried to infuse my gaze with all the hatred I could summon. My heart pounded as I tensed my body, preparing for a fight. After a pause that lasted an eternity, Colt's shoulders slumped. He stepped aside in silent permission to let me go.

I'd won. *I'd won?*

A strange sensation shot through my heart, almost like disappointment. I shook it away, but before I could act, someone interrupted.

"Beggin' your pardon," Sedge called out coldly. Despite his words, there was no hint of pleading in his deadly voice. "But what we do next is no longer your decision."

I wasn't sure he could have been called a *friend,* but as Robert's closest companion, the bald shipmate looked as if he wanted to murder me for hiding the Crimson Eye and Colt for killing Redhands.

Sedge's eyes pinned me to the deck and the hair on my neck stood on end. Colt didn't move but he returned Sedge's stare with enough menace to make me think he might kill him first. Johnson immediately stepped into the circle of shipmates and spread his arms wide in a gesture of calm to everyone.

"You killed Robert," he said gently to Colt. "And while he's not missed by many of us, this isn't a lawless ship. You cannot execute men at your discretion. Not to mention, you've been hiding this gem from us for years," Johnson accused, as if he wasn't aware of the fact all along. Was he lying to gain favor from the crew? I watched Johnson with cautious, nervous interest.

"I'm sorry but your captaincy is on hold until we decide to reinstate it or to vote a new captain in your place."

I raised my brows in surprise. *What a quiet, clever little backstabber Johnson is.*

"I suppose you think you're the man for the job?" Colt asked between gritted teeth.

"Aye, maybe he is," came the cry from one of the men.

Colt and Johnson stared at one another as if they might come to blows, which was ridiculous because Johnson, slight and bookish, would never beat a man as strapping as Colt. But Colt couldn't win against all the men gathering at Johnson's back, either.

How fast fortunes can change aboard a pirate's ship, I marveled.

The clouds broke and light raindrops pelted the wood with an ominous, musical cadence.

"We can't sail anywhere until this storm passes," Conks announced, interrupting the tense stand-off. "I say we get out of this rain and convene below deck to vote on what to do next. Colt will be temporarily relieved of his captaincy. Anyone who's interested in taking over the job will have his turn to speak, and we'll take a vote on who will fill the role," Conks declared, spinning to address everyone.

Conks's suggestion was met with proclamations of support. They kept coming until he asked, "Any nays?"

When he was met with silence he said, "Then it's settled. After, we can have a fair trial to judge Colt for his actions."

Conks looked at me and it was impossible to read his expression, but my heart sank at his next decree.

"And we'll keep Charlie in the brig until we decide what to do with her in the morning."

My head spun wildly and my pulse raced with fear at the change in fortunes and leadership.

What would become of me?

I barely heard Conks tell Miguel, "Stay here a moment, please. We'll be down there awhile and I'll need you to prepare some food for everyone while we debate."

CHAPTER 42

CHARLOTTE

COLT SAID NOTHING, but he was the last to leave the deck, gazing at me with his dark eyes as if he tried to memorize every part of my body, my face.

How dare you even look at me? I thought.

He continued to stare.

You, who murdered my father and stole me. You have no right.

His eyes glistened, slick like water on pitch.

I despise you.

Colt didn't leave until Conks gave him a firm, but gentle, nudge.

Once the men were assembled below deck only Conks, Miguel, and I remained above. I braced, preparing to be dragged to the brig, but their demeanor immediately changed.

"Hurry, get the ropes," Conks ordered Miguel, and the two men sprung into action. "Charlotte, help us, quickly."

Help you?

Seeing my confusion, Conks explained, "Of course we're not locking you up. You'll escape in the jolly boat. Miguel can row you to shore. Find Mrs. Penningham and hide yourself. Leave town. Some of the men down there want you for the murder of Maurice and the rest will want you contained—or worse—for stealing the Crimson Eye. They won't let you go. This is your only chance to escape. Hurry!"

My mind quickly caught up to the fact that the captain, Conks, Johnson and Miguel had all just performed a ruse they were in on together, without even speaking. I wasn't sure what was happening below deck, but above, their plan involved getting me off this ship as quickly as possible.

With no time to ask my many questions, I raced to aid in my own escape, loosening ropes. Miguel and I prepared to climb inside the boat, leaving Conks on deck to finish lowering it to sea.

My hair began to stick to my forehead as the rain pelted the ship with increased force. What had been a sunny morning had turned dreary after my fall and the skies were quickly darkening as the storm progressed. There was no time to do anything other than hug Conks goodbye and whisper, "Thank you."

Tears of gratitude pricked my eyes. As I leaned into the gray-haired man, he said in my ear, "He loves you, Charlotte, and you must believe he'd take it all back if he could. Even if it meant putting his own life at risk."

I knew who he meant, of course, and the tears turned bitter before they fell. Ensuring no one could get a good look at my face, I wiped them away and climbed into the boat.

"Hide alone in the woods if you must, but hide," Miguel instructed as we rowed across the bay toward the place I'd once called home. "Everyone knows Arbuckle won't stay in Nassau long. The crew will eventually give up the search for you in order to catch him before he departs. But it could be a day or two."

Nodding vigorously, I clutched the side of the boat's rail, riding increasingly tumultuous waves as we made our way to shore.

"What about you and Conks? Won't you be in danger for helping me?"

Miguel smiled, though not widely enough to flash his dimples. "Trouble, yes, danger, no. They depend on me to take care of each growl in their stomachs and every scrape on their skin. And Conks is like a father to all. He's too beloved by the crew for them to punish him harshly."

Something hung in the air as Miguel trailed off. Something unspoken.

"Unless?" I prodded.

Miguel gave a small smile. "Unless things turn out very badly down there and Sedge takes command."

I swallowed. My stomach lurched and it wasn't just from the increasing waves.

"Come with me," I pled, already knowing he'd refuse.

"My loyalty is to the captain. Always has been. Same as Conks."

I didn't want to ask. I didn't care.

"What—what will happen to him?"

Miguel shook his head. "Nothing that would be worse than seeing you hurt. So if you care about him, you'll do as we instruct and run. Hide."

Bristling, I lifted my chin and replied, "I don't care about him."

A small, sad smile played at Miguel's lips.

When we reached the beach, Miguel couldn't pull the boat ashore by himself, and especially not against the force of the rising waves. Not to mention, he needed to save his strength for the return trip to *The Dread Night*.

"Hurry," Miguel warned. "I don't know what will happen back on the ship."

He pulled me into a tight hug as he said goodbye, and I was forced to trudge toward the beach through cool waves that rose nearly to my waist.

What should I do now? Where should I hide?

My feet sunk into the wet sand as I stood with indecision. My heart thundered, matching the booming sky behind me. My upper half grew slick from the rain and my lower half was soaked from the sea. My dress stuck to my skin and my hair was a tangled fright.

Where should I go?

I couldn't run to Mrs. Penningham. Not only was I completely opposed to putting her in danger, it was the first place the crew would expect.

Daniel, I thought. He might have been disappointed in my recent behavior, but he would protect me from harm at the hands of the pirates he so hated. His lashing out had been a response to my betrayal and I couldn't blame him for that.

I gathered my sodden skirts and raced up the beach, heading toward Daniel's elegant home on the outskirts of our settlement. The muddy path squished under my feet and I was thankful for the sturdy boots I wore.

I knocked on Daniel's door and I was surprised that he opened it himself, and to see that he had company. Four other men stared back, just as startled to see me—likely from my shamefully bedraggled appearance. I recognized the men as business acquaintances of Daniel's, though I had never been formally introduced.

"Charlotte?" Daniel shook his head and as if remembering himself, he opened the door wide, ushering me inside. "What are you doing here?"

"I need your help," I said, sloshing into his home and feeling guilty as I dripped water on the fine carpets. The air hummed with tension and the back of my neck tingled as I studied the assembled companions. Somehow, being alone amongst this elegant gathering of gentlemen felt more foreboding than when I'd been on a boatful of murdering pirates.

"Where are your servants?" I asked.

"I sent them home so that my friends and I could chat," Daniel replied, enigmatically.

Daniel can help, I reminded myself, shaking my odd feeling.

"I need to hide from Captain Colt and his men," I announced, hoping he wouldn't tell me I deserved whatever fate was to befall me.

Daniel's pause was oddly long, and I worried I'd been mistaken. But then his eyes lit in a familiar manner and I relaxed. He turned to his friends and announced slowly, "Gentlemen, this is the girl I told you about."

I shifted my weight. *Told them what?* Not of my relationship with Colt, I hoped. *Did that mean he was still upset with me?*

"We saw *The Dread Night* in the harbor," Daniel explained. "That's why we've gathered. To see if we can do something about it this time."

A man with a short beard and wavy black hair leaned

forward and announced, "He's stolen from every merchant I know."

"Aye," another man agreed.

"It's time we put an end to his piracy once and for all," the third man said.

The fourth only stared, darkly.

We're on the same side then, I thought with relief. *Except, wait...*

"It's not really Captain Colt I'm running from," I corrected. "It's some of the other men. Colt actually tried to help me. Which isn't to say he's a good man, he's terrible. But in this instance, it's the crew, you see. The captain, well, he cares for me-" I cut off my rambling, bringing a frustrated hand to my head. "It's hard to explain right now, but some of the crew might be after me. Can you help me find a place to hide?"

Daniel crossed to his table and poured a steaming cup of tea. He and the other men looked at one another for long moments and I hoped they were coming to an agreement on how to assist.

"Please," I whispered. "I don't have much time. Perhaps you could help me hide in the woods? I just need some blankets to stay dry and a bit of food and water to last for a day or two. And if you could let Mrs. Penningham know I'm safe—but not yet," I said quickly. "I wouldn't want the crew to take her and try to force my location out of her."

"You need to calm down and warm up," Daniel said. Irritation pricked at the back of my neck. I'd always hated it when he spoke to me like that, and didn't he understand that there wasn't time?

Daniel pressed the cup into my hands, insisting. I relented and took a few fortifying sips of the hot tea.

"Have a seat," Daniel urged, patting my shoulder. "I'm going to discuss with my friends how to take care of you."

My pulse raced and every bone in my body protested the time wasted, but with no other choice, I sat. Unable to force myself to take another sip, I clutched the teacup so tightly I feared I'd break the delicate porcelain. Daniel turned his back to me, speaking in a low, urgent tone with the men.

Finally, he turned around, smoothed his sandy hair back into his ribbon and said, "We can help you, Charlotte, but more importantly, you can help us."

A chill raced up my spine at his measured tone. *What did that mean?* Two of the three men moved, blocking the door behind me. Sweat mingled with the rainwater dripping from my hair and down my neck.

"Help you how?" I asked, cautiously, clinging to a hope that went against what my instincts were screaming.

Find a weapon. Run. You shouldn't have come here.

"We're going to take a trip to the woods, like you wanted, Charlotte," Daniel declared. Before I could feel any relief over his words, he said, "But some things are going to happen that you may not want."

With my free hand, I clutched the chair's armrest. Licking my dry lips, I croaked, "What are you talking about?"

Daniel nodded to the men behind me and said, "Since you wouldn't be our spy, my darling, you must be our bait."

Hardly anyone moved an inch during the tense pause that filled the air. Then my teacup clattered to the ground as I sprung from my chair and bolted toward the back of the room. Two of the men grabbed me, though they needn't have bothered as Daniel aimed a pistol at my head, halting my attempted fleeing easily enough.

"Daniel, *please*. What's happening?" I whispered, trying to calm my pounding heart. Everyone in the room was dressed in gentlemanly attire and had, until this point, acted with civility. I desperately clung to what I hoped wasn't a façade.

"This is your doing, Charlotte. I would have liked it if you'd stayed on our side," Daniel said. Though his face seemed sad, regretful, his eyes danced with glee. The contradiction was diabolical. "Reported back on Colt, sung for us. Instead, we have to make you scream."

Daniel's proclamation quickly came true as he stepped forward and tore my dress, not stopping until he'd ripped it from me and I was clad only in my chemise. Rage filled my breast, and when I managed to get an arm free from one of the men, I lunged for Daniel's pistol. Not only did he avoid my grasp, but as the brutes recaptured my arm, Daniel turned the weapon around and casually slammed the butt into my head. Hissing in pain, I tucked my head into my shoulder. Daniel's nonchalance at harming me sent waves of alarm coursing throughout my body. Tears pooled in my eyes but I couldn't even rub the injured area, which would surely swell in no time.

"Why?" I cried.

"Captain Colt cares for you. I've seen it myself," Daniel replied. "We're going to bring you into the woods and you're going to help us send him a message. When he comes to respond..."

"We'll ambush him," the dark-haired man behind me concluded as his hands tightened on my shoulder and wrist.

"You're setting a trap," I whispered, pain squeezing my heart. Daniel nodded, confirming my fear as his gaze lingered on my body.

In that moment when my heart screamed, I knew. *Oh god, I was a fool.* Faced with Colt's imminent death, I knew I didn't want it. It didn't matter what he'd done to my father, to me.

I still loved him. More than anything.

He'd tried to tell me how sorry he was, I realized. He believed I'd forgiven him and he was humbled and grateful. But I thought he'd been talking about past punishments, not the death of my father and his part in it.

Daniel seemed to be debating something as a few quiet seconds passed.

"I've stripped you naked before," Daniel said, still eyeing my breasts, barely concealed beneath my chemise. "When you washed ashore like a siren of the sea."

Stripped me? Chills ran up my spine again.

"I took your clothes that day and I might have had the opportunity to take more, but we were interrupted by Mr. Penningham's bloody morning stroll along the beach."

My stomach dropped to my feet as I pieced it together. *That's why I had no clothing when I was found.* Recalling how I escaped Colt's ship, I now knew it wasn't the captain or any of his men who'd stripped me. But I didn't know what had happened between when I'd fallen into the sea and when I'd awoken, naked, on the beach. Maybe I could have thought more on it, made some guesses, but there hadn't been any opportunity considering recent events.

Daniel's fingers traced my décolletage, lifting my locket. With a sharp tug, he yanked it clear off my neck, making me jump.

"I didn't have time to secure this," he said, pocketing my locket. I gulped as Daniel leaned into my ear and whispered,

"Though I never got the chance to thank you for the gold I did have the time to acquire."

My eyes widened and my heart skipped a beat. *Colt's missing bag o' bits.* The one I'd stolen to fund my new life off his ship. I'd assumed it had been lost at sea...

I gazed at Daniel's elegant home, set amongst his rich farmland and adorned with beautiful art, tableware, and knickknacks. Everyone knew he'd come into wealth about the time that I was found, but no one knew how. Perhaps he'd doubled or tripled the money with wise investments, but it had all started with what he'd stolen from *me*.

Even the pink dress Daniel had gifted me—the one I wore the day Colt attacked our settlement. It was all with my gold. I'd bought my own dress.

Well, I supposed I'd first stolen the bag from Colt. But that was beside the point.

"Thank you, Miss Charlotte." Daniel leaned back and with a sweep of his arms, he declared, "None of this would have been possible without the gold you provided."

Fury at Daniel's deception made my blood boil. He'd robbed me of a new life; one I deserved for all I endured. I struggled with the men holding me, determined to scratch out Daniel's eyes the moment I had the chance.

"Remember, you brought all this on yourself," he said, and from his disappointed tone I could tell Daniel was convinced it was true. "You were determined to be a pirate's whore. We're only obliging you."

Dizzying fear threatened to take over my mind and I tampered it down because I needed to stay alert, to pay attention. Being alone with five men, the possible horrors they could inflict upon me were endless.

Determination to stay alive kept me struggling, however.

Daniel jutted his chin in the direction of the door, indicating to his friends to begin walking.

"Go to *The Dread Night* and tell Captain Colt we have his whore," he instructed one of the men. "If he wants her, he comes alone. Otherwise, she's as good as dead."

To two of the men he ordered, "You'll hide in the woods. Shoot him when he gets close." Turning to address the fourth man, he said, ominously, "And you'll help me with her."

At last his gaze came to rest on me.

"And you, Charlotte, will scream for your lover. Save your strength, girl," Daniel advised cruelly. "You're going to need it."

One of the men opened the door and shoved me forward, into the stormy night and towards the dark woods behind Daniel's manor.

I clamped my mouth shut, determined. No one from our settlement could hear me above the rain.

You must not make a sound, I warned myself.

My screams would only bring about Colt's demise.

CHAPTER 43

COLT

I'D LOST HER once, I could suffer it again. Couldn't I? But the last time, I hadn't lost this much. I'd focused on losing the crew's future and all the freedom entailed for myself and my men which the Crimson Eye could purchase. At least, I'd tried. Now, after those nights with Charlotte... after holding her, loving her, safeguarding her... I'd lost so much more. I'd lost the her—the us—I'd only ever dared to imagine in the darkness of my cabin after several cups of rum.

Devil in hell, what could I do about it?

Nothing. She despised me all over again and for even greater reason. *All that time I'd thought she'd been a willing participant in a game she'd constructed,* I thought, wincing, *and all that time she didn't remember...*

Conks had joined our gathering and the look in his eyes told me it was done.

She's gone.

Charlotte had been delivered to shore by Miguel, who stayed on deck for watch duties while we debated below.

Twice I'd tried taking her, forcing her to stay with me, and twice I'd failed. A third time and she'd slit her own throat, just as she'd sworn.

And if I didn't pay attention right now, Sedge might slit mine.

The crew had divided between Sedge and me, but I had a few tricks up my sleeve he couldn't predict, not to mention Johnson's subversive eloquence in swaying men to my side. It was remarkably subtle every time Johnson brought up a point that seemed, overtly, to be in Sedge's favor, but secretly raised concerns giving way to the men questioning his ability to lead. Though we were evenly matched, the men supporting him were all muscle, no mind.

Sway over sabers, dear Sedge.

This was my ship and he wasn't going to take it from me.

You conniving little bastard.

I'd planned on being merciful, but after his suggestion to maroon me for slaying Robert, I'd debated what sort of accident would befall the eager climber once this matter was settled. Perhaps when he scaled the rat lines I'd cut the ropes, and he'd have a physical downfall to match the metaphorical one he was about to experience. Sedge marched around the hull, grandstanding about his abilities. I sat, letting others speak on my behalf. I did my best to appear thoughtful, if not contrite.

I needed it to be believable, after all.

Once the vote is cast, I can allow myself to consider how to survive without Charlotte…

The pounding of rain upon the ship's wooden sides dimmed sounds of whatever commotion ensued above deck. It wasn't until the door swung wide and Miguel sloshed down the steps that everyone turned to take stock of an unexpected guest upon our vessel.

I froze. Something in my bones told me it had to do with Charlotte and a chill raced down my spine.

"Beggin' your pardon, the man said, swiping a cap from his head and holding it near his chest. "But I was made to send you a message. My name is John. Please don't hurt me. If I didn't tell you, they said they'd take my wife and children and-"

"Spit it out now!" I growled, springing to my feet.

"He's taken Miss Charlotte, he's hurting her," the man supposedly named John announced, trying to appear shaken and so clearly a part of whatever scheme was happening that I was certain that even the dimmest man on my crew could see through him. "Said he's making her scream to make you scurry."

I broke out in a panicked sweat because those words rang true. A fear like I'd never known set my heart racing, pounding. The room disappeared and nothing mattered but getting off my ship and getting to Charlotte.

"She's not in the brig?" James asked. "How'd she escape?"

Sedge snorted. "Wouldn't be the first time the bitch gave us the slip. Or the second."

"Who has her?" I demanded, ignoring everyone and fisting my hands against the urge to clutch this man's collar and to shake him, to lift him off the ground and dash his head against the wall.

"Daniel," John replied, confirming my suspicions. "He said to come alone or he'll kill her. He said the longer you take, the more he'll hurt her."

I'm going to kill him. You. Everyone involved.

"It's a trap," Conks said behind me, announcing what we all knew to be true.

"A trap?" John asked, with false, wide eyes. "I wouldn't know anything about that, I'm just the messenger. I only saw Daniel take her into the woods. Said I was to bring you to him."

"It's a trap," Johnson said, sagely. "And one you have no choice but to walk into."

"You're not going anywhere," Sedge interrupted, stepping into the center of the circle and raising his hands. My stomach knotted and my head began to throb. *"She's* not going anywhere."

At his words, a few of the men on Sedge's side brought their hands to their swords, tensing. A chorus of *"ayes"* echoed around the rocking hull. It was too many men to fight through.

Fuck. I closed my eyes and re-opened them, determined.

"You can have her. My ship. Command of *The Dread Night,"* I announced, words tumbling from my lips. "Let me go to Charlotte and I'll end this debate now. I'll give you my captaincy, no vote required."

The men behind me sucked in a collective breath of surprise. Lazily, wasting time, Sedge paused and replied, "No."

I can't fight my way out of this, I thought again, eyeing the men at his back. Even those supporting me supported justice. Killing Robert might be excusable, with the right persuasion. Attacking half the crew to do as I pleased, like a tyrant king, would not.

"You can have the Crimson Eye!" I shouted, not caring how desperate I looked. "My share, all of it. Just let me leave, now."

"We need her to find the Eye," Sedge countered. "Maybe we should all go get her together."

Grumbles rose up from the men.

"I'm not walking into a trap," someone protested. "What if they've got the whole town waiting to grab us and make us dance the hangman's jig?"

"We're not risking our necks to rescue her," James agreed, facing Sedge as he stepped into the circle. Turning to me he said, "And even if we did, we're not setting her free. Her only use is in leading us to the Eye."

"She's of no value to you, she's already confessed where it's hidden!" I raked my hands through my hair, frustrated and growing more panicked with every passing second. Visions of Charlotte being cut and raped invaded my mind, torturing me. I felt like I might do something foolish if I didn't get off this ship soon, like drawing my sword to begin cutting down men, which would only lead to them restraining me and ending all hope of saving her.

"Let me go and you can have it all," I swore, looking Sedge dead in the eye. "Use my ship to capture *The Dark Blade*. Take the Crimson Eye for yourself. I renounce my claim on any of it. Take my gold and whatever's in my cabin. Everything is yours if you let me leave now."

My offer struck the crew into stunned silence. Long seconds passed with no sound but the rain beating the deck above. Sweat gathered at my neck as I tensed to fight a losing battle if we couldn't come to an agreement.

Sedge let his lips curl into a bastard's smile. He looked over his shoulder and nods were exchanged between him and the men on his side.

Turning back to me he said, "Go now. Take nothing and never return."

A surge of relief swept over me. I immediately shifted mentally into imagining potential scenarios in which I might find Charlotte and how to get her out of them, safely. My mind still raced as Johnson grabbed my arm.

"Captain, wait," he said, speaking on behalf of Conks as well. "We're coming with you."

"As am I," Miguel piped up, stepping forward.

I wanted to protest; they weren't my best fighters and I didn't want to get them killed. But they wouldn't fare well on a ship under Sedge's command and I needed any help I could get, knowing I walked into an ambush of some kind.

With a cocky grin and a wave of his hand, Sedge showed that he was happy to get rid of what he deemed the least able-bodied of the crew.

I had no time to argue with anyone.

"Let's go," I said, already storming up the stairs and into the rainy night.

CONKS, JOHNSON, MIGUEL and I boarded John's small boat, leaving *The Dread Night* behind forever. I didn't think about my books, my clothes, my gold, or any worldly possessions. I didn't care about my ship or the Crimson Eye. My only focus as we fought the waves on our ride across the stormy bay was getting Charlotte away from Daniel and somewhere safe.

The biggest asset I possessed was that the bastard sitting before me didn't know that *I* knew he was in on it.

I laid a hand on his shoulder and said, "Thank you for your help in saving Miss Charlotte. I imagine this must be frightening for a simple man such as yourself to be so regrettably tangled up in."

"Terrifying," John said, nodding. "I'll take you where Daniel's hiding her in the woods and then, if you don't mind, I'll be getting back to my wife and kids."

You'll be dead within the hour. Enjoy your last few moments alive.

"Of course," I lied. My men and I exchanged a glance, wordlessly communicating our intentions.

We play this game at sea and we're by far better players than you.

"She's not far from his manor," John said. "'Bout a five-minute walk."

By the time we reached the shore, my men were soaked and wary, fingers twitching on the hilts of their swords. We trudged up the beach and into the woods, breaking into the quickest pace possible that still allowed us to listen for any enemies approaching.

My head and heart pounded in a war to be the first to explode.

Charlotte, Charlotte. I'm so sorry. I'm coming.

Only the barest glow of moonlight shone through the clouds and the foliage, hindering our progress in the thick woods and making me feel as if I'd go insane.

After a few minutes a sound carried through the trees and I was forced to halt to listen.

Was it —

Yes. God help me and God help the man who caused it.

Over the beat of rain onto the earth, I heard Charlotte scream. Beside me, the man called John twitched.

Quicker than he could react, I grabbed him and brought my blade to his throat. With his back pressed to my chest, rain dripped from my hair onto his shoulders. I didn't know his plan and didn't care. He wouldn't live long enough to enact it.

"Your next words determine your fate. Don't waste your breath lying. I know you're a part of this."

Charlotte's screams were meant to distract me and by God, they were. I could see how torn my men were too, instinct calling them to run in her direction but wisdom telling them to stay put.

Struggling to breathe, I demanded, "Where are the others hiding and how many are there? Lie to me and you're dead. Think carefully before responding. Your life depends on it."

I heard a rush of liquid as the man, unwillingly and full of fear, relieved his bladder onto his breeches. I almost felt bad for the coward. I doubted he'd lived an honorable life and he wasn't going to be given an honorable death.

"Two men in the woods," John confessed, voice shaking. *Thank God,* I thought, *it's not the whole town.* But a different panic rose within me because if Daniel didn't want others involved, that meant what he was doing to Charlotte was unspeakable.

"Behind the boulder before you approach. It's up the slope there on the left," John continued in a rush, pointing into the darkness. "I was supposed to signal our approach and they'll shoot you before you even get close. There's four of us in total as he's got one man with him. Now let me-"

I sliced his throat in one clean swipe. It could be considered a mercy to put him out of his misery before he knew it was coming, but in truth I didn't have the time to waste either way.

"Take care of the men at the boulder," I ordered Conks and Johnson. "Miguel, with me."

We raced forward while Conks and Johnson veered left, heading to the boulder and hopefully taking out the two men with the element of surprise. Miguel had no problem keeping up with me as we raced on, leaving them to their fight.

There was no need to be silent as Charlotte's screams increased, covering any noise. My blood raced and my hands tingled, desperate to beat Daniel's face until it was unrecognizable and then to tear the flesh from his limbs.

When the screaming stopped, so did my heart.

What had happened?

My heart began working again when I heard a struggle. I faltered, tripping over my own feet as I picked up speed.

She's fighting back. That's my girl.

I heard a man shout, and from the volume I knew I was only seconds away.

Hold on, Charlotte. I'm coming.

I burst into a rain-soaked clearing and my eyes widened. Daniel had raised his pistol, pointing it at Charlotte who, on her knees, looked up with defiance.

It was a scene from the worst possible nightmare, etched forever in my brain.

I saw Daniel's hand move, finger tightening on the trigger, and every fiber in my being screamed in agony.

Because I knew I wasn't going to make it in time.

CHAPTER 44

CHARLOTTE

"OPEN YOUR MOUTH and call to him or I'll be forced to cut it wide open and make you scream."

Hunched above me on one side, Daniel's man growled the command. Daniel took the other side, holding me to the sodden earth despite my frantic kicking.

"Or maybe we'll cut out your tongue," the man added.

Rain from both men's hair splattered my face, making it difficult to see, but I couldn't miss the twin sets of glistening blades held to my face with evident threat. I clamped my lips tighter and braced for pain.

"How can she scream if you cut out her tongue?" Daniel asked, huffing. I wasn't sure if he said it because it raised a good point—or if because some part of him deep down didn't want to hurt me too badly. I hated the gratitude and relief that washed over me.

"Fine. There are other sensitive parts," the man said ominously. He slid down my body and stabbed his dagger so quickly into the mud between my legs that he would have managed to cut me if I hadn't squirmed out of the way. The temporary relief I had felt was replaced by sheer panic and I regrettably let out an instinctive cry.

"That's it, girl," the man praised. With his dagger lodged in the dirt, he attacked with his bare hands instead. Gripping my arms, Daniel's man squeezed like he wanted to break my bones, then twisted my skin as if he aimed to tear the flesh from my body.

"Stop!" I shouted, between garbled screams of agony.

It only made him hurt me more.

My skin was soaked from a mix of the cold rain and my own hot sweat. It was an advantage.

In my thrashing against Daniel's grip, I managed to free my arms and throw Daniel's man off balance. The slippery grass helped too, as did our motives.

They wanted to keep me alive—at least a little while longer. I had no such compunction.

I couldn't wrest control of either blade. I couldn't overpower either man. All I could do was maneuver myself.

With a cry, I rolled away on the wet grass, hearing the tear in my skirts as they were freed from the dagger. Daniel's arm plunged downward as he tried to stab my body or my skirt—I wasn't sure which. Either he aimed at wounding me or pinning me back to the ground. Fortunately, his man also lurched forward, attempting to use his body weight to detain me. In the synchronized tussle, Daniel's man quickly collapsed on the ground, taking my place —

—and Daniel's own dagger, already in motion, stabbed the man right in his unprotected back.

I gasped as the lackey gave one cry and slumped, dead in the grass or unconscious on his way there.

Oh my god, I've done it, I thought, scrambling away. *He's dead. One man down and one to go.*

Daniel stilled, eyes widening in shock at having slain his own companion.

My victory was short-lived.

Tangled in my sopping skirts, I'd only made it to my knees before Daniel came to his senses. Instead of drawing his sword, which I'd at least have had some chance of fighting, Daniel grabbed his pistol from his belt and aimed it at my head.

I froze, mouth parted in horror.

He wouldn't really shoot me. Would he?

Daniel leapt to his feet. Keeping his weapon trained on me, he stepped closer, until he stood above me with vicious fury in his eyes.

Yes, he would. He's going to shoot me.

I tried not to weep. My heart pounded so rapidly in my head it drowned out the sound of rain beating on the trees.

I'd nearly done it. I had been so close.

It made the taste of defeat all the more bitter in my mouth. It made me rage against death that much harder. Yet in the end, all I could do was clench my fists and try not to cry. I saw the desire to retaliate in Daniel's eyes. I hated that I was going to die on my knees.

Daniel's hand moved, his finger positioning on the trigger.

At the same time, I heard a roar through the trees.

"No!" Colt burst into the clearing, shouting, rain-soaked

and wild with madness, making my heart swell with love at the sight of him even as I thought, *No! Run away!*

Were Daniel's men waiting in the trees to shoot him? Or had he thwarted them somehow?

Colt and I were both going to die in this wet, dark wood. Colt was too far away to save me, and it was all happening too fast. Had Daniel thought it through, he might have turned and shot at the captain, or stopped and used me as leverage against Colt's attack. But either Daniel counted on his men to intervene, his emotions overrode his logic, or he just couldn't halt as his finger was already in motion, squeezing.

Goodbye, Colt. I love you.

The thought was all I had time for before —

Click.

Click.

Click and…

…nothing.

"Dammit!" Daniel swore.

Oh my god.

I could scarcely breathe as I realized the pistol hadn't fired. Either rain had soaked the necessary mechanisms or it was just the ever-poor odds that the weapon would properly function.

A pistol was never as reliable as a sword.

As a captain.

As *my* captain, wielding *his* sword, and barreling down on Daniel with deadly intent. I scrambled backward before Daniel could grab and use me as defense.

Colt, face twisted in rage, drove his sword directly through Daniel's midsection. My abductor fell to his knees, then flopped, face-down in the grass.

Dead.

Neither Colt nor I paid him any mind as Colt reached out his hand and pulled me to my feet. The world disappeared as he swept me into his wet embrace. Smoothing my hair from my face he asked again and again, *"Are you hurt?"* Despite my frantic and repeated reassurances, Colt continued to examine my body, apologizing for being too late, for letting Daniel take me, and for a host of other things he wasn't responsible for.

"I'm alright," I panted, pushing my hands against Colt's chest to cease his fussing. "Please, let me speak. There's something I need to tell you and it can't wait any longer."

Colt quieted, but he looked as if he wouldn't stay that way for long. Out of the corner of my eye, I noticed Conks, Johnson, and Miguel in the clearing. I wondered how long they'd been there whilst I'd been so focused on Colt.

Breathing deeply, I said, "I want you to know I understand now. The decision you had to make in the heat of the moment all those years ago. I forgive you for what happened with my father. For…" I trailed off, still panting for air. It was too much to discuss right now. "Everything."

Subtly, Conks, Johnson, and Miguel stepped back, giving us space.

"Oh god, and there's so much to tell you about what happened that night," I continued in a rush. "Maurice… he might be, likely is… my father."

Colt's eyes widened and he shook his head in denial.

"Yes," I insisted, interrupting before Colt could speak. My heart continued pounding and I struggled to even my breathing. "But it's too much to get into now and none of that is important. I will explain it all later, I promise. The important thing is, I want you to know that I remember everything and I forgive everything. And I love you. Do you forgive and love me too?"

"There is nothing to forgive," Colt swore, cupping my cheek. "And there has never been a moment I haven't loved you. Only moments in which I love you more, because I have, with each passing day since the day I saw the real you… and maybe even before."

Colt furrowed his brow in frustration and shrugged. I laughed at the implication. There was a touch of hysteria to it, given my overwhelming relief from escaping recent death, but it felt good to laugh and even better to be in Colt's arms.

"I'm never leaving you again," I said. I brought his hand to my lips and kissed it. "I want to return to your ship and stay. This time, forever."

A shadow passed over Colt's face and he shook his head. After a pause, he said, "We can't return to *The Dread Night*. She's no longer mine. I gave command to Sedge and we don't have enough men to take her back."

Searching Colt's pained face, I saw the truth in his eyes. A captain who lost his ship lost a part of himself. In my stunned silence, it dawned on me that I had something to do with it. That, somehow, he must have given up his vessel to gain me. Colt had enough men to reclaim me, but not enough to retake his ship.

"She's gone. As is my gold and any hope for the Crimson Eye. I have…" Colt sighed, "nothing of value. And soon, the rest of your townsfolk will come looking for us and we'll all be hanged, unless we leave now. But, Charlotte," he said, releasing my hand to grab my biceps, "I have nowhere to go and nothing to provide for you, nothing but the life of a wanted criminal. Worse. The life of a beggar."

Colt's voice slowed and deepened with grief by the end of his speech, and I realized he was confessing. This was Colt's way of offering me a chance to depart, believing he had nothing to give me but empty pockets and a target on our backs.

I was temporarily speechless. More than saddened that he thought I'd leave his side at this moment, I bristled at the insult.

Who was this man before me who let himself be so easily defeated? Had Colt's love for me caused him to give up, believing it to be for my benefit?

I'd never known Captain Colt to be the self-sacrificing type. At least, not before. But I now understood that was what he did when he tried returning me to my old settlement. He'd wanted to let me go before I remembered.

Too late, my love. I remember and I will never again forget.

A plan began forming in my mind.

"Captain Colt," I admonished, and my sharp tone snapped the curious crew to attention. Even Colt dropped his hands from my arms, taken aback.

"You have your sword," I said.

Miguel, Conks, and Johnson glanced down, wondering why that made any difference against the angry mob that would descend upon us by morning's light.

"You have your wits. You have your courage," I continued, lifting my chin. Meeting Colt's eyes, I concluded, "And you have me."

I marched to Daniel's body, sprawled on the sodden grass. "Lucky for all of you," I said, drawing Daniel's sword from its sheath and not sparing him a moment's thought, "I too possess all three assets." Turning to face the men, I announced, "And I intend to use them to our advantage."

Colt looked at me with a twinkle in his eye and that faith was just one of the thousand reasons why I loved him. With a grin he prompted, "Tell us what we need to do, Lady Charlotte."

I met his smile with my own and declared, "Daniel's men are here, slain. His estate is unguarded as he's sent away his servants for the evening."

"You propose we rob him." Colt said, quickly catching on.

"I propose we reclaim what should be yours, by rights," I amended. "All of Daniel's worldly possessions were first gained by your bag o' bits. I stole it from you and he stole it from me the day I washed ashore. That he used his own abilities to grow that small fortune into a larger one doesn't change the fact that it began from your coin, and it doesn't change that fact that you can't rob a man who forsook all rights to his holdings the night he became a monster. Maybe not in the eyes of the king's law, but I no longer live by that law," I pointed out. "I live by a pirate's law. By yours."

I am yours, I thought, staring up at Colt's wickedly hand-some wet face. *Do you believe me now?*

"So what say you, men?" I asked, blinking away the rain from my lashes. "Shall we raid the manor and run?"

Colt looked over his shoulder. Conks, Johnson, and Miguel nodded, drawing their swords. Colt grinned back at me.

"Lead the way."

I started to walk and abruptly halted.

"Wait!" I said, darting back to Daniel's corpse and fishing around in his pockets. I retrieved my gold locket and handed it to Colt.

"He tried to steal this too," I said, turning and brushing aside my slick, stringy hair. "Will you put it back on? I vow never to take it off."

Colt's fingers grazed the back of my neck as he fastened the chain. His lips tickled my ear and I heard the smile in his voice as he whispered, "I vow to make you beg for mercy if you do."

Spinning to face Colt, I threw my arms around him, sealing our vows with a long, hungry kiss.

CHARLOTTE

UNDER THE COVER of night rain we raided Daniel's manor and claimed everything we could carry. Selling Daniel's finery bought our new life—the ship, the pardon. The governing heads that needed to look the other way when questions were asked about the deadly scene in the woods behind Daniel's manor. Something nefarious had obviously been going on, authorities reasoned. Perhaps there had been a squabble between business partners, they decided, leading someone from within their association to set up the gruesome murders and robbery.

A bit of digging into Daniel's finances revealed that all of the men had been cheating one another from time to time, making it an easy theory to apply.

For a group of gentlemen supposedly so incensed by the immorality of piracy and yet so willing to injure me, I found the irony unsurprising. So did Colt.

And if it *hadn't* been an inside job, the townspeople gossiped, perhaps it was the work of Captain Sedge, who'd taken command of *The Dread Night* that same evening.

Unfortunately, no one could ask, because *The Dread Night* had been captured, plundered, and all her men put to the sword in a battle with Captain Arbuckle of *The Dark Blade,* mere days after the gruesome murders in the woods.

Colt and I never learned what became of the Crimson Eye.

We turned to legitimate merchantry now, sailing boundless horizons without any targets on our backs and free in every sense of the word.

Well, maybe not one sense.

Colt and I were as bound to one another as any two people could be.

Claiming the authority of captain, Colt married us as soon as we set out to sea. The legality of such unions were already questionable to the crown, and adding to it the fact that Colt was both officiant and participant in the ceremony made it even more dubious. Moreover, it wasn't quite a ceremony but rather Colt coaxing all sorts of sordid vows from my lips whilst I was tied to the bed.

I couldn't even think of those promises without blushing.

With the legitimacy of the union thus suspect, we married, more properly and officially, in Port Royal a few weeks later. But because I'd deliriously promised Colt all the submissive and obedient delights of his heart (his loins) the first time, he always claimed the private ceremony as the *true* one.

Conks, Johnson, and Miguel stayed with us, though Colt offered to give them whatever share of the spoils they wanted to start a life elsewhere.

"When you've been at sea as long as we have, you become like a creature of the ocean yourself," Johnson said. "We've got to keep in motion with the waves to stay alive. We need the spray of the sea upon our skin to keep our old joints lubricated. And salt air is the only kind to breathe life into our lungs."

Miguel just smiled and said, "I like to cook fresh fish."

And so it was settled. We stayed together on our newly acquired ship and gained a reputation as shrewd, but trustworthy, merchants for hire. Once potential partners got over their suspicion about having a female amongst the crew, Colt said my unusual presence actually helped.

"You've a sweet and honest face," he told me one night in bed, smirking and half-rolling his eyes. "If they only knew."

"But only you do," I whispered in his ear.

"Only I ever will," he added, grabbing my waist possessively.

"I must admit, I like being in the open ocean without the constant fear of attack," I confessed, settling my head into his shoulder. "I don't fancy a sword through my belly or being strung upon the gallows."

"You were never *truly* one of us," Colt sighed thoughtfully, stroking my neck and arms. "Always between worlds, one foot in ours and one in theirs."

"Well, then, it's good you've come 'round to changing your world for me," I said, lightly smacking his chest. "Now everyone is pleased."

Colt's fingers caught and encircled my wrists. He gently raised my arms above my head and pinned them with one hand.

"We're not completely safe. There are still pirates sailing these seas," he warned.

"And lucky for me, you know the best ways to evade them," I reminded.

"Lucky for me," Colt grinned, pulling the lace on my blouse and exposing one plump breast to his eager hand, "you don't."

THE END

ABOUT THE AUTHOR

Una spends her free time revel-
ing in fantasy. Nothing snaps her
attention like a dominant male
in single-minded pursuit of a
headstrong female—except when
those same lovers initially despise
one another. She reads and writes
these angst-filled pairings (and

their happy endings) from the East Coast of the U.S.

Romance? Dark. Characters? Gray. Cheeks? Flushed pink
as you read, I hope.

Didn't Austen say something like, "It is a truth univer-
sally acknowledged, that a dominant man in possession of a
powerful will, must be in want of a brat." (Or did I get that
wrong? ;)